# PROMISE OF SILVER

# PROMISE OF SILVER

A NOVEL BY

## Michael K. Brown

INGALLS
PUBLISHING GROUP, INC

INGALLS PUBLISHING GROUP, INC
PO Box 2500
Banner Elk, NC 28604
www.ingallspublishinggroup.com

2014 © Michael K. Brown
Cover photo by Jeff Breiman
jeffsfineartphotos.com
Book design by Luci Mott

LIBRARY OF CONGRESS CATALOGING-IN-PUBLICATION
APPLIED FOR

ISBN; 978-1932158465

*To Judy,*
*for all the wonderful memories of our life together and*
*the promise of our future.*

*Love is the flower of life,
and blossoms unexpectedly and without law,
and must be plucked where it is found,
and enjoyed for the brief hour of its duration.*
~D.H. Lawrence

# PROMISE OF SILVER

# *1*

Dae Whitehead gazed beyond the real estate agent and re-called the day she had stepped into the house forty-three years before.

John opened the door and she walked in with two-year old Julie in her arms. Stopping in the foyer to look around, she was reminded of the spaciousness of her new home. After two years in a cramped apartment, the Georgian Colonial with four bedrooms and three baths seemed like a palace.

"Whew, it's going to take a lot of furniture to fill this place," she said.

"That'll take a while," John replied. "We just signed our life away for three hundred dollars a month, you know."

Dae walked into the living room, ignoring his comment as if in a trance. "Take her please."

After handing the baby to him, she started her tour through the rooms one more time, explaining to him where things would go. She labored up the stairs, carrying an extra twenty pounds that would become Justin four months later.

"This will be the nursery," she said, entering a room across the hall from the master bedroom. "I want to paint it yellow," meaning she wanted *him* to paint it yellow.

The house had been well kept by the former owners, a banker and his wife who had perished in a private plane crash. The lone heir, a son living in California, had no interest in owning property in Savannah other than obtaining some quick cash. So it was, in the words of the executor, "a steal" and, though it stretched their budget to the limit, Dae wanted the house badly. She would hardly consider any of the other places presented by the realtor and had nothing good to say about the few she looked at. Finally, she coaxed John into making an offer. When the counter-offer came back, it was surprisingly close to the original and the deal was closed.

"It's our house," John said. "I can paint it whatever color you want."

"Our house," she said, as if repeating the words made it so. She reached to him and they shared an awkward embrace with two babies snugged between them, one in his arms and one in her stomach.

It was their house and it became a home to four people, the only home Julie and Justin ever knew until they left the family nest. John and Dae worked hard at keeping it in good condition and the market value continued to increase until the neighborhood began to decline. After the kids grew up and John had gone, Dae was left alone in the big house. As the surrounding area became less desirable, she refused to part with the only thing she had left to hang onto.

Now, she knew it was time to let go, but it was hard. She turned to the pretty real estate agent who held a contract in her hand. "The offer is still less than what I think the house is worth," Dae argued.

"It's been on the market for two years. I don't think they'll come up any." The agent paused with a sympathetic look on her face. "It's in line with comps in the neighborhood."

*Comps?* Dae thought. That's all it came down to. The house was just a pile of bricks and mortar and sheetrock to anyone else. To her it was walls that echoed with the sounds of laughter and crying; floors that held invisible prints of soft feet and heavy footsteps; ceilings that trapped the odors of fresh linens and burnt toast. It was her life.

Yet even though each room was full of treasured possessions, the house felt as empty as her life had become.

"I'll take it," she said.

The agent broke out in a glad-that's-over-with smile. "Good. Sign here and I'll get the ball rolling."

At last, she had let go of the house and, like a bird released from its cage, she felt liberated. As soon as the real estate agent left, Dae was on the phone with another one. She desperately hoped that cluster home at Seaside Village was still available.

———❦———

Braxton Donovan sat in the quiet solitude of early morning, staring at a crossword puzzle in the newspaper. Setting his reading glasses and pen aside, he leaned back in the chair and let his mind drift into the wispy shadows of his life. At seventy-one, he didn't feel like an old man but when middle-aged people addressed him as "sir," he was reminded of that fact. Yet he wondered exactly when that had occurred. What happened to all those years between young and old? They had flashed by like a meteor leaving only a trail of memories. Settled into that time of life when the mind and body slows down but the world speeds up, he felt disconnected from the present.

As in his favorite song, "Stardust," Brax often found himself in reverie. Dreaming of the times when he played his trumpet and led the band while people danced in rhythm to the music; when he could run seven minute miles for three hours; when he was the life of the party and people laughed at his jokes; when he wrestled with one of his sons on the floor until Daddy said "I give;" when he came home after a hard day's work and walked into a house that felt like family. Those were the days when he was neither young nor old but simply full of life.

Now, the in-between years were gone and he longed to be alive again. Maybe he was past his prime, but he could still feel the music and he needed a new song; something to believe in, something to grab hold of, something to make the days meaningful. Something to ... love.

*Ah love; an often abused word.* He liked a lot of things—a good cigar, smooth whiskey, his trumpet—but he could never love "things." Jane had been his one true love but she was gone, leaving him with only those dusty memories. *But maybe there's a different kind of love,* he thought. *A kind where the past remains a haunting melody and the present is played in a beautiful new tune. To love once more, that would be something. Even an old man can dream.* Then he smiled at the absurdity of the notion. *There I go again.*

Brax took his pen and leaned back down to the crossword puzzle as the light of day began to seep through the windows of the clubhouse at Seaside Village.

———✦———

# 2

After finishing the crossword, Brax turned to the front page and looked at the headline one more time: **Development Plan for State Owned Island Gains Momentum.** Then he wadded the newspaper and angrily tossed it into the trashcan.

Stepping outside, he was calmed by the fresh air and the sight of the ocean in the distance as if he had walked into a different world. Behind the building he picked up the folding beach chair with his name stitched on the canvas back. With the chair in tow, he walked through the exit gate and past the sign that marked the entrance to Seaside Village, An Active Adult Community. He crossed the quiet road and onto the sandy path that led to the beach.

As he emerged from the dunes, Brax could see the sign just beyond the high tide line:

## LOGGERHEAD TURTLE NESTING AREA.

In smaller letters, the sign warned of fines and criminal prosecution for disturbing the hatchlings of the endangered reptile. The sign was an ominous reminder of the encroachment upon his little piece of paradise and he felt as if he, like the loggerhead, was a specimen of an endangered species.

Determined not to dwell on that depressing prospect, he tucked the thought away and set the chair on the firm sand beyond the receding surf. With his left hand cupped around the lighter to ward off a light breeze, he lit up a cigar. It was just past daybreak, following an hour devoted to two cups of coffee and the crossword puzzle in the clubhouse. Dr. Mathews wouldn't approve of the cigar, but Brax considered it a deserved wicked pleasure. He exhaled a big plume of smoke that quickly vanished in a whiff of wind.

He settled into the chair to absorb the gentle roar of the surf and the salty smell of the sea. Here, removed from the bustle of the world, his mind was free of clutter and a comfortable feeling settled into his well-worn bones. It was that feeling of serenity which had brought him to live on this island off the coast of Georgia three years before.

The beach was empty, a rarity even for a weekday in late April. Others would soon arrive, but now he was alone except for the winged creatures. He watched the seagulls flitter and squawk overhead before diving down for their sea-bound prey. Sandpipers followed behind the waves in tippy-toe haste looking for tiny sand crawlers. There was something oddly peaceful about being alone amongst the commotion of the busy little birds.

The day began to brighten when Brax heard someone approach from behind. Turning his head slightly to the side he could see just enough to recognize Jim Hawkins approaching with a folding chair in one hand.

"Good morning," Brax said out of the side of his mouth.

"Morning," Jim replied as he settled his big body in the chair beside Brax. Wearing a bright yellow shirt draped over his ample belly, tropical design shorts, and deck shoes, Jim looked sportier than most of the retirees that shuffled around the complex in their Velcro strapped sneakers and mismatched clothes.

Jim looked at the cigar in Brax's mouth and said, "You need to cut those damn things out, they'll kill you."

"This is my last one," Brax said. "I'm quitting today."

"You're a lyin' scumbag. I've heard that before."

"No, it's no problem to give up smoking. Like Mark Twain said, I've done it hundreds of times."

The two men exchanged small talk for a few minutes before Jim said, "All right, enough of this b.s.—let's go before my fat ass gets too settled." He pushed against the arms of the chair and grunted as he slowly lifted himself up. Stepping out of his deck shoes and standing barefoot in the sand, he made a couple of crisscross motions with his arms in front of him, arched his back, and uttered a drawn out "Aaaah."

Brax rose from his chair, took a draw from his cigar, blew a puff of smoke, and then said, "I've got to get rid of this." He walked to the water's edge, doused the embers of the cigar and stuck it in his pocket.

In the middle of the beach Jim spread his arms out and asked, "Which way?"

Brax silently lifted his right arm and began walking toward the south end of the island. The two men strolled at a leisurely pace with Brax leaving tread marks in the sand from his sneakers beside the footprints of Jim's bare feet.

"This beach will be a lot more crowded after they get through with the development," Jim said.

"Uh huh," Brax mumbled.

"We've got to go to that meeting next month and speak our piece," Jim continued. "I've got a friend who works in the Capital and he knows what's going on with this whole project. It's a lot bigger than we thought. They're talking hotels, condos, gated communities, all kinds of garbage. The politicians just want to keep it from the public as long as they can. They know a lot of people aren't going to like it. Not just us or the turtle lovers either."

"It won't do any good. They don't give a rat's ass about us. They ... hey, let's not talk about it now. This is our time to forget crap like that. Remember?"

Jim looked straight ahead as he walked. Finally, he nodded and said, "You're right."

For about a mile they spoke sparingly as the early morning sun bathed the shoreline in a warm amber glow. Before they had gone far, the beach began to come alive with other walkers, people fishing in the shallow waters, and an occasional bicyclist. More fishers dangled their lines from a wooden pier that jutted into the ocean in the distance ahead of them.

They walked on until they passed the pier, sharing small talk and offering "good morning" frequently as more people arrived on the beach. After a half-hour they turned around and headed back to where they started.

"How did it go with your check-up, yesterday?" Jim asked.

"The doctor told me not to buy any green bananas," Brax responded.

"Okay, funny guy. So it's none of my business."

"No, I'm just being a prick, as usual. I'm okay. I just have some … issues."

"Hell, everybody our age has issues. But you look in good shape. I'm sure you're a lot healthier than I am. Talk about issues—I've got high blood pressure, fifty pounds of extra blubber, and a family history of heart problems. Hell, I could keel over right here on the beach."

"Yeah, and so could I." Brax paused, then added, "Or we could both live another twenty-five years and be so senile that we wouldn't know our own name and have to wear a diaper to keep from messing our pants. That would be worse."

"Damn, that's a great way of looking at it," Jim said in a sarcastic tone. "I'm going to keep spittin' and gettin' as long as the old ticker holds out. That's all you can do, man."

"Do you know how many old farts our age have dementia?"

"Hey, we said we weren't going to talk about depressing stuff. Remember?"

Brax acknowledged with a grin and a tilt of his head as he noticed a woman in the distance heading toward them from the opposite direction.

The woman, walking at a brisk pace, approached the two men and smiled. "Good morning," she said as she maintained her stride.

"Good morning, Dae," responded Jim.

"Good morning," echoed Brax.

As soon as the woman passed, Brax turned to Jim and laughed. "What kind of talk is that? Good morning day?"

"Hey, that's her name. D-A-E. It's really Daedre, but she says that everyone calls her Dae. I think her last name is Whitehouse or Whitehall or something like that."

"How do you know her?"

"She just moved in yesterday. I saw them unloading the truck and I went over to introduce myself and see if she needed any help. But she had a daughter and a son-in-law and some other guy helping her so we just talked for a few minutes. She moved from Savannah and said she'll be safer here. She's pretty sharp—an ex-school teacher. A looker, too."

"Yeah, she's not bad for an AARP Mama." Brax turned to get another glimpse of the woman as she strode away.

"You better believe it. She's a ten on the granny scale."

"Ha! Bo Derek on Medicare," Brax added.

They had a good laugh over that one, but privately Brax perked up over the prospect of an attractive widow in their midst. They finished their walk back at the spot where they had started and settled into their chairs.

"This is something else, isn't it?" Brax asked. "No work, no worries. Life is just a walk on the beach." His words dripped with sarcasm.

"Hey, this is a pretty good deal," Jim responded. "I worked all my life for this. I wish Helen was still alive to enjoy it, too, but that's just the way things are. A lot of people would give anything to be in our position."

"Yeah, I know. I'm not bitching. It's just that things are never exactly like you think they're going to be."

"It depends on how you look at something. It's all in … perspective."

Brax nodded agreement. The two men focused on the scenery in front of them as a few swimmers braved the cold water while others waded knee deep in the surf or casually strolled the beach.

Then Brax spoke again, the irony of perspective stuck in his mind. "When I was a kid, my mother made a German chocolate cake one year for a holiday. Maybe it was Thanksgiving or Christmas—I'm not sure. Anyway, I had never eaten that kind of cake before and I told Mom that it was the best thing I had ever tasted. So a few days later she made another one and she said that it was just for me. Well, I don't think she meant for me to eat the whole thing in one day, but that's exactly what I did. And I got sick as a dog. I never ate German chocolate cake again."

"What the hell brought that up?"

"I don't know. Maybe just thinking about how things that seem so good can turn out bad."

"Damn it, there you go again. You told me to cool it about the developers and you keep coming up with this woe-is-me stuff."

"I know," Brax said.

"Besides," Jim added, "I don't think that was the cake's fault."

Brax was struck with the simple wisdom of the remark. "No, you're right," he said with a laugh.

They relaxed in their chairs for a little while longer with occasional small talk about politics and sports. Then Brax removed his sneakers and joined Jim barefooted to walk to the water. Wading in up to their knees, they let the small waves splash their shorts. On the beach they saw the new woman approach again, this time from the southerly direction. Jim waved at her and hollered, "Come on in, it feels great."

Dae was wearing a short sleeved pullover and pants from a warm up suit, but it wasn't uncommon for some of the women of

Seaside to wade in the water with long pants rolled up.

"No thanks," she replied with a smile. "Maybe later."

She continued at a brisk pace past them toward the north end of the island. With short-cropped brunette hair that framed a fresh face and a trim figure, Dae appeared to be the picture of vitality.

"She doesn't even look to be fifty-five," said Brax, referring to the minimum age required to live in the complex.

"Young blood," Jim responded.

"Okay, Bela Lugosi, calm down."

The two men laughed as if they were teenagers sizing up a new girl at school.

They returned to retrieve their chairs and begin the short walk back home. On the way, they passed the warning sign for the turtle's nesting site and the dark mood returned to Brax. The folding chair felt like an anchor as he trailed Jim through the beachside dunes and across the blacktop road. A macabre thought hit him, one he should avoid, but it loomed over him like a dark cloud. Maybe, unlike the loggerhead, he would be extinct by the time the island was swallowed by development.

Then he remembered the woman on the beach and, like the sun breaking through a cloudy sky, his mood shifted again. She was pretty and had an interesting name. He needed to meet her.

"C'mon, old man" Jim said, as they approached the gates of Seaside Village.

After they placed their chairs in the rack behind the clubhouse, Jim started in on the issue of development again. He clinched his jaws and spoke through his teeth. "We've got to fight the sons-of-bitches."

"Yeah," Brax said, weakly. But his mind was on a name that kept swirling in his head; *Dae.*

# 3

Dae and her daughter, Julie, busied themselves unloading boxes and putting the small things away while showing the guys where to put the furniture. The cluster home was new, with two bedrooms, two baths, and a two-car garage connected to an adjacent unit. In the back, a patio faced eastward into a thicket of oleanders, pines, and live oaks with a glimpse of the ocean in the distance.

"Mom, this is really nice," Julie said.

"Oh my gosh," Dae replied, "I am so glad to get out of that big house. This will be much easier to take care of."

After living in the same house for most of her adult life, she had mixed feelings about leaving the rambling two-story home in Savannah. At first, she wasn't sure she had done the right thing. The house had become a part of her. Or maybe it was the other way around. The neighborhood had matured well past its prime, though, and the upkeep on the house and yard was costly as well as stressful. Her logical nature convinced her she had made the right decision, but it didn't stop the tears from flowing when she walked out the front door for the last time.

But now, Dae stood beside her daughter and looked around at her new place feeling as if she had gotten younger. Seaside Village was only ninety miles from the house in Savannah and she had visited the island many times over the years, but the newness of the surroundings made it seem like a whole new world.

"This house is so bright and fresh," she said to Julie. She walked through the kitchen and gazed out the patio door. "I can see the waves from here." Turning back, she said, "I'm glad this unit was available. It was the only one left with an ocean view."

"I think it's perfect for you and I'm glad you have the extra bedroom. We can come and stay with you sometimes."

"Yes, I can't wait. But it's not a prison. I can still visit you in Charlotte. I have to see my darlings."

"We're always glad to have you and the girls love to see Grandma. You can come as often and stay as long as you wish. You know that."

Julie's husband, Ben, and his brother, Jeff, emerged from the second bedroom where they had just finished moving the furniture and setting-up the computer. Sweat spotted the T-shirts of both men and their faces reflected the signs of two hours of physical labor. Dae offered them a beer from a six-pack she had bought for the occasion.

They didn't stop with one beer. In thirty minutes, the brothers finished off the six-pack along with a pizza Julie picked up at the convenience store.

"Ben, don't you guys drink another beer," Julie said after the second one. "We've got to get the truck back today and one of you has to drive." She said the same thing after the third one.

"Don't worry Babe," Ben said. "I'm sober as a judge."

"And I'm sober as the jury," chimed Jeff.

Julie rolled her eyes with obvious disgust. "Mom, I hate to leave but we've got to get the truck back to U-Haul in Savannah, and it's another four hours to Charlotte. I have to work tomorrow but I can come back next week-end."

"You don't have to rush back. I'll be fine. You have been so much help."

After a round of goodbye hugs, the brothers climbed into the truck cab and pulled away. Julie followed close behind in her car.

Dae stared at the Georgia Tech logo on the license plate of the car as it disappeared and she could see Julie standing beside her father after the graduation ceremony. That was the day she let her daughter go. Her little girl had become a woman. A smart, beautiful woman in full bloom, like a flower that blossoms when the time is just right.

———◆———

John Whitehead sat quietly beside Dae among the audience of parents and friends as the graduates filed across the stage in their caps and gowns to receive their diplomas. Grouped by major and alphabet, the procession continued for over an hour as the respective department heads called out the name of each graduate. Finally, the professor said slowly and clearly, "Julienne Daedre Whitehead," as Julie took her diploma. Dae had made sure that the name she and her daughter shared had been spelled phonetically—DAY-DRA—in the professor's notes. In the audience, Dae felt John's grasp tighten in her hand and they smiled at each other. For a moment, she remembered how it used to be. Then she took a tissue from her purse and wiped the moisture from her eyes.

After the ceremony, the family took pictures outside in the bright sunshine of a hot June day in Atlanta. Wearing a white corsage with yellow ribbons pinned to her blue dress, Dae felt a sense of accomplishment as if she, herself, had just graduated. She was very close to her daughter and sometimes felt almost like a big sister instead of a mother. Julie inherited Dae's vibrant personality as well as her good looks, but her talents were totally opposite those of her mother. Dae was a reader, a writer, an historian, a student of words and people while Julie inherited her father's genes with a facility for numbers and technical things. So when Julie was accepted as a freshman at Georgia Tech, Dae was full of maternal pride but felt a distinct separation of intellect. In recent years, more and more women had begun to choose technical careers and Dae was thrilled when her daughter succeed in a curriculum that was beyond her own comprehension.

Though Dae could not have been prouder of her daughter, she knew this day had a special meaning to her husband. John had always hoped there would be a Tech grad in the family. Their son, Justin, had tried but he wasn't suited for the rigors of academic life. Instead, he joined the Army where he found contentment in Buddhism and a Korean wife. Stationed far away, he sent his sister a graduation gift and a poem expressing how proud he was of her.

On the drive back to Savannah the next morning, Dae tried to share her thoughts of the previous day with John. But he spoke sparingly as usual.

"Wasn't that a beautiful poem Justin wrote for Julie?"

"Yes, it was."

"He really has a gift for words." She paused but he didn't respond. "Isn't it funny how different they are? He's so sensitive and unconcerned with material things and she's so career driven."

"They're different all right." Without a hint of emotion, he added. "But you raised them well."

She could feel the distance in his voice. It was true what he said, but it was painful to hear him say it as if it were a confession of guilt. The attempt at conversation died and Dae withdrew into her feelings. The euphoria of the graduation ceremony was replaced by the realization that letting Julie go was like breaking the last link in the family chain. Julie would be moving on to a new job, a new city, a whole new life. Dae knew it was a life that included her only on the periphery, just as she was no longer in the center of the lives of her son and husband.

She looked out the window of the car at the lonely landscape of South Georgia and the feeling began to settle in.

Dae stood alone for a minute outside her front door after Julie and the brothers left. Then she went inside and introduced herself to her new home. She walked slowly through each room. Looking at the walls, the floors, the ceilings, the furniture, and how everything seemed to fit together. It made her feel comfortable as if she had just made a new friend that was pleasant and interesting. There was a stimulating aura about the surroundings that refreshed her sense of being alive. Tonight she would rest and start a good book and tomorrow she would discover more about her new world. A world where she would meet new people and feel safe at night and go to the beach whenever she wanted to.

Dae slept restfully and woke up earlier than usual. A long, hot shower opened her eyes to the first full day in her new home. Still in her robe, she grabbed a glass of orange juice and walked onto the patio. A speck of early morning sun peeked over the water barely visible in the distance and slivers of light sneaked through the trees. The temperature was mild and the scent of the ocean floated in a slight breeze. It was too beautiful to resist.

Quickly, she dressed and donned her walking shoes. She stepped outside with a sense of urgency as if the ocean might disappear before she could get there. "Good morning," she said, passing an elderly couple on the sidewalk.

They responded pleasantly as the old man helped the woman along with a hand on her arm. Dae felt safe walking alone here, unlike in her old neighborhood where cars passed through with radios blaring loud obscenities from open windows and strange new neighbors entertained visitors at all hours. So she didn't hesitate to walk past the entranceway and across the road onto the short path to the beach. There, she encountered only a few people scattered about.

She couldn't recall being on that part of the beach before, away from the main public area, and it was refreshing, as if she had wandered onto a different island. Although the beach was not as wide or as clean as in the more frequented spots, the relative seclusion made it all the more appealing. Still, she couldn't resist an urge pulling her back to a familiar place. She walked briskly toward the south end of the island, to the spot where she once danced in the arms of a soldier she loved more than the promise of her next breath. The memory filled her mind and every stride took her closer to a day forty-five years earlier.

⎯⎯•⎯⎯

John was on a week-end pass at his parents' home in Brunswick and Dae came from Savannah to be with him for one last time before his deployment to Vietnam. They went to the matinee at the Ritz Theatre to see the Beatles in *A Hard Day's Night*. John loved the Beatles.

"What do you think?" he asked. "Probably not an Academy Award, eh?"

"The music is kind of catchy and … infectious," Dae replied. She liked John too much to say what she really thought; that the mop-haired boys from Britain were a fad sure to fade away and the music was more about noise that feeling. She would think differently one day but Lennon and McCartney were yet to pen their love songs.

"Yeah, that's what it's all about," John said. "The movie is just a campy excuse for the music."

"Kind of like an Elvis movie, I guess," she said playfully.

He laughed. "No, it's not that bad."

"Well, anyhow, it was fun."

"But not as fun as this." He stopped right on the sidewalk, put his arms around her, and kissed her long and passionately to the amusement of people walking by. She didn't mind that they were in public and when he pulled his head back, she leaned forward on her tiptoes and kissed him again.

"I love you," he said.

It wasn't the first time he had said it, but it felt different to her this time. "I love you, too." She pulled herself tighter against him and buried her head into his khaki uniform shirt, as their bodies fused together on a sultry afternoon.

After a long embrace, he pulled his head back and looked at her with a gleam in his eyes. "Hey, I want you to go somewhere with me."

"Where?" she asked with a surprised grin.

"You'll see. C'mon, let's go." His eyes widened and he spoke with a flash of urgency.

The two lovers walked to John's car, entwined with his arm on her shoulder and one of hers around his waist. He drove through familiar streets to a place only a mile away. There, he parked near the nine-hundred-year-old tree that locals call "Lover's Oak." As he led her to the big tree, she suspected something special was about to happen and she began to feel airy. Standing under the long, arching branches, he reached out to hold each of her hands in one of his.

"I'll be gone for a year, you know. But I'll be back, I promise." His serious face turned to a grin. "I love you too much to get my ass killed."

She winced at the thought. "And I love you too much not to worry about that. But I'll wait for you and miss you every day." His intention was obvious now and she became flush with anticipation.

"Are you sure?"

"I've never been so sure of anything in my life. You know I love you." She knew what was coming next and she knew what she was sure of.

He pulled her closer, still holding her hand in his. "You're the most beautiful woman God ever made and I'm the luckiest guy in the world." He took a deep swallow and opened his mouth to speak, but she interrupted him.

"And I'm the luckiest girl."

"Shh," he hissed, playfully. He paused and looked down as if to gather his thoughts as she waited patiently with a smile. Lowering the timbre of his voice, he said slowly, "Daedre Maureen Spencer, will you marry me?"

She closed her eyes and started shaking as the tears began. "Yes," she said through the sobs. "Yes, yes!" It was something she thought might happen one day, but the emotion of the moment was more overwhelming than she ever imagined.

"That's good. So now I can give you this." He pulled the ring from his pocket and tried to put it on her finger, but his hands were shaking.

She smiled and slipped the ring on. Then he kissed her and she tasted the sweetness of fresh love. When they embraced, she no longer felt like a girl. Instead, she was a woman now and she held snugly to him with the warm feeling of promise in her future.

After that she was in a daze and the afternoon faded into ice cream cones and peering into storefront windows and falling asleep in his arms on the grass in the park.

When she woke, she turned to him as he opened his eyes half-way. "I feel like a different person now."

"Umm," he said sleepily. Still holding her as he rose up on his elbows. "I hope not, I want you to be the girl I asked to marry me."

"I am. That's what made me different. I'm so happy I could float away into the clouds."

He smiled and turned his head sideways. "Well, if you do, take me with you. I'd rather be there than where I'm going."

"I'll be with you wherever you go. God will be with you, too." She raised her left hand and looked at the ring. "And someday, I'll be Mrs. Whitehead."

In the evening they drove out to the island. At the pier they joined the crowd of young people on the open-air dance floor as music from the jukebox blared out over the water. Spurred by the furious beat of the fast songs, and her inhibitions numbed with beer, Dae danced with an unbridled feeling of freedom. Even in the frenzy of full motion, she was conscious of the ring on her finger as if everyone noticed it and she imagined the crowd around her as a private celebration. When the first chords of "When a Man Loves a Woman" began, the dance floor quickly filled. The lyrics of the song seemed to be written especially for them and, with their sweaty bodies pasted together, they sang the words as they swayed to the music while barely moving among the throng of amorous couples. John moved his hands from the base of her back to the soft flesh below and she pressed closer to him. The music ended and she lingered in his arms as they shared a long kiss, becoming the last couple to leave the dance floor.

Before the next song began, he led her outside and to his car, parked among dozens of others in an unlit patch of grass and sand. In the darkness, he caressed her willing flesh and she yielded until two bodies became one. Consumed by passion and sexual desire, she discovered a new dimension of love.

Afterward, they walked the beach in bare feet and cooled in a gentle breeze. The jukebox was quiet in the distance and, as they moved further away, the noisy din of the crowd on the pier became a murmur.

"A year is a long time," he said.

"Not when you have something to look forward to," she replied.

They shared a long kiss. Then he turned her gently and embraced her from behind, her breasts resting softly against his arms. A fresh wind stirred her hair and, wrapped warmly in his clasp, her heart was so full of the moment she felt as if she were in a dream. The moon bathed the starless night in a silvery glow and she could see her future in the clouds as they slowly drifted overhead like a gossamer promise. He pressed his cheek to hers as they looked out at the sea and listened to the surf lapping ashore.

There were no more words to say.

The dance pavilion on the pier was now gone, but this morning Dae stood at the spot where she had nestled in John's arms many years before. A year later, he returned from Vietnam and they were married a month after that. She stopped to linger for a while and looked out at the ocean, recalling the wonder of young love.

Scenes of the past raced through her mind like her whole life was being replayed in fast forward. Sometimes the past was bittersweet, but today was different. It was a day to remember how good life can be. Shading her eyes, she peered at the early sun and smiled as she thought, *It's a new Dae.* Then she began walking back to where she started.

"Good morning," she said to others, as she passed. A few times she stopped to chat briefly before quickly marching off again as if in a hurry to get somewhere. It was her habit to keep a swift pace when she walked, a pace most her friends found hard to maintain.

*I may be a senior citizen,* she thought as she hustled along, *but I've got a lot of life yet to live.*

# 4

After leaving Jim, Brax walked slowly to his house. Beyond the larger homes, he reached his street with the single-level complex that included eleven other one-bedroom units. Each residence had a small swatch of tidy landscape, a one-car garage, and a patio in the rear.

When he opened the door and stepped inside, he looked around as if he had never been there before. He ignored the light switch and, with the door closed, the only sign of daylight leaked around the edges of the blinds and poured through the high windows in the kitchen. The intriguing vision of the pretty woman on the beach faded away in the darkness and he was alone again. He walked as if in a trance to the bedroom and lay down on the king-size bed.

He closed his eyes and there, lying beside him, was Jane.

---

The cancer had eaten away until the wrinkled flesh no longer hid the bones that poked from her shriveled body and her eyes stared out in silent torment. For months Jane had seemed barely alive, suspended in a fog of drug-induced sustenance. It was excruciating to see her like that and the struggle to survive without comfort or hope seemed crueler than death itself. He felt helpless and, somehow, guilty for not being able to alleviate the misery. *Take her, God,* he prayed, *she doesn't deserve this.* All day he lay beside her until each breath was weaker and further apart than the last.

Then she was gone.

He stroked her hair and kissed her cheek and, for the first time in years, he cried. Really cried. Not just with silent tears, but with unabashed sobbing, his face scrunched in despair. Her body was lifeless but he felt that her soul was still alive. He spoke the words that had been held captive inside of him, released by the jolting blow of finality.

"Jane, I love you. I love you for being there, my wife, my every-thing. For loving the boys and being the best mother. It hurt me to see you suffer. I wanted to comfort you, but I didn't know what to do. Now that the pain is gone and the journey is over, go to rest, my love, in the world of eternal peacefulness. Someday I'll be with you. I promise I will."

It wasn't enough. The words didn't match his feelings and he seemed to be speaking to himself more than to her. How can you make your heart be felt? How can you keep the flame of love inside without it consuming you?

He lay beside her withered body for a long time before he opened the door and let his three sons in. That was the last time he would lie on the big sleigh bed they had shared for more than half of their forty-eight years together.

Jane's final days tested Brax's already fragile faith. There was no doubt in his mind of the existence of God, but he had never fully embraced the orthodoxy of any religion. He wasn't sure there was a heaven, but he knew there was a hell because he had seen his wife endure it. He could accept the finality of death, but not the cruelty of it. There was no way to ignore the hurt, but he eventu-ally came to accept the fact that it's just the way things happen. Life happens and then death happens, and no one knows why. It would have been better if he had been the first to go—better yet go quickly—but there was no way to design for that. His greatest fear was that someday others would suffer because of him or, worst of all, suffer with him, like he did with her. The time would come when he'd have to deal with that fear. That's why he hated the next visit with Dr. Mathews.

There were no tears now, only memories that he tried to keep tucked away like the special little keepsakes that stay in a drawer because they mean nothing to anyone else. He rose up and removed a dusty, black case from under the bed. Sitting on the side of the bed, he placed the case across his legs, opened the lid, and removed the trumpet. He licked his lips as he wiped the mouthpiece on his shirt. Lying back down, he looked up at the ceiling with the horn to his lips.

He closed his eyes again and it was 1960.

⊱━━━⊰

On a sunny fall day in Athens, Georgia, Brax stood at midfield in Sanford Stadium, surrounded by the rest of the band. He watched the fans milling in and out of their seats as he blew his trumpet in solo to "Stardust." It was halftime at the homecoming game, and the Dixie Redcoat Marching Band was performing a medley of tunes in tribute to Hoagy Carmichael.

He missed a note, but otherwise played the song well and finished to a smattering of applause from the bustling crowd. He moved back into the pack with the rest of the horns as three hundred Redcoats scurried to form the word GEORGIA in big block letters. The band closed out the medley with "Georgia on My Mind." Then the tempo revved up several notches and the stands erupted at the first chords of the raucous fight song, "Glory, Glory, to Old Georgia," set to the familiar tune of the chorus from the "Battle Hymn of the Republic." Despite the many times he had been a part of that scene, it still gave him chills.

Leaving the field, the band passed the players coming back from the locker room. Brax looked at the big athletes, their muscular bodies accentuated by the padded uniforms, and envied the way they carried themselves with a manly swagger, like proud warriors heading to battle. The fans, fueled with smuggled booze and buoyed by a big lead against an overmatched opponent, cheered contentedly as the players streamed onto the field. The day would be measured in the glory of victory for the men in red jerseys and "silver britches."

Brax imagined the thrill it would be to play the game at that level, proudly representing his school and, in many ways, his home state. He had always dreamed of himself in that role. But in high school he had learned that the "want to" in his heart did not match the "can do" in his body and his love of the game was not enough to realize that dream. Instead, he had become the lead trumpet for the Redcoats which gave him the honor of playing his favorite song in front of forty thousand people.

He looked toward the student section and saw Jane waving a pompom at him. Even the football players would envy him for that, he thought. In his eyes, Jane was the best looking girl on a campus full of good-looking girls. She had once gone steady with the star halfback, whose picture appeared prominently in the game program, but that night she would be with him. He couldn't top that if he had won the Sugar Bowl single handedly.

Brax and Jane had been a steady couple for three months but he wasn't absolutely sure of her feelings. They had engaged in heavy petting and she returned his affection, but each of them had avoided the L word. But while playing "Stardust," urging the notes from his trumpet with all the air he could summon, he had made up his mind. From that very moment he knew what he had to do before the day was over.

At the country club that night, Brax fronted a six-piece dance band sharply dressed in red blazers, gray pants, white button-down shirts, and narrow black ties. In the process of working his way through business school with a co-op job, Brax had just turned twenty-three. The other five in his combo, all music majors, were younger. He had recruited them from the Redcoats and led them with a passionate, if technically imperfect, feel for the music.

Brax knew that the crowd, composed largely of gray-haired alumni and boosters with deep pockets, had a taste for music from their college days of the thirties and forties. So he played some old classics, mixing a slow one, "Mood Indigo," with an up-tempo number, "In the Mood." The enthusiastic response was measured by a pile of bills in a tip jar near the stage.

During the first break Brax sauntered to the bar and an older gentleman pressed in beside him.

"It's on me," the man said, as he ordered a drink for himself.

"Thanks."

"You're the one that played that solo at halftime today, aren't you?"

Brax looked at him in shock. "Yes sir. How did you know?"

"Your girlfriend over there told me." He looked behind him in the direction where Jane was sitting. "You better hang on to that young lady. I can tell by the way she looks at you when you're up there what she thinks of you."

Brax smiled and took his drink from the bartender.

The man continued. "You don't find a woman like that every day. I know—it took me three wives to figure that out." He laughed, cocked an eye with a glint of self-proclaimed wisdom, and walked away with his drink.

Brax made his way to the table where Jane sat with two middle-age couples. After the conversation warmed up, he subtly placed his hand on her thigh under the table. She smiled at him and didn't resist. Wearing a black dress that clung to her shapely figure, she was the most beautiful woman in the room. Her fair skin, blond hair, and bright red lips completed the image that seemed an invitation to ecstasy.

After the second break Brax called her to the microphone for her only song of the night. She wasn't a member of the band but she had a feel for the music and she could sing a pretty decent rendition of "When I Fall in Love." At twenty-one, there was a convincing plea in her voice as she finished the first line—"it will be forever"—as if longing for that perfect someone. Brax accompanied her with his horn muted and the dance floor filled with couples clinging to each other and swaying to the slow, romantic tune.

When the song ended, Brax stepped to the mike and extended an arm toward Jane. "Ladies and gentlemen, the beautiful Miss Jane Cummings." A nice round of applause followed.

Beaming with radiance in the center light, she thanked the crowd with a smile and held it as she turned to Brax with a nod. All eyes were on Jane as she returned to her table.

A woman stuck an arm out as she passed by and said, "That was lovely."

"She sure is," said a man sitting beside her.

"All right, that was nice and easy," Brax said to the crowd. "You know, I think that one day there's going to a mighty lucky guy somewhere." Without thinking, he added, "Forever." He didn't mean to say it, but the word tumbled out of his mouth just as Jane looked back at him.

The band fiddled with their instruments in a brief interlude before Brax returned to the microphone. "Now we're going to change the pace a little. With this number you might say we're going from the beauty to the beast. Here is our take on a song about one mean son-of-a-gun." With that he started blowing his horn and the familiar tune of "Mack the Knife" was instantly recognizable. Halfway through the song he lowered his trumpet and began singing the lyrics, joined by the piano player in a rowdy duet. An older couple danced to the entertainment of the onlookers with some well-preserved jitterbug steps. Jane joined the younger crowd on the dance floor with one of her male friends in an energetic version of the shag.

A little after midnight the crowd emptied the dance floor after the last slow song. "Well folks, thanks for having us out tonight," Brax said. "We hope you've had a good time. Before we leave though, we're going to play one last song for you and don't forget—Go Bulldogs!"

Immediately, the band began playing "Dixie" so loudly that it seemed like the room had exploded. After the first few notes everyone in the audience stood up, presented their drinks in a toast then began singing the words to the Southern anthem in a boisterous chorus. Brax played his horn with fervor as beads of sweat ran down his face and his shirt became soaked into a sticky body wrap. When the song finally came to an end the room erupted with cheers and whistles, and he could feel the appreciation of the crowd. Maybe scoring a touchdown in a red jersey and silver britches might feel better, but this was a damn good second.

The room soon emptied and the band packed up their instruments to go back into the world. Brax carried his horn in one hand as Jane clung to his other arm on the way to his car. He tossed his coat in the back seat and pulled his shirt out of his pants in an effort to cool off.

"Sorry, I don't smell so good," he said as he settled into the driver's seat. She moved next to him and snuggled to his cheek, arousing him with the sweet scent of womanhood. "You smell just fine to me," she said. Then she kissed him with a tenderness that penetrated deep inside him. He didn't want to let the feeling go. It was after one a.m., but as far as he was concerned, the night was just beginning.

"I thought you might be all puckered out," she said when their lips parted.

"I'll never be too puckered out for that," he said, kissing her neck.

"Promise?" she asked playfully.

"Promise," he said as he found her lips again.

She hummed the tune in his ear and then sang the words in a

whisper. "When I fall in love, it will be forever."

"Are you sure?"

"I'm sure," she replied. "I already have."

He couldn't believe she said it first. He was all worked up to express his love, like a proper suitor but she beat him to it. Overcome by the moment, he hugged her so tightly that it felt like she was a part of him. "Jesus, I love you. I love you more than I know how to say."

"I love you, too," she said through her tears. She kissed him again.

His body felt an electric tingle of pride and he knew that nothing would ever match the power of those words. He didn't expect it to feel that way. It was overpowering, as though he had just been enveloped by an earthly rapture. He knew how good it felt to love her but he never imagined how good it would feel to be loved by her.

It happened just as the song said. She fell in love forever. And he did too, but he couldn't know that her forever would end before his.

⸺◆⸺

Brax opened his eyes and the Homecoming day of more than fifty years earlier faded away. With the trumpet in one hand and a more upbeat attitude, he walked into the shadowy living room. He took a CD from a stack, placed it in the player and sat down in the leather recliner, holding the instrument silently in front of him. Suddenly, the unmistakable raspy voice of Louis Armstrong singing "Hello Dolly" filled the room. Armstrong, known as Pops to musicians, sang the lyrics as if they were filtered through charcoal, sometimes slurring words. After a short riff of scat singing, he began playing his horn in the way that only he could.

Brax lifted his instrument, with both hands in the playing position, and put it near his lips and closed his eyes. He felt a smile grow on his face and he could feel the energy, the uninhibited joy that seemed to flow directly from the pores of his body as if the sounds were coming from him. He couldn't play his trumpet like Pops but he could still feel the music as intensely as ever. It was a good feeling to remember.

When the song ended, he turned off the CD player and settled back into the deepest position of the recliner. With the horn still in his lap, he soon drifted off to sleep.

An hour later, Brax awoke and set the trumpet on the floor as he groggily arose from the chair. He went into the kitchen, opened the door to the refrigerator, unzipped his fly and stared straight ahead, dumfounded. Then he remembered: he meant to go to the bathroom. *Just a senior moment*, he told himself. *Or maybe not. I won't know if it's happening.* It was a grim thought.

From the counter, he grabbed a bottle of Crown Royal that had just enough left to mix with a jigger of water for a stiff belt. He mixed the drink and took it with him into the bathroom. There he took a good swig in one end as he pissed out the other, like the little cherub in the water fountain on his patio. Returning to the kitchen, he casually dropped the empty glass on the tile floor and watched it shatter into countless pieces. He wasn't sure why he did that and he looked down at the scattered shards with no feelings of anger or regret.

After watching the late news on television, he went to bed and tried to forget the melancholy thoughts churning in his mind. Sleep would come uneasily and interrupted by brief spurts of semi-consciousness, but it was time to wait for another day. Another day that would begin with a walk on the beach with Jim and nothing else but idle hours. Maybe they would see the woman with the strange name on the beach again and strike up a conversation. Then in a bit of random silliness that pops up when you're trying to sleep, he thought of the word play on her name.

*Maybe I'll talk to Dae tomorrow.*

# 5

Brax closed his eyes and he could see the familiar face, but the name of one of his favorite actors remained hidden in the darkness of his mind. A simple four-letter word was all he needed to fill in the spaces. The clue: Connery of the movies. What is his first name? Bond? No, no, that doesn't fit; the third letter has to be an "a."

He sat racking his brain when an older couple entered the clubhouse. He looked up and greeted them with a brisk "Hi" as they sat down at a nearby table.

"Morning, Brad," replied the man.

Brax knew the couple, but for the life of him, he couldn't remember their names, nor could they remember his. He had told them his name several times, but they always called him Brad, so he just went along with it.

The old man opened a crossword puzzle book and began making marks while the woman busied herself with a lap full of knitting.

Brax turned back to his puzzle, still unable to put the right letters to the word he was looking for. Sometimes he would forget the most familiar things, like his own telephone number or address, but once he spit out the first digit the rest would tumble out of his brain as if they were linked together genetically. Other times, a micro-part of his mind was mired in blankness and seemingly no amount of concentration could extract the right word from his memory bank. It would drive him crazy until finally the word came to him as if it popped out of a jack-in-the-box in his head. The brain locks were occurring more frequently lately and it was scary. *What the hell is happening to me?*

When he filled in one of the other words going in the opposite direction, the first letter of the name was revealed as "s" and suddenly the lights came on. Sean! That's it; Sean Connery. How in the hell could I forget that? Frustrated with himself, he looked up and stared out the window, trying to come up with a word to fit another clue.

"Did you finish your puzzle, Brad?" the old man asked.

"Not yet."

"Well, don't give up. We have to keep our minds in shape, just like our bodies, don't we?"

"You're right."

Brax looked with amusement at the old man, whose body was so frail it didn't look to be a match for a stiff wind. Then he stared intently at the pen in his hand and his thoughts turned back to his memory lapses. At his physical, he had mentioned his concern to Dr. Mathews, whose words, at first, were comforting.

———◦—◦———

"It's probably nothing to get too worried about," the doctor said. "Our minds are like our bodies. As we age, we begin to lose some of the suppleness that we take for granted."

"But my memory seems to be worse than most people's, even those of my age. And my body seems to be in better shape."

"I can run some tests for neurological signs. But if it's random, and no more frequent than you've described, the tests may not show anything." The doctor paused, then resumed with an edge of concern in his voice. "There is something else, though, that we need to look at further."

"What's that?"

"Your prostate. When I examined you I felt a hardness that's not normal. We should get the blood tests back tomorrow and we'll see what the PSA level is. We just need to check everything out."

"Yeah, that would be good. Check things out." Brax exhaled deeply as he pursed his lips and arched his brows. The concern about his short-term memory loss instantly evaporated.

"Don't be alarmed," the doctor said. "It's not a definitive exam, just a preliminary indicator. And, if something needs attention, these things are treatable if detected early."

"That's very comforting. My head is okay, but my butt might be killing me."

A slight grin grew on the doctor's face. It was one of those times, Brax thought, when a little dark humor seemed to be the best medicine.

Dr. Mathews turned serious again. "No, as I said, don't jump to conclusions."

But that's exactly what Brax did. When he left the doctor's office, he was convinced he had cancer. Without the test results he had no way of knowing it for sure but he assumed the worst case.

Brax had almost completed the crossword puzzle when he looked up to see Dae enter the main room of the clubhouse. The only other people around were the elderly couple. The old man stared intently at his crossword puzzle and the woman continued to work on her knitting without looking up.

"Good morning," Dae said as she approached.

"Good morning," Brax replied.

"Don't let me interrupt you. I was just looking around."

"No, that's all right." He put down his glasses and pen. "You're new here aren't you?"

"Yes, I just moved in a couple of days ago. My name is Dae Whitehead."

"Glad to meet you, Dae Whitehead. I'm Brax Donovan." He stood up and pulled a chair from the table. "Here, have a seat."

"Thank you."

"Welcome to our little piece of heaven." He laughed. "I think you'll like it here."

"Yes, I love it."

"Would you like some coffee? I just made two fresh pots."

"No thanks, I'm not much of a coffee drinker. I just stopped by on my way to the beach."

"An early riser, eh? Me too. I'm usually the first one here, before I go for my walk. I saw you on the beach yesterday. I was with Jim Hawkins."

"Yes, I think I recall seeing you fellows. I saw so many people and I can't remember everybody's name right now."

"Well, that's kind of normal around here. If you have a good memory, you're not old enough to live in this place." He smiled as he closely observed her features. She was even more attractive than he had recognized from a distance. Late fifties, he guessed. Very well preserved.

She grinned and looked at the newspaper in front of him. "I see you're working on a crossword puzzle. I like crosswords, too."

"Yeah, they're good for the brain cells. It's the first thing I do each morning. The paper doesn't come early around here so I save the puzzle for the next morning." He caught himself babbling on like a boring old geezer. Embarrassed by his exposition of too-much-information, he looked at her sheepishly. "Pretty fascinating stuff, eh?"

A broad grin on her face signaled amusement at his self-inflicted jab. "It looks like you're almost through. Don't let me keep you from finishing."

"I've got all day." He folded the paper and laid it in front of him. "Would you like to join me for your walk on the beach?" Nothing else could have torn him from that crossword puzzle.

"Yes, I would love to. Thank you for asking."

"Just a sec." He stood and carefully ripped the puzzle from the paper, then stuffed it into the back pocket of his shorts. Extending his hand as a gesture for her to go first, he followed her out of the clubhouse.

On the beach, they found Jim Hawkins sitting in a folding chair at his regular place and Brax called to him as they approached.

Jim turned his head and returned the greeting, then repeated it with emphasis when he realized Dae was there as well. He looked at Brax quizzically. "Where have you been, man? It's almost seven o'clock."

"I slept in a little this morning. And I kind of got hung up on the puzzle. I met Dae in the clubhouse. You two have met haven't you?"

"Yeah. Nice to see you again," Jim said, looking at Dae.

"My pleasure." Dae tilted her head with a slight nod.

"So are you ready to go?" Brax asked Jim.

"No. You know what? I think I'll just hang here. You guys go ahead. I'm not feeling a hundred percent this morning."

"Oh, come on." Brax tried to sound sincere.

"Yes, do," added Dae.

"No, really, y'all go ahead." Looking sternly at Brax, he added. "Just don't gross the lady out with one of those stinking stogies."

"Gave 'em up for good."

"I'll bet."

As Brax and Dae turned to walk away, Jim hollered at their backs. "And don't bore the hell out of her with that crap about eating too much cake."

Brax smiled at Dae and asked, "This way?" He pointed northward where the beach disappeared at high tide leaving a rocky, drift-scattered shoreline.

"That's fine."

She walked at a faster pace than he was used to and he hustled along beside her, hoping she didn't notice his heavy breathing. At first they spoke sparingly, finding a common rhythm with their footfalls in the sand, enjoying a conversation without words. Almost immediately, Brax was attracted to Dae by the chemistry that occurs between a man and a woman that defies reason and he sensed she might have the same feeling.

"I like your name," he said. After taking a breath, he added, "Dae ... that's pretty." He talked louder than normal since they weren't facing each other.

She spoke haltingly while maintaining a brisk stride. "Thank you. ... It's short for Daedra. ... It's hard for some people to spell, much less pronounce. ... It's been in my family for six generations. ... My maiden name was Spencer. ... My great-great-great grandfather ... came from England in 1763. ... Georgia was still a colony. ... We've been here ever since." She talked in short bursts through the exertion of her pace.

He spoke between breaths as well. "That's something else ... I don't know much about my family tree. ... They came from the backwoods of north Georgia ... mostly illiterate farmers and railroad men."

"Your full name is Braxton, isn't it? ... Braxton Bragg I would guess."

"Yeah, that's me ... Braxton Bragg Donovan. ... How'd you know?"

"As I said, I'm a native Georgian. ... And I taught history for thirty-seven years . ... I know all about Braxton Bragg ... and the Battle of Chickamauga. ...That's not such an uncommon name ... for Southern boys."

"I guess not. ... Glad I wasn't born a Yankee. ... they might have named me Ulysses." He turned his head and looked at her with a grin and she smiled back.

"Or worse, Tecumseh," she added, as she stopped walking.

He looked at her curiously.

"That was Sherman's middle name."

"Oh yeah," he said with sudden recall. "My people had another middle name for him. I won't say the whole thing, but it's SOB for short."

She laughed and they began walking again.

They reached a place where the shoreline narrowed down and a pile of driftwood and debris stretched the width of the beach. He took her hand to steady her as they stepped over the jetsam. Her hand felt small in his yet her grip was firm and she stepped nimbly. But he clumsily snagged his foot and had to let go of her hand, struggling to keep from plopping face down into the sand.

"Are you okay?" she asked.

"Yeah," he replied, somewhat embarrassed. "I was just practicing my pratfalls."

She smiled at his humor in a way that made him feel glad he had stumbled.

When they resumed walking she asked, "Do you mind if we take it easy for a spell?"

"No, that's okay with me. Do you want to stop and rest?" They had been walking for almost forty-five minutes and he was hoping she would answer "yes."

"No, I'm fine. I just thought we might slow down a bit."

"Sure. You saw the way Jim and I walk. We don't get in a hurry."

They continued for another ten minutes before deciding to turn around and head back.

"They told me there are quite a few singles at Seaside," she said. "That surprised me. I would figure that to be the case at a nursing home, but not at a place like this."

It sounded like a probe. It never occurred to him that she might not be sure of his status.

"Yeah," he said, "a lot of us have outlived our better half."

"I'm learning to be on my own," she said.

"My wife passed away six years ago. You never get used to it." He walked a few steps before adding, "I'm sorry. That was a dumb thing to say."

"It's okay. I know what you mean."

They again reached the place where the debris was strewn across the beach.

"Hey, watch this," he said. He walked quickly through the pile, stepping over a knee-high piece of driftwood and then made a three-hundred-sixty degree spin. When he reached the other side of the pile, he turned around and looked at her with his arms spread wide apart.

"Voila!" he shouted. "I'm King of the driftwood!"

She laughed and shook her head. "And sometimes you're the klutz of the driftwood." Then she started picking her way through the pile.

He grabbed her hand as she reached him and, with a flourish, bowed in front of her like a knight before royalty. Rising up, he extended an arm, bent at the elbow. "May I have the privilege, milady?"

She put her arm in his and for a few steps they walked, linked together, with their grinning faces held high as if they were the King and Queen of the Island.

On the way back to their starting point they met a man wearing a waist length African dashiki shirt and round kofia hat. The man was stockily built and his shiny brown skin made him look as if he were made of chocolate.

"Hi, Jaws," said Brax.

"Hello," the man replied politely, looking at Dae.

"Hi," said Dae.

After the man passed, Brax said, "He lives in Seaside. He's another one of us—what do you call us—singles?"

"Widower," she said, mocking his wryness. Quickly, she changed the subject. "Is he from Africa?"

"Nah, he's an ole biscuit eatin' homeboy from South Carolina. His real name is Willie Simmons, but he changed it to Momadou Jawara. He told me once that he felt attracted to this island because it's where the last slave ship landed in America."

"The Wanderer," she said.

"Yeah. I think it makes him feel closer to his roots somehow. It's a sad piece of history, but he doesn't dwell on it. He's a good guy. We call him Jaws for short. You know—from his adopted last name and us being on the beach near the sharks and all. He's real sociable and everybody likes him. When I told him I was named after a Confederate General, he just laughed and said, 'Well, hell, I guess that makes you another lost cause.'"

"That's funny," she said.

When they returned to the beach in front of the clubhouse, Jim was gone. Brax walked Dae to her unit and invited her to join him for another walk the next morning. She accepted and they agreed to meet at the clubhouse at seven.

Brax walked away looking forward to the next morning for something other than the crossword puzzle.

⟫•⟪

# 6

Dae entered her house with mixed feelings. She couldn't deny the enjoyment of meeting Brax and the anticipation of seeing him again in the morning. Relaxed by his friendliness, she had quickly felt at ease with him. He seemed like a pleasant gentleman and rather attractive in a mature way; neatly trimmed white hair and a lean face warmly weathered by the sun and age. Seventy-ish, maybe. Something drew her to this man, a titillating reminder of her womanhood.

But she had hedged her comments about living alone. Maybe Brax would never get used to it but she was "used to it" long before John had gotten sick. Not that she wanted it that way, but that's the way it was. She didn't want to tell of her personal struggle just then and she couldn't decide if she envied his faithfulness or resented it.

Still, she had never known a man of his age with such spirited abandonment and she felt an undeniable tug of attraction. It was a feeling she hadn't experienced in a long time and she wasn't used to it. Even the comment about missing his wife was overshadowed by the impression she had of her new friend.

*He's still young at heart.*

———◆———

A couple of hours after she returned from the beach, Dae received a phone call from Justin. She had not heard from him in several days and, though she knew he was heading back to Korea soon, she wasn't sure of his whereabouts.

"Where are you?"

"I'm in Seoul. We just got here yesterday. Well, that would be tomorrow in the States. Ha! We're fourteen hours ahead, you know. It's almost midnight over here. Anyhow, I'm back at Yong-san for a while."

"Are Seon and Snow there, too?"

"Yes, they're with her parents."

"I just moved into my new place yesterday," Dae said.

"Yeah, I thought so. That's why I called. Is everything going okay?"

"It's going great. Julie was here to help me get moved in. And Ben and Jeff. They really worked hard and everything is all set up. I love it. It's so new and it's just the right size for me. It's close to the ocean, too. I went for a long walk on the beach this morning." Without a pause, she shifted directions. "How are y'all doing?"

"We're doing fine. I guess I'll stay in the Army unless they kick me out. It's kind of rough sometimes moving around to different places, but it's a good thing in some ways. I don't know what the hell I would do in the real world."

"Whatever you decide to do, I'm proud of you. I just hope you don't have to go back to Afghanistan, or one of those places where the terrorists are."

"Yeah, that was not a lot of fun. But there are terrorists every-where these days."

"The world is so scary now," she said.

"Yeah, it is. You know, it's kind of weird being a pacifist in the Army. A soldier that doesn't like to fight—that makes me an oxy-moron doesn't it? Or maybe just a moron is more like it. I'll fight if I have to, but I'm no Rambo like Dad. I'm a real wuss."

The self-deprecation in his voice irritated her. Firmly, she said, "Your father was proud of you."

"Hmm," he mused, a hint of doubt in his voice. "Well, anyway, I'm glad you're in your new place. Stay in touch and send me some pictures."

She had not seen Justin in over six months and his phone calls as well as e-mails had become less frequent lately. At forty years old, and a man by any reckoning, he remained a boy in her mind, the young blond-headed kid with the bright smile and the penchant for taking sidetracks on the path to adulthood. He was cute, and funny, and lovable, and stubborn, and irascible, all wrapped up in one package of confusion. School didn't settle well with him, though he was bright enough. It was the emphasis on subjects that seemed useless to him that turned him off. Why did he need to learn calculus, or physics, or some crazy foreign language? And why would anyone want to spend their whole life in some boring job in an office, like his father?

He would be different. He would own a bar, a cool place where people would come to drink and watch the games on big screen televisions and listen to the band. No; he would get into sales, traveling around to college campuses selling travel packages for Spring Breaks and holidays. All college kids go on big party trips. No; he would learn how to build things—walls, floors, ceilings, and, finally, whole houses. That's where the real money is; building houses and selling them to rich people. He tried them all and none worked out, each one melting under the heat of reality.

"Mom," he said one day, "I'm broke. In fact, I'm worse than that. I've got some big time debts. I've decided to join the Army. At least then I'll have a steady income. It will take a long time but I'll pay them all off."

Dae cringed at the thought of her son following the path that had left her husband scarred by the hell of war. But the sense that, at long last, he had faced up to the real world was a relief.

"I think the Army will be good for you," she said. "How much money do you need?"

"I've borrowed too much from you guys already. I can't take anymore."

They talked on before she, once again, "loaned" him some

money that John would never know about.

That was ten years ago and now she realized how hard it must have been for her son to decide on the ultimate conformist's career. But he told her he had come to realize that duty has its own rewards and there are a lot of things worse than the regimen of discipline. So for the first time in his life, he stuck with something and, in time, was promoted to sergeant. In her heart, Justin was still her boy, but Dae had seen her son become a man in full measure.

It always amazed Dae that even John found a new sense of pride in his son that somehow penetrated his invisible cloak of stoicism.

———

After Vietnam, John was a different person. He appeared well adjusted at first, but within a year, he began to have fits of moodiness. When Dae tried to talk to him, he would dismiss her with no explanation. "I'm just learning to be a citizen again," he would say.

After the fall of Saigon several years later, he became even more withdrawn.

Finally, one day she wouldn't be denied. "John," she said harshly, "what is the matter with you? You've got to talk to me. I can't stand it when you get like this."

He answered her with a blank stare.

"Do you not love me anymore?" she asked. "Is there another woman?"

"No, no. I've never touched another woman and, of course, I love you." He sighed deeply, then added, "but I don't love anything else." His voice was soft, muffled with a tone of desperation.

She waited silently for him to continue before he turned his head and looked away, his entire body as rigid as a corpse. The distance between them was like an invisible curtain that allowed them to see, but not touch, each other.

"I don't feel anything," he finally said. "Nothing I eat tastes good. Even the booze doesn't work anymore. I'm just … here." He closed his eyes and leaned his head back. "I don't know why we were there or what good it did."

She knew it. It always came back to that damn war that had been over for years. "You were serving your country," she said.

"Maybe." He paused, seeming to search for the right words. "But it felt like we were just serving the politicians. Everybody else in our own country was against us. They didn't want us being there and they didn't appreciate anything we did. It was all a waste."

"That war's over." For him to be haunted by a war that had been over long ago was maddening to her.

"Yeah, for everybody else, it's over. Like it never happened. Like the guys that died in my company never happened. Like I never saw my buddy with his brains coming out the top of his head or guys hit by land mines and nothing but pieces of their bodies left. Or women and children slaughtered like cattle and their village burned to the ground. All of that and then we just left. What the hell good did it do?" His voice became louder with each word and his face roiled with anger.

She couldn't answer that. All she could do was be there for him, try to comfort him, try to help him adjust. When the nightmares came in the night, she would hold him and tell him everything was all right. But she knew it wasn't.

The doctors at the VA hospital counseled John and gave him medication. For long stretches, he would be okay, then the nightmares would come back and the fog of depression would be even thicker. Sometimes his mind blanked out and his actions became erratic. He lost the management job at the paper mill along with any desire to be a "company man." More than a year went by with nothing but a few odd jobs. It was hard times. Finally, he got a job as a computer tech with a small company at half his former salary. That, and Dae's teaching position, kept them afloat. She supported him in every way she could, but he remained withdrawn and her love eventually wilted like a rose cut from the stem.

When Justin joined the Army, it seemed like *deja vu*, but things were different now. The American people supported the troops, if not the war. Since nine-eleven, it had become fashionable to be patriotic and a wave of national chauvinism made military service a badge of honor. So despite his bitterness and even though he knew Justin's service to be more out of necessity than patriotism, John spoke proudly of his son.

Yet Dae knew that John never forgot the hypocrisy of anti-Vietnam sentiments in the sixties and seventies. Nor the fact that he fought in the only war his country ever lost. "It tears your guts out," he told her, "to fight like hell and then watch your country just give up".

For John Whitehead, it was a war that never ended.

That evening, Dae made a cup of tea and took it to her desk in the spare bedroom. She settled in front of the computer and stared back at the document entitled *Georgia, The Thirteenth Colony.* Slowly scrolling through the pages, she read each word carefully as she had countless times before. Typos always drove her crazy and she knew how hard it is to edit your own work. The proof-reader would find the mistakes, but she wanted the manuscript to be as perfect as she could make it. Her years in the classroom had taught her that the textbook was not as important as the teacher, but she knew what the students needed to know and, more than that, what they would remember.

With a lot of material to cover in one semester, she wanted the text to accurately reflect the evolution of early American society with some reference to current times. Only in that way would it be meaningful to the students and help them understand history beyond memorizing dates and names.

She felt satisfied with the manuscript in the way that one can only be when they know their work is complete and substantial, yet imperfect. But would students find her text interesting and challenging, or would it just be another weight in their backpacks? More importantly, would the publisher think it worthy of the advance?

Scrolling through the pages, she stopped at the chapter titled "Race and Slavery." She thought of the chocolate-colored man in the African garb she had seen on the beach that morning. The casual reference Brax had made to the slave ship named *The Wanderer* reminded her of a commitment to insure the chapter be presented in complete honesty and thoroughness.

———

Dae was a young teacher fresh out of college when she found herself in an integrated class for the first time. Some fights had occurred between black and white students and there was outward hostility. The tension in the school was palpable. After class one day she spoke with a black female student who was unresponsive when called upon. Only a few years separated them in age, but there was a chasm of understanding as wide and deep as the Atlantic Ocean. She asked the girl to sit in a chair beside her desk.

"Denise, why won't you speak when I call on you?"

The young student looked at Dae defiantly and said, "Because you think I don't know nothing."

"Why do you think that?"

"Because all white people think black people are stupid." Denise stared at Dae intensely as if to burn her thoughts into Dae's soul. "I hate this school. They only let us go here because the law made them."

Having been insulated from the raging fire of the racial divide, Dae was shocked by the boldness of the girl and the venom of her words. Looking straight into the eyes of the girl, she gathered herself and tried to mask her uneasiness before speaking again.

"Denise, please don't think that way. I know you have a good mind and all white people don't think black people are stupid."

"I ain't no black person. My skin is light brown 'cause a white man done put some cream in my mama's coffeepot. And I ain't no nee-gro 'cause that's just a fancy word for nigger. And that's all I am to these lily white honkeys. They hate me and I hate them." The fiery words spewed from the girl's mouth as if the door to a furnace had been opened.

The air was thick with animosity and uncertainty tugged at Dae as she looked at the girl, pondering what to do next. She thought the girl might stand up and walk away, but she didn't. Dae moved her chair from behind the desk and positioned it beside the girl.

"Denise, I don't hate you. I'm sorry for the way things have been to make you feel the way you do. There are some bad people in the world, but there are many more good people. Don't hate everyone."

The girl didn't respond but she looked down as a tear trickled from one eye.

Dae reached out and put a hand inches above one of Denise's hands. She wasn't sure what would happen if she touched the girl, and she let her hand down cautiously, as if she was testing a hot iron. Then slowly, white flesh met brown. Denise kept her hand still and her head lowered. Touching the girl's flesh brought Dae a sense of calm and she felt a connection as if their veins shared the same blood.

"You're a beautiful young girl and I know how smart you are. Hate is a disease that's born from ignorance. I'll try as hard as I can to help you fight that disease, but I need you to do your part." She paused before asking, "If I call on you tomorrow will you say something?"

Denise remained silent and didn't look up.

"Please," Dae pleaded.

The girl wiped her eyes with her free hand.

Dae removed her hand, retrieved a tissue from a box on her desk, and handed it to Denise. "You don't have to answer now. Will you think about it?"

The two women sat silently frozen in their seats. Finally, Denise rose from her chair. With dry eyes and no sign of emotion, she faced Dae and, without looking directly at her, made a slight nodding motion before walking out of the room.

Dae remained seated for several minutes, completely drained of emotion. Then she stood and slowly began to organize her desk for the next day.

The following morning in class, she called on Denise and anxiously waited for a response. All eyes turned to Denise and the room stopped still as if on pause. After a few excruciating seconds, Denise responded calmly and correctly. Dae's pulse returned to normal and the tension in the room dissipated.

When the bell rang to end the class, she carefully observed the faces of the students as they filed out of the room. She didn't see hatred, only a group of teenagers slogging their way through another day at school. A sense of relief settled in and she looked forward with anticipation to the rest of the year.

Later as Dae left the building after the last period, she looked back at the big, brick edifice that rose three stories high with the imposing sturdiness of a fortress. She realized it wasn't just a building, rather a sanctuary for hearts as well as minds, and she felt just as much a part of it as the bricks and mortar. It was a good feeling.

Denise became an above average student and the hard edge of her personality softened a little. At the end of the year Dae gave her a big hug out of sight of other eyes. It was a tiny step, almost imperceptible but edged in the right direction. The next time the two shared a hug was when Denise came back fresh out of Spellman College. Her classroom for ninth grade math was only a few doors down from Dae's.

Dae never forgot that talk with Denise. Nor did she forget many other incidents where a bond was formed between teacher and student. There were no miracles in the classroom and frustration often trumped satisfaction, but she had lived a good part of her life doing something that she felt was worthwhile; she was a teacher. She loved her students and, in her heart, knew that she had influenced many of them in a positive way. Some even returned years later to tell her so. And, in return, she had received a gift from them; warm memories of small moments threaded together like pearls on a necklace. A beautiful keepsake.

The textbook would be a connection to her past, a learning tool for students she would never know. It would be the culmination of small triumphs into a lasting legacy. And she had promised herself she would finish it if it were the last thing she ever did.

Dae labored over the pages of the final draft for three more hours, making an occasional minor change. Finally, when she thought her head might burst from the concentration, she pushed her chair back from the computer. The manuscript was as ready as it was going to be. She pulled the flash drive out of the port and cradled it in her palm as if it were a little pink ball of flesh that had just been pulled from her womb. Too much work had gone into this to chance a crash of the hard drive. Closing her eyes, she leaned back in the chair with an overwhelming feeling of fatigue.

*Oh Lord, this is hard. I need a glass of wine.*

# 7

The crossword puzzle was hard the next morning but Brax completed it without blanking out on a familiar word. The old couple that he normally saw in the clubhouse had arrived before him and they left as he waited for Dae.

When he went to the men's room, he noticed the man had left his crossword puzzle book on the counter beside the lavatory. Out of curiosity, he opened the book and looked at one of the puzzles. All of the blanks had been filled in but most of them didn't make words. Many of the spaces had markings with two letters written on top of each other at the intersection of the vertical and horizontal words. He flipped through the book and each of the completed puzzles was marked in the same way with letters randomly connected like a mysterious code. There were some unfinished puzzles in the book, so he returned it to the table where the couple always sat, wondering how long it would be before he stopped seeing them there.

When Dae arrived they walked to the beach. This time Jim wasn't in his usual spot and Brax wasn't sure if his absence was purposeful, but he was glad to be alone with Dae again. It was a windy day and cooler than the previous day, so they were dressed in light jackets and long pants. Dae's pace was much slower than the day before and that suited him just fine. The walk became more of a moving conversation than an effort of exercise.

Before they had gone far, they approached the sign designating the loggerhead nesting site.

"I noticed that yesterday," Dae said, "and I didn't see anything except where the sand was stirred up in little piles. How did anyone find the nest and know what it was?"

"The turtles come to this same place every year," Brax said. "The Fish and Game people know where to look."

"When will they hatch?"

"About a month from now. As the time gets closer we can come here and watch for the hatchlings."

"Oh, that will be exciting."

Talking about the endangered turtles renewed in Brax the dark thoughts about the impending development of the island. That could completely destroy their nesting sites. But now, more interested in the company of his new companion, he cast those thoughts aside and turned the conversation back to Dae.

"Are you settled in?" he asked. "Is there any way I can help you?"

"No, I'm fine." She grinned and added, "Unless you're good at editing text books."

"I'm afraid not. Is that what you do?"

"I've just completed a history textbook, but it needs some polishing. I feel pretty good about the material and the organization, but I'm not great at punctuation and sentence structure and the technicalities of writing."

"Me either. But writing a book—that's impressive."

"It's taken a while. I've been working on it ever since I retired seven years ago. It's kind of a hobby, but I think it turned out pretty well. Oh gosh, that sounds like I'm tooting my own horn. It's just a boring book taken from the works of a lot of other people smarter than me."

*Tooting her own horn—that's funny,* he thought. *I used to toot my own horn, too.*

"I'd like to read your book. I watch The History Channel a lot and that was my favorite subject in school. It's boring to some people, but it fascinates me."

"That's nice to know. Of course I love it, too. Otherwise I would have been bored out of my mind for thirty-seven years if I hadn't liked what I was doing."

"I sold insurance in my former life. Pretty dull stuff, but it kept food on the table and I met a lot of interesting people. That's all it is, a people business."

"I'm sure. I worked with a really diverse group of people in my job also, but they were all teenagers. That is, except for the other teachers and some of them were crazy as bedbugs." She laughed.

"I know; I sold insurance to a lot of them. But teaching is a noble profession. I couldn't deal with the kids the way they are these days. They don't have respect for anybody or anything."

"Yes, it's not the way it was when we were growing up."

There was something about the way she spoke, the way she carried herself, the way that she seemed comfortable in his presence that created a spark in him that had been missing for a long time. It was as if his chemistry had changed. That was the phrase his boss had used once years before.

---

"Brax, your numbers are down." His boss sat in a high-back leather chair behind a big wooden desk, peering over a stack of papers.

"I'm still one of your top producers, though," he replied.

It wasn't true. There were plaques and framed awards on his office walls, but for the last two years he had gotten off the path and into the weeds. He looked at the man who was not only his boss but also his best friend. His boss didn't respond but continued to look at the reports in front of him as if that would change the numbers.

"Some of the new guys are coming on pretty strong," his boss finally said.

"So what are you saying? I'm Willy Loman, or something?"

"No. You're still Brax Donovan, the best salesman I've ever worked with. But your chemistry has changed."

He didn't need an explanation. He knew exactly what his boss meant, but he didn't realize it was so obvious. It was no longer exciting to wine and dine clients, to be a sycophant for corporate brass, to be the life of the party, to keep climbing, keep pushing. He had settled into the place where he was going to be and had become the person he was going to become. It wasn't complacency or boredom as much as it was resignation. It was the knowledge that there was nothing more. He could almost hear Peggy Lee singing in his head, *Is that all there is ...?*

"Don't worry, I can still get the job done."

"I know you can."

They both lied.

Before the year ended he retired. They gave him another plaque. After the most miserable year of his life, he found another company that gave him a chance. He fell in with guys half his age and gave just enough effort to get by for another three years.

After he finally retired for good, he and Jane shared five of the best years of their marriage. The love that once burned white hot in their youth returned with the warmth of embers as if stoked by a gust of wind. When she died the emptiness seemed unbearable before he eventually settled into the ashes of emotional inertia.

Being with Dae affected his chemistry for the better. He could feel the depression and malaise being exorcised as he walked beside this woman he had only known for a couple of days.

When they were leaving the beach and heading back to their units, he asked, "Tomorrow?"

"I'll be here," she answered. Then as he walked away, she said, "Uh, would you like to have dinner with me tonight?" She had a funny look on her face as if surprised by her own boldness. "At my house," she added. "I can put together a little something. Of course, if you have plans, I'll understand."

"No, no," he said quickly. "That sounds great. I appreciate the offer."

"Is six o'clock okay?" she asked.

"Yes, that's fine." If she had said midnight, it would have been fine with him.

"I'll see you then. I'm in unit ninety-eight."

"It's a date," he said with a grin that might have embarrassed him if it hadn't felt so good.

———————

After he returned from the long walk with Dae, Brax was energized. He turned the lights on and, with the blinds open for the first time in weeks, the sun glared through the windows with a warm brightness. The words of Dr. Mathews were still fresh in his mind and the thought of prostate cancer was sobering, but somehow he didn't feel down. Even the possibility of being the victim of development receded into the realm of a distant future. Instead, there was a certain vitality coming back to him. Remembering how it felt to enjoy living, not in the past or in the future, but in real time.

He retrieved the black case from under the bed and took out the horn. He contorted his lips and tongue on the mouthpiece, seeking that old feeling of the embouchure. When he forced the air from his mouth, no sound came out. His lips felt stiff and he blew harder. Nothing. Then he remembered to relax and his lips quivered as he let out a small stream of air. A few notes came out weak and out of focus. Slowly, the sound came back and he warmed up with long, slow notes.

It would be a fitful, dispiriting process like an athlete trying to get back into shape after years of being a couch potato. Ten years; that's how long it had been since he played his last note. Even then he was just fooling around. Sometimes, at holiday parties he would play a little, and a couple times at church. It was a welcomed respite from selling insurance, but it got to a point where he couldn't hit the notes anymore. Now he decided that perfection didn't matter. He knew that, like singing in the shower, it's the personal connection to the music, though raw and far from perfect, that provides satisfaction.

Closing his eyes, Brax began to play "Stardust," then stopped. After several false starts, he finished the first verse of the slow, melancholy song. Following that, he picked up the pace , playing random notes with no particular tune.

After the last note he whispered, "More practice." Then he placed the trumpet back into the case and slid it under the bed.

*That's a start*, he thought.

Yes, that's what it felt like: a start.

---

When Dae arrived home she saw the message light on the telephone blinking. Julie had called to see how things were going. It was still early and Dae called right back, hoping to catch her daughter at work before she got tied up in meetings.

"Are you busy?" she asked, when Julie answered.

"Not right now. I've got a meeting in an hour but I can talk for a few minutes. How is everything going?"

She told her daughter about her conversation with Justin and reiterated how much she was enjoying her new home.

"That sounds great. I wish I was there instead of sitting in a conference room in a boring meeting all day. Have you met any of your neighbors?"

"Yes, a few. I walked the last couple of mornings with a nice man. He's a widower from Atlanta and we enjoy talking to each other."

"That's nice. You mean he's not like Dad used to be?" Julie said, her voice laced with derision.

"Julie!"

"I'm sorry. Anyhow, I'm glad you're settling in. Tell me more about this man. He sounds … interesting. You told him about Dad didn't you?"

"Of course." It wasn't the truth, but Dae intended to correct that soon.

"Good. Sounds like y'all hit it off."

"As I said, we just walked on the beach and talked. Julie, you know I wouldn't—"

"Mom, it's okay. Dad's not with us anymore and you need to move on. Justin and I understand that."

"Well, maybe it's the new house or being near the ocean. I don't know, but I do feel ready to move on with my life. I invited him over for dinner tonight." It was an impulsive comment as if a newly found sense of self had been included with the purchase price of her new home.

"All right, Mom! I knew getting out of that big old dark house would be good for you."

"Don't get all excited. We're just having dinner, for heaven's sake."

"Okay, but it's a start."

"Oh, come on. Quit making such a big deal out of it. You're embarrassing me. But the last few days *have* seemed like a new start in a way."

"I'm so happy to see you be you, again."

"Yes, the move has been a good change for me. Everything is going well, but I know you've got to get back to work. Tell the girls I said hi."

When she hung up the phone Dae, felt a sense of relief. It was comforting to sort out some of her thoughts with Julie, knowing her daughter could sense her uncertainty. And she found satisfaction in her daughter's approval even if it did seem as if their roles had been reversed.

Even though she had all day, she began right away planning for the meal, making a list for the supermarket, and how much she had to do to get her brand new home ready for a visitor. Despite downplaying it to Julie, it was a big deal.

The textbook could wait for another day.

# 8

It was almost noon when Brax went to pick up Jim at his house to go to lunch. He rang the doorbell twice and started to walk away before the door opened. Jim was in his underwear, red-eyed and grim-faced.

"Geez, you look like you just got run over by a train. Did I wake you up?"

Jim ran his hands through his thin, tousled hair. "Nah," he replied. He looked at Brax with no explanation.

"Did you forget we were going to lunch?"

"Mmm," Jim mumbled, "I guess so."

"Are you all right?"

"Yeah," Jim said, without moving from the door.

Brax was startled to see Jim like that in the middle of the day and he knew something wasn't right. "Can I come in?"

"Uh, ... okay. We can be all right together."

Once inside, Brax became more concerned. Everything was a mess. Clothes, magazines and empty glasses were scattered about the living room. In the kitchen, dirty dishes were piled in the sink and the counters were littered with open containers of food. A half-empty bottle of vodka stood on the table.

"I need to take a leak," Brax said.

"Help yourself."

As Brax walked away, Jim asked, "Something wrong with your toilet?"

"I just went at my place, but the old bladder likes an encore." Brax spoke with his head to the side as he opened the bathroom door. "Put it on my bill."

"Just don't take a crap," Jim hollered. "That's extra."

The bathroom was as unkempt as the rest of the house and there was urine on the toilet seat.

"You need to aim a little better," Brax said, returning to the kitchen.

"Just a little *projectile* dysfunction," replied Jim nonchalantly. "You want a Bloody Mary?" He grabbed his drink from beside the bottle on the table.

"No."

It was obvious that Jim had forgotten about lunch and Brax wondered if he should stay. Jim was his friend and he wanted to help him, but he had his own problems and he wasn't sure if he could handle someone else's.

"Well, how about a beer?" Jim asked. "And some chips? Sorry, I'm all out of caviar."

"No, I'm good."

"You want to sit for a spell?"

"Yeah, why don't we?"

They went into the living room where Jim gathered a sweat suit from the sofa and put it on. He grabbed his drink again and sat down facing Brax.

"So how are you and the good looking granny getting along?"

"We just walk the beach and talk, like you and me. You weren't there this morning so we went on. You can join us tomorrow."

"Maybe. I've been a little under the weather lately. I'm sorry things are kinda messy".

Brax nodded his head.

"That's a bullshit excuse," Jim added. "I've just been lazy as hell."

Brax looked at Jim and felt like he was looking at himself. At least the person he had been before he met Dae. Loneliness, emptiness, malaise; he knew all about it. But he had never seen that in Jim. He knew about the alcoholic past and the weekly visits to AA, but this was a side of Jim he had never seen.

"I'll help you clean up."

"No, I'll do it." Jim spoke with a tone of tired resignation.

"Something you want to talk about?" Brax asked.

Jim rubbed his eyes and took a sip of his drink. The room became stone silent.

"Nine years," Jim finally said. "Nine years, three months, and seventeen days. That's what I told them this week at the meeting. But yesterday I fell in the big black hole where this son-of-a bitch lives. That would've been the eighteenth day." He talked slowly and wistfully as if he were talking to himself and the words tumbled out of his mouth with a slight alcohol induced slur. He didn't seem to be stinking drunk. Maybe a little high, a little loose tongued, but apparently not totally out of touch with reality.

Brax didn't say anything. He didn't know any words that would make things better.

"What do we do now?" Jim asked childlike. He said "we" as if the alcohol was just a part of a bigger question.

Brax knew what he meant. "We" were people like the two of them. People that looked at their lives in the rear view mirror as if everything was in the past. People without life partners and nothing to really look forward to except the inevitability that comes with the last years. Brax put his hands together as if praying and rested them under his chin. He gathered his thoughts before replying.

"We keep on living."

Jim brought the drink to his mouth and took a big swallow, draining the glass. His eyes winced as he rolled the red liquid around in his mouth and absorbed the words from Brax.

"Yeah. Yeah, I guess we do. Some of us do, anyhow."

"I know how you feel," Brax said. "I lost my wife, too. And sometimes I think that she took a big part of me with her, but—

like they say—life goes on. You've got to keep spittin' and gettin'. That's what you told me and you were right."

Slowly the sorrow faded from Jim's face. Brax looked at his friend and thought he saw a glimmer, just the faintest promise of hope in Jim's eyes. Maybe he was only imagining it, maybe only wishing it, but that was enough to make him glad he had come.

"Why don't we get some lunch?" Brax said.

Jim seemed to wrestle with other thoughts as he considered the question. Finally, he said, "Okay." He slowly rose from the sofa. "Let me put on some decent clothes. I'll clean up the place when I get back."

"I'll help," Brax said.

"You already have," Jim said with a ring of sincerity.

Jim's mood brightened during lunch at a little hole-in-the-wall sandwich shop. "Tell me more about your new friend," he said.

"You mean Dae?"

"You know good and well who I mean. Yes, Dae."

"She's nice. Not as nice as you, of course, but she's better to look at."

"You're hurting my feelings. But look, seriously, you guys seem to go together. You know, like butter and grits."

"I don't know about that, but I guess I haven't scared her off because she invited me to dinner tonight."

"See. I knew it. You can't have grits without butter."

"Jim, you're so full of bullshit it's coming out your ears."

"There're worse things to be full of." Jim's mood suddenly turned somber again.

*That's an odd thing to say,* Brax thought. He guessed that Jim was still thinking of his personal war with alcohol, a war that they say is a daily battle. Still, Jim was his best friend and Brax decided he needed to tell someone about his own situation.

"I need you to be sober tomorrow. Okay?"

"You don't need it near as much as I do, but okay, that's the plan. What are we going to do, rob a bank or something?"

"I need you to take me somewhere. It's not far, but I need a driver." Then he proceeded to tell Jim where he needed to go.

"You've got to be crazy. Why did you wait 'til the last minute to tell me?"

"I was going to drive myself, but I guess somebody else needs to know where I'll be. And I don't want to leave my car."

Jim cursed Brax for being such an idiot in keeping things secret, but he agreed to be his chauffer just as Brax knew he would. They made their plan and Jim reluctantly agreed to Brax's request not to talk about it to anyone.

When they got back from lunch they began to clean up Jim's place. Brax went to work on the living room while Jim started in the kitchen. The drawer on one of the end tables beside the sofa was ajar and, as Brax went to shut it, he got a glimpse of something shiny. He pulled the drawer out and saw the revolver. Picking up the gun carefully, he noted the bullets in the chambers. Brax stood motionless with the gun in his hand and turned to see Jim looking at him from behind the bar in the kitchen.

"Expecting a home invasion?" he asked, in an effort to break the tension.

Jim walked into the living room. "You never know." He took the gun from Brax, opened the cylinder, removed the bullets, and put the gun back in the drawer. "It was my Granddad's," he said. "Been in the family for years."

"Jim, you don't need this," Brax said.

"It's just for hunting," Jim said with a smirk. "You know, thinning out the herd of developers."

Brax noted the sarcastic attempt at humor but he could see a side of Jim that he had never seen and it was unsettling. Still, he didn't want to overreact and he guessed Jim wasn't the only retiree that lived alone with a gun at the ready.

As they finished the cleanup, Jim gathered all of the unconsumed liquor and beer and put it in a plastic garbage bag. "I'm getting rid of this," he said.

"I'll take it to the dumpster," Brax volunteered.

"No, I will. I have to do it myself. But you can go with me."

"I trust you."

"I know you do. I might need a little help though. It's broad daylight but that son-of-a-bitch in the black hole might still be looking for me."

Brax didn't know whether that was funny or sad but he walked across the parking lot with Jim and watched as he tossed the bag into the dumpster. Jim stared into space for a second before he turned around to go home. Brax gave him a friendly pat on the back and began walking to his own unit. He could only hope that Jim would keep the gun in the drawer with the bullets removed.

"Get a good night's sleep and drink a lot of coffee in the morning," he said, turning back. "Don't forget, I'm putting my life in your hands tomorrow."

"Don't worry, I haven't had but three wrecks this year. Ha!"

Brax knew Jim was kidding and he trusted him to sober up. If push came to shove, he could drive himself. Of more concern was the gun in Jim's house. Something told him there was more to it than Jim had admitted to.

On the way back to his unit, Brax was passed by a white mini-van with the words Evergreen Gardens on the side. In the back of the van he could see the elderly couple that had been in the clubhouse each morning. And he realized he would never see them there again because he knew where they were headed. It was a place where he never wanted to go.

He looked at his watch and it was after one o'clock. In a few hours it would be time to break out that shirt in the plastic bag from the cleaners that had been hanging in the closet for at least six months. He had a dinner date with a pretty lady.

# 9

As Brax approached Dae's unit he realized he was fifteen minutes early. He kept walking, hoping she wouldn't see him from a window. It reminded him of his first date as a teenager when he had arrived ridiculously early.

———◆———

When challenged to a dare by one of his buddies, Brax called Mary Ann Gillingham, a cheerleader and one of the prettiest girls in school, and nervously asked her for a date. To his surprise, she accepted and, for the next week, he thought about little else. Then the big night arrived.

He was sixteen years old and it was the first time he had driven his mother's car by himself. Feeling like a grown-up, he wanted to act mature which meant being on time. But the drive to Mary Ann's house didn't take as long as he expected so he circled around the neighborhood until he finally decided it was okay.

He was still half an hour early when he knocked on her door. Naturally, she wasn't ready and he was too naïve to be totally embarrassed. It took him a while to realize what a giveaway it was but Mary Ann acted as if it was perfectly normal. In short time, she made him feel relaxed in her presence and before the night was over he was hopelessly snared. More dates followed and, in time, they became a steady couple. Mary Ann's affection stoked his ego and she made him feel special even when he did goofball things.

Eventually teenage infatuation ran its course, but Brax never lost his affection for his first girlfriend who helped him discover something he had never known before. Confidence.

⸺◦⸺

Brax felt like a teenager once again when he rang Dae's doorbell at six o'clock on the dot.

She opened the door with a cheery "Hi." Then her voice slowed and her smile widened as she looked at the bundle in his hand. "Come on in."

He stepped inside and handed her a dozen red roses. "Thanks for inviting me over."

"Oh, my gosh, you shouldn't have. Thank you, they're lovely. They match my outfit. You must have ESP."

Dae was dressed casually in white slacks and a red printed blouse. Everything about her, including the bright red lipstick and nail polish to the slight blush of makeup on her cheeks, was perfectly coordinated.

"You look very nice," Brax said. "As usual."

"Thank you." Her smile widened. "You look sharp, too. I like your shirt. Now we know what we look like when we're not beach bums. Come, make yourself comfortable. I'll put these in a vase."

She led him into the living room before proceeding to the kitchen with the flowers in her arm. Beyond the pass-through counter top, he could see her place the roses in a tall, clear vase and fill it with water in the sink.

As soon as he entered her house Brax knew he was in a woman's world. The furniture and accessories were carefully placed within the limited space and arranged in an eclectic, yet complimentary, way like he had seen in Jane's Southern Living magazines. There was no hint of a man's presence. No ugly, overstuffed, lounge chair, golf trophies, mounted fish, or collegiate knickknacks lying around. Beyond the vision was the smell. The house possessed the unmistakable fragrance of a woman. It was not the overpowering odor of too much perfume, rather a pleasant bouquet as if the rooms had been given a bath and spritzed with a scent of freshness.

Then catching the aroma of food wafting from the kitchen, he felt a total sensory awakening that evoked the warmth of a home that was not just a set of walls, but bore the fingerprints of someone's life.

He took a seat on the sofa in the living room. She returned from the kitchen to place the roses on the mantle and then sat facing him in a high back chair.

"Um, they smell so good. They are beautiful."

"Beautiful flowers for a beautiful lady." He didn't mean to be so bold but struck by her simple elegance and the attractive surroundings, he couldn't resist the comment.

"Such flattery."

She modestly downplayed his compliment, but Brax was sure she savored his words. He was comfortable in Dae's presence when they walked on the beach but now, despite the light atmosphere, he felt like he was on display and he sat more upright than was his custom, almost stiffly. Glancing around the room, he observed the décor more closely: an oriental vase filled with long-stem dried grasses, an oil painting of a coastal marsh, a mahogany colored accent table with intricate carving and gilded accents, a sisal rug in a herringbone pattern. It reminded him of one of Seaside's meticulously staged model homes.

"Your home is well decorated. Did you do it yourself?"

"Yes, with some help from my daughter. Thank you."

"My unit looks more like the 'before' picture in one those home improvement shows on TV, but it works for me." Muffling a laugh, he added, "I don't have a lot of guests."

"I have more space than I need. This unit is really designed for a couple. I certainly don't need a double garage."

"Well, I'm sure you've seen all those golf carts running around.

That's where they put them. I'm not ready for that. I think the more sedentary you become, the faster you get old." He smiled and added, "I guess old is a matter of perspective. I think it has as much to do with your mind as your body."

"I agree," she said. "Those morning walks are a great way to stay in shape and I'm sure the crossword puzzles are good exercises for your brain. I think you're still young at heart."

He felt a blush of self-consciousness and crossed his legs, then set his hands on his thighs. "Not always, but I try." Realizing his penchant for fatalism, he felt like an imposter, but he was glad she saw the good side of him.

"Yes, I think it's true that age is a state of mind. But more importantly," she added slyly, "are you ready to eat?"

"Sure." Her abrupt segue from the small talk was a relief and, as he rose from his chair, he faked a smile to hide a grimace from the stiffness in his knees. He stood straight and tall, as if on inspection, before following her to the dining area.

During the meal, the conversation revolved around the state of the world and stories in the local news. Brax didn't bring up his concern about development and kept his pessimism under control, not wanting to come across as the naysayer Jim accused him of being. He even ate the salad and refrained from calling it "rabbit food."

When he finished the last bite of his key lime pie, he took a sip of decaf coffee, and leaned back in his chair. "That was delicious," he said. "I haven't had a home cooked meal since I don't know when, and I love pork chops. You're a good cook, just like Jane … uh, my wife." Embarrassed by the reference to his deceased wife, Brax quickly tried to square things "Of course," he added, "I'm sure your husband told you that many times.".

She stared at him for a moment. Then she said, "Yes, he is … I mean, *was* very thoughtful, like you." She patted her mouth with a napkin. "I'm glad you enjoyed the meal"

Brax felt a little uneasy when Dae began to refer to her husband in the present tense, but being familiar with the bond that lingers beyond the grave, he didn't dwell on the thought. He attempted to help her clean the table but Dae protested. She removed a bottle of red wine from a small rack above the counter and he dutifully uncorked it before they returned to the living room to chat.

Warmed to Dae's company, Brax finally brought up the issue of development. "I hate to say it, but I'm afraid the State is going to give in to the developers. If they do, it will really change the island. And not in a good way." He took a swig of wine, which, like all wines, tasted like mouthwash to him, but the tingle of alcohol kicked in immediately.

"Oh, we'll still have our little patch of Eden," she replied.

"Maybe, but they'll build a bunch of high rise hotels and condos and shopping centers and stuff. The beaches will be packed with people from who-knows-where and the roads will be backed up with traffic."

"You really think it will be that bad?"

"Look at all the other islands. Once they start there's no stopping the bastards." He gritted his teeth, then raised his voice a notch as he set his wine glass on the end table. "They can't let us have one simple place free from over-damn-development." He caught himself getting carried away and quickly lowered his tone. "I'm sorry. I didn't mean to get on my soapbox."

"It's okay. I knew about the plans for development when I decided to move here, but I still thought it would be a good place for me. "

"Yes, I'm sure it will be. Like you said, we'll still have our little patch." He began to backtrack, feeling guilty for creating doubts about her new home. "Besides, it may never happen. Even if it does it could be a long time before it's completed."

Dae looked around and stared at a wall as if she could see through it all the way to the ocean. "I hated to move away from my friends in Savannah. I still go back every Thursday to visit a friend who can't drive. But I love this place."

"I do, too. Don't pay any attention to me. I'm just an old curmudgeon."

"No, I've been around you long enough to know better."

He took that as a compliment, especially from someone who had only known him for two days. The little ego boost felt good, but he moved the focus of the conversation away from himself.

"It's funny. Seaside was only built a few years ago and now we don't want any more building. We want to draw the line right here. I know it's hypocritical and that's the *Catch 22*, but the kind of development they're talking about is just too much." He spoke more calmly. "Oh well" he added, "I guess you can't hold back progress."

"No, I think not. Of course, progress is just another word for change. We've seen enough of that in our lifetime—some good, some not so good." She exchanged blank looks with Brax for a second. "Oh my, that was profound, wasn't it?" she said with a grin.

"Yeah." He returned the grin. "Did you put that in your book?"

They both laughed and the specter of development faded away.

Afterward, the conversation flowed smoothly, but there remained a veil of reserve that kept each of them from delving into the past. Except for the awkward comments about Jane and John after dinner, there was no further mention of their former marriages.

Then Brax made a clumsy comment.

"It's taken me a good while to get used to living alone." He stared into space for a second before turning on a grin. "Now, I don't have anyone to argue with except myself."

Dae opened her mouth as if to speak, but then simply nodded with an affected smile.

"I'm sorry," he said. "That was self-indulgent. I'm sure you've—" He cut himself short, realizing he was digging the hole deeper. "Don't pay any attention to my gibberish."

"Brax, I need … ," she began. There was a serious look on her face, but she turned aside and the words seemed to be stuck in her throat.

*What she needs is for me to change the subject,* he thought. "You need another glass of wine."

Dae turned back and looked at Brax with squinted eyes as if looking straight into his mind. Then she seemed to snap out of a trance and said, "Yes." She stood up. "Why don't we go outside? Get some fresh air."

"Sounds good."

He knew he had touched a nerve. Maybe he was the first man with whom she had shared a social evening as a widow, her "first date" in a sense. He had experienced a couple of short-lived relationships since his wife's death seven years earlier and remembered having, at first, a spooky feeling that Jane was watching over him. And the thought that Dae's deceased husband's ghost might still be hovering over her head was unnerving. Yeah, some fresh air, that's what they both needed.

She refilled their glasses in the kitchen on the way to the patio. Sitting at a table under the shade of an umbrella, they made small talk while the warm day slowly ebbed away. As Brax sipped the wine, it seemed to bypass his throat and go directly to his head with a warm flush. His attraction to Dae was undeniable and he steeled himself against the numbing effect of the wine to keep his inhibitions in check. Beyond her looks, there was a certain bearing about her that mesmerized him. Her voice carried a pleasant tone, the proper English of an educated woman blended with the unmistakable Southern flavor of her roots. As they talked, he sensed that the wine loosened her up as it did him.

"Has anyone ever told you that you look like Lee Marvin?" she asked. "You even sound a little like him."

"Ah, you've found me out," he said with a feigned look of surprise. "That's just my stage name."

"He's dead," she said with a smile.

"Uh, I guess that's a giveaway. You might call it a dead giveaway." He felt a tinge of satisfaction in the little touch of humor.

For a few seconds he stared at her as if he were assessing her features. "Has anyone ever told you that you look like Bo Derek?" Her eyes opened wide and she started to speak, but before she could get any words out, he added, "I mean the way that she looks now." He thought of the banter he and Jim had when they first saw Dae on the beach and calling her "a ten on the granny scale." It was a ridiculous comparison and obviously a way to deflect her comment about his looks.

"Oh, you know that's not true. I haven't seen her in a long time but I don't think she looks a thing like me."

"She should," he said. That embarrassed him, and he figured it did her as well, but he wasn't sorry he said it.

After an awkward pause, she said, "Well, I promise you won't see me running out of the surf in a form fitting one-piece bathing suit to the tune of … what was it … "Bolero"?" She laughed at the thought.

"And I promise not to sic the Dirty Dozen on you," he said. "But really—Lee Marvin? I was thinking more of John Wayne." With a drawn out imitation of the Duke, he added, "P-i-l-g-r-i-m".

The silly bantering was a tonic for Brax, a shot of his old self, but after they emptied their wineglasses for the second time, he decided it was time to go. Not that he wanted to go, but he was cautious to keep his attraction in check. He wasn't sure if she felt the same and he didn't want to be too bold.

"I'll be gone for the next few days," he said, as he readied to leave. "There's some business I have to take care of. So I won't be able to walk with you in the morning. I'll miss that."

"I'll miss it, too," she said. "When will you be back?"

"I'm not sure, but I'll catch up with you as soon as I can."

"I'll be here."

Her words sounded like a promise. Now he really didn't want to go, but he had already started. As she walked him to the door he frantically considered how to say good-bye. A kiss on the cheek seemed a little too forward, a handshake too formal. He turned to her, hesitated, then impulsively embraced her loosely with a friendly hug.

"Thank you, again, for the meal. Thanks for the conversation, too. I've had a very nice evening."

"It's been my pleasure."

He took her hands in his, looked into her eyes and nodded, as if to say yes, it was a pleasure.

"I love the roses," she said as he opened the door. "Please call me when you get back."

"I will." *You better believe I will.*

After Dae closed the door behind him, Brax could still feel the cool softness of her hands. He walked to his house thinking about how good it felt to be with her and how much he wanted to see her again. His outlook on the future had completely changed.

*I'm not giving up. I may be an endangered species, but I'm not ready for extinction.*

———·◇·———

Dae watched through the sidelight as Brax walked away, then retrieved her wine glass and refilled it with just enough for a couple of sips. Standing in the middle of the quiet living room, she could still feel the warm strength in his hands as she stared down into the glass. She took a sip and reflected on her thoughts about the evening. In a way, she felt liberated by the mutual attraction of a man and the sense that she was still a woman in full, rather than just another senior citizen living out the years.

However, when she walked into the bedroom, she couldn't shake her concern about the reference to Bo Derek. It was fun at the time and she went along with the banter good-naturedly but to her, the comparison was more sobering than absurd.

John had called her "my ten" when they made love after seeing the movie years before. Now she looked at him in their wedding picture on her dresser. He was handsome and a big smile let the world know he was a lucky man.

John stared back from inside the frame as if he were standing there in front of her. Then her gaze moved from the picture to the mirror. She looked at herself for a good while before putting her hands over her eyes. She felt guilty, but all she could think about was Brax.

"I'll tell him soon," she whispered.

# *10*

Dr. Mathews told Brax that prostate cancer is increasingly common as men age, but it's very treatable when detected in the early stage. Brax had always felt strangely invincible to physical maladies, even though the stamina that once carried him through marathons at a seven minute pace was now just a distant memory with an artificial knee as a reminder.

His fitness level was better than most men his age and he had kept his weight reasonably in check. Still, there was no way to ward off the effects of heredity. Both of his parents as well as his brother had succumbed to cancer, so he knew that his odds were not good. It even consumed his wife and, though Jane shared no genes with him, it was another signal that the cancer vulture was circling overhead looking for another carcass.

It was his spirit, though, that betrayed Brax more than his body. Sometimes he felt transparent, as if people could look at him and see that he had lost his enthusiasm. They didn't realize he had once been the vibrant, self-assured life of the party, the leader of the band. Perhaps they thought he had always been that guy who sat quietly alone in the clubhouse, hovering over his crossword puzzle, someone who seemed polite but showed little inclination to join in the social life of the close knit community. Maybe that's what they thought. Sometimes he felt that way, too, like he had always been that person instead of the Brax Donovan that he used to be.

Meeting Dae had changed all of that. At first, he had tried to put up a front, acting more casual than he felt. But he soon felt a stir of optimism, a sense of anticipation that he hadn't felt in a long time. Even the thought of prostate surgery didn't totally dampen his sprits. The sooner it was over the sooner he could get back to spending more time with her. He wouldn't allow himself to consider the alternative.

———⊷———

Jim picked up Brax at six a.m. and they spoke sparingly until they neared the hospital in Brunswick.

"I think your sons are going to be mad that you didn't tell them about this," Jim said.

"It would just make them worry and feel like they had to come down here to be with me," Brax said. "I don't want them to feel that way. You've got their telephone numbers, just in case."

"You can count on me," said Jim.

"I know I can."

In depending on Jim, Brax trusted his friend had recovered from his relapse and wouldn't fall completely off the wagon. Still, there was a sliver of question in his mind, knowing that alcoholics are never totally in control of their actions.

At the hospital, Brax checked in at the registry desk before taking a seat awaiting the nurse to take him to the prep station. "I'll see you later," he said to Jim.

Jim sat down beside Brax. "I'm not going anywhere."

"You don't need to hang around. There's no telling how long this will take."

"It doesn't matter. I'm an old retired codger—remember? I can read my book here just as well as I can at home." Jim lifted a hardback novel in one hand.

"This might take longer than it takes you to read that book."

"I'm a slow reader. Besides, I've got another one in the car." Jim looked at Brax sternly. "I'm not leaving."

Brax nodded. "Okay." He leaned back in his chair, nervously

bouncing one leg and, with his fingers entwined, he began twiddling his thumbs. "The cafeteria is just down the hall on the left," he said.

"Don't worry about me," Jim responded. "I can take care of myself. You're the dadgum patient."

Within a few minutes, a cheerful nurse in a floral print scrub top appeared from the hallway. "Mr. Donovan?" she said, looking at the two men.

"That's me." Brax stood and said a final, "See you later," to Jim.

He followed the nurse through the door and into the corridor. The spotless, shiny floor led past rows of rooms identified with the patient's name. Beyond the closed doors he imagined a variety of poor souls suffering from God-knows-what and whose lives begged the mercy of modern medicine and the grace of The Almighty.

He was about to be one of those poor souls and the reality of the situation began to sink in. For the first time, he worried about the possibility that the operation might not be a cure-all, and even so, the effects it would have on his normal bodily functions. The thoughts were unsettling and he wished he were back on the beach with Dae.

———

Dae took the flash drive from her computer and looked at it, wondering how such a small thing could hold all the words she had written. Five years of work was wrapped up in a neat little package that seemed so insignificant. She had checked and rechecked to make sure all of the changes dictated by the editor had been made. The manuscript was so familiar to her now that she couldn't stand to go over it again. The exciting prospect of getting the book published had dimmed in the exhaustion of details. Beyond any tangible results that might follow, simply completing the task was the only reward she now sought.

She wished she'd been able to complete the book before she lost

John. In the last years he had become more and more withdrawn into a world of his own. Spurred by a failed career and haunted by memories of the insane horror of a war many years before, he had faded into deep depression. He carried those memories inside and they ate away at his soul as surely as Agent Orange had ravaged the vital organs of some of his buddies. Even as he fell deeper into an abyss of darkness, he was never cruel or spiteful and he always told her he was proud of her. Unrequited, her love withered like a beautiful orchid thirsting for water, but she never thought of leaving him. Instead, she buried herself in her book and hoped that someday he would come to a reckoning with his demons. That day never came.

She opened a desk drawer and pulled out a picture from a family vacation long-ago. They were at Lake Tahoe, all four of them bundled in their insulated suits and wrap-around helmets, looking puffy and bulky like astronauts. Behind them the big, black snowmobiles sat starkly against the powdery white snow that covered the ground and clung to the limbs of the pine trees. The picture was taken seventeen years earlier, so Julie would have been twenty-five and Justin twenty-two.

She sat behind John as he dutifully followed the guide in the caravan of snowmobiles. They couldn't go too fast on the winding mountain trail, but once they got to the open meadow, the guide let them open up at full throttle. Dae held on as John propelled the big Yamaha across the meadow at seventy miles an hour, bouncing off the high spots like jet skiing on an ocean of snow. Julie and Justin were on individual snowmobiles and they raced back and forth across the meadow, their excited screams drowned out by the noise of the machines. The air was brisk and clear and the pristine countryside gave them the feeling of being in another world.

In the evening the family had a Christmas Eve meal in town. Afterward, they walked the streets in their new sweaters and hats and scarves, warm clothes they seldom needed at home. Later they gathered in front of the fireplace in their cabin and played Scrabble like they had when the kids were young. Dae and Julie drank hot chocolate while John and Justin swigged from bottles of dark German beer. Christmas music spilled from the radio.

"Boy, was that snowmobiling fun or what?" John asked.

"Yes," Dae responded. Her eyes opened wide with excitement. Seeing the contentment on John's face was almost too much to bear and she had to hold back tears of joy.

"Can you believe it?" Julie said. "We're having a white Christmas."

"It's cool," Justin agreed.

Dae felt as if she were in a make-believe setting, like a feel-good movie. "It's wonderful," she said.

It was the only white Christmas she had ever experienced and it *was* wonderful. The setting was idyllic; the change of scenery, the beautiful snow, the Christmas season. What she remembered most, though, was the ultimate feeling for a mother and a wife—the feeling of a family in love. That was the wonderful part.

John's words echoed in her mind for a long time. *Boy, was that snowmobiling fun or what?* It was the last time she remembered him expressing the joyous exuberance of the young man she had married. On the plane coming home he peered silently out the window and his mood changed as if he was leaving a world of fantasy and returning to the real world where the new year looked just like the old one.

Dae put her hand over his on the armrest. *Yes, John, the snowmobiling was fun.*

A lot of things had changed since then, but sometimes seventeen years ago seemed like yesterday. The John she had known was gone now. Visits to him were a painful reminder that he would never experience the joy of life again.

She put the picture back into the drawer and the magical Christmas at Lake Tahoe disappeared. As she stared at the little flash drive again, she knew John would be proud of her if he were still himself instead of an empty shell who no longer knew who she was.

*Maybe Brax will be proud of me too.*

# *11*

When Brax woke up he wasn't sure where he was and it took a few seconds to focus his eyes. Then he recognized Jim as the drug induced haze began to clear.

"Am I still alive?" he said.

"Yeah, but the morgue is just down the street. So you won't have too far to go if you keep smoking those damn cigars."

"I told you I'm through with those."

"Well, I know about being through with things. You can't just say it. Anyhow, they're still checking your dipstick, but I'll let the doc tell you about that."

"How long have I been here?"

"It's been almost eight hours since you left the lobby."

"You've been here all that time? You don't have to stay any longer. I'll be fine."

"I know I don't have to, but you helped me when I was screwed up. Besides, actually, I did leave for a couple of hours to go home and take a shower."

"Good."

"I ran into Dae as she was coming back from the beach."

"Really?"

"Yeah. When I told her you were in recovery, she was surprised to know that you're in the hospital. I figured you had told her about this."

"Not really." Brax was fully alert now and he listened to Jim patiently, if somewhat annoyed.

"Sorry if I opened my big mouth. I knew you didn't want your sons to worry but I assumed you had told her."

"So she knows where I am?"

"Yeah."

Brax rolled his head on the pillow and moaned deeply. "I just didn't want her to be bothered."

"Come on. What's with all the secrecy? You can't just pretend nothing happened. It's going to take a while to get over this, and there's no use in trying to deny it."

Brax was beginning to regain his bearings. "I know," he said.

"Why don't I tell Dae she can come with me next time. Maybe she could perk your ass up." Then Jim began to laugh. "Well, maybe that's not a good way to put it."

"Boy, you really know how to make a guy feel good. Anyhow, I don't want to gross her out with this damn piss bag. It feels like my plumbing is a little messed up right now." He added nervously, "Did they get it all?"

"You need to talk to the doctor," Jim said, matter-of-factly. "They said he would be in here in a few minutes."

Brax closed his eyes and remembered when he was strong and healthy. It didn't seem that long ago when his physical fitness was at its highest pitch, the closest he would come to hitting the perfect note, athletically.

---

He had trained for five years—fifty, sixty miles a week for months on end—to get in top shape. After long hours at work and a grueling commute home, the day wasn't complete without a run around the neighborhood. When he traveled on business, an early morning run in a strange city was the normal regimen. Saturdays might call for a leisurely ten-mile jog followed by twenty miles on Sunday while Jane was at church.

Competition began with short races, three miles or so. Then

came six miles, after that half-marathons, and, eventually, full marathons that required nothing more than an entrance fee to participate. It was all in preparation for the ultimate goal: the Boston Marathon. At first, it seemed like a faraway dream, but at age forty, he finally ran a qualifying time in a sanctioned race and his application was accepted for the event that amateur runners consider the quintessential test.

Three hours, that was the magic figure. Less than seven minutes a mile for more than twenty-six miles; it would have to be his best race.

On a warm day in April he headed out from Hopkinton among a throng of runners with Jane and his three sons waving to him. Through the streets of suburban Boston the crowds cheered him on as if he was the lead runner instead of a middle-aged guy plodding along in the pack of weekend warriors. He was right on pace as he checked his time through the first eighteen miles. The course began with a long stretch of gentle downhill miles, luring the runners like a siren to a series of short, steep rises known as Heartbreak Hill. A strong uphill runner, Brax passed people on the ascent and thought to himself how easy the famous hills seemed compared to his training runs around Stone Mountain.

Then it happened. Somewhere beyond the hills, the bear jumped on his back and he felt like an engine gasping on one cylinder. His eyes watered in pain and his legs felt like they were made of lead. As he slowed down to a tortuously sluggish pace, spectators urged him on from the sidewalks. "Only five miles to go," one said, as if that was encouragement. He kept plodding along until the Prudential Building appeared in sight, the location of the finish line.

From the loud speaker in the distance he could hear the times being called out. Three hours. Still almost a half mile away, he urged his legs to go faster but he was like a jockey putting the whip to a dead horse. Finally, he crossed the finish line with spittle flying from his mouth, his chest heaving in triple time, and his eyes blurred with teary sweat. He grimaced at the big digital clock as he passed under it, overcome with a mixture of relief and disappointment.

Three hours, three minutes, and eighteen seconds. No cigar.

Afterward, he collapsed onto the bare concrete of the Prudential parking garage for more than thirty minutes, surrounded by his family. Other runners sprawled around him in various stages of exhaustion. When he rose and tried to stretch his calves, they began to seize and, it became impossible to negotiate steps without going backward. The next day, he went with Jane and the kids to visit the historic sites around Boston. Walking the Freedom Trail, he was as stiff as the bronze statue of Benjamin Franklin and felt almost as old. In time, the sense of accomplishment overcame the "agony of defeat" and he took pride in himself as if he had won an Olympic Medal, even if it wasn't gold.

---

After Boston, Brax never ran another marathon. That was more than thirty years ago, but it was still etched in his mind as if it were on a DVD that he could insert into his brain and relive the moment. *How great it would be,* he thought, *to be able to run twenty-six miles again.*

Now he lay in a hospital bed, feeling nothing like an athlete, and wondering what had happened to his body. The fear of uncertainty welled in his mind, like the distant rumble of a storm. When could he walk on the beach with Dae once again? How soon would he be able to resume practicing his horn?

Soon he would learn what the doctor had to say and he wasn't sure he was ready to hear it.

Jim was in the room with Brax when the doctor arrived.

"Hi," the doctor said, looking up from the chart in his hand. "How are you feeling?"

"I'm fine," Brax answered. "I think."

The doctor lifted the sheet and took a quick look at Brax, then lowered the sheet and glanced at Jim.

"Dr. Eisenberg," Brax said, "this is my friend, Jim Hawkins."

Jim began to rise from his chair. "Want me to leave?" he asked, looking at Brax.

"No, I want you to stay."

The doctor looked at Jim and smiled.

Brax glanced at Jim, then back at the doctor. "We're not that kind of friends," he said, emphatically.

In pre-op meetings, Brax had become comfortable with the doctor, whom he guessed to be in his early forties at most. He found the young urologist to be pleasant enough and had the confident demeanor that doctor's assume.

"What's the verdict?" Brax asked. "Am I eaten up with it?"

"I don't think so. I think we found it in the early stage. You can thank Doctor Mathews for that. We'll check your PSA again in a couple of weeks when we remove the catheter."

"You mean I have to keep this thing in for two weeks?"

"Yes."

"When can I go home?"

"On Friday if everything looks good."

"Friday?" Brax looked at Jim with a grimace. Then he looked at the ceiling and muttered, "Three more days." Finally, he turned back to the doctor. "When can I walk?"

"Now, if you feel like it. I want you to walk every day for a little while unless it begins to hurt. You need to keep your circulation up. But for the next two or three weeks don't do any lifting or anything real strenuous. I'll give you a prescription that will help keep the pain down."

The doctor stayed for only fifteen minutes or so, discussing the potential side effects of the surgery and advising Brax about life style changes. "Eat a balanced diet, avoid a lot of spicy food, drink lots of water, and—especially—don't smoke," he said. "And make sure," he added, "to keep a positive attitude."

"Do you have a prescription for that?" Brax asked.

"No, but it's the best medicine there is and it's free." The doctor made a few marks on the chart and started to leave. He turned and looked at Brax with a pleasant, self-assured expression. "We're here to help you through this."

After the doctor left, Brax sat up and rolled his legs over the edge of the bed. He gently stepped down and stood motionless for a few seconds to make sure he was steady on his feet. He slowly walked from the bed to the door and back again, carrying the catheter bag while Jim followed, wheeling the morphine drip suspended from a pole. It wasn't painful but he moved gently due to mild soreness and a psychological fear that he might injure himself.

"So how does it feel?" Jim asked.

"Not too bad. It just feels … strange, like something is missing."

"That's a good thing. What's missing would have killed you."

In the bathroom Brax looked at himself in the mirror and glared at his matted hair, baggy eyes, and white bristles of a two day growth of whiskers. Lee Marvin on a rough day, he said to himself. A real rough day.

He walked back into the room and eased onto the bed. "I don't feel too bad, but I look like shit."

"You'll look like your senile old self after you get some rest," Jim said. "I'll get out of here now, but we'll be back in the morning."

"We?"

"Dae wants to see you. She didn't say that in so many words but she didn't have to. You said it was okay, didn't you?"

"No, I didn't say that, and you know it." Brax thought about it for a couple of seconds. "But I guess it's all right."

It would be good to see Dae, even if he did look like death warmed over. Just seeing her would make him feel better.

Besides, he knew damn well that, even on his best days, he wouldn't be mistaken for any movie star. Especially Lee Marvin.

Earlier that morning, when Jim went home to take a shower, he had met Dae as she returned from the beach. He casually mentioned that Brax was in recovery and she appeared stunned by the comment.

"I had no idea," she said. "He told me he would be gone a few days to take care of some business." She stared at Jim with a pained expression.

"I know he doesn't want people worrying about him, but I figured he'd told you." Jim exhaled a puff of air. "That's the way he is, though."

"I hope everything goes well."

"Yeah, me too."

"Give him my best wishes, please."

Dae had known Brax for only a few days but she found herself being more concerned than one should be for a casual acquaintance. She tried to ignore the feeling and debated with herself about the wisdom of visiting him in the hospital. Maybe that was too forward considering his desire for privacy. Besides, surely he had relatives visiting and she didn't want to crowd him.

Later that evening, Dae answered her doorbell and found herself, once again, speaking to Jim. She invited him in and asked, "How is he?"

"He's doing well. He'll be in the hospital for a few more days and he'll have to take it easy for a while."

"That's good to hear. Thanks for letting me know." Dae tried not to show how relieved she was. "I know he appreciates all you've done for him. You're such a good friend."

"Well, he doesn't have any family here and he didn't tell anybody. That's the way he wanted it. You and I are the only ones who know about this. He hadn't planned on telling you, but I spoiled that. He doesn't mind though."

"I'm glad."

"Would you like to go with me to visit him? He said it was okay."

"Oh, I'm not so sure. He might not appreciate it."

"Don't worry, he will." Without a trace of subtly, he added, "He likes you."

Dae knew it was true but hearing Jim say it was more than nice to hear. It was comforting. She stared at Jim and paused as if she were considering the offer. "Are you sure he won't mind?"

"Dae, quit being so damn like a woman. I told you he wanted to see you."

"Fine, then. What time do we leave?"

———❖———

Brax got up early to shave and wash himself to be ready for Jim and Dae's arrival.

"Hey," he said when they walked in. The greeting was meant for both of them, but his gaze hung on Dae.

"Hi," she said, smiling.

"How're you feeling today?" asked Jim.

"Better."

"Good. You look a hell of a lot better, too."

Brax looked directly at Dae. "Thanks for coming. You didn't have to, but I appreciate it. The doctor told me it's important to keep a positive state-of-mind. Seeing a pretty woman sure helps that."

"Whoa!" Jim said. "It's getting thick. I see they didn't cut the B.S. out of you."

Dae laughed. "You guys are such cards." Then she said to Brax, "I'm glad you're feeling well."

"Yeah, I'm still kickin'. I'm not ready to run a marathon but I guess I'll live a few more days." The other two didn't respond and Brax felt the atmosphere turn sober. "Hey, come on, y'all don't worry about me. I'm good to go."

Dae handed him a crossword puzzle book. "I thought you might like this."

"All right! This will make the time go a little faster. Thank you."

"You're welcome," she said.

"Is there anything else you need?" Jim asked.

"No, I just want to get out of here as soon as I can. I need to suck some of that salt air into my lungs. "

"Don't rush things," Jim said. "In a few weeks you'll be back walking on the beach."

"A few weeks? Damn, that's a long time."

"The beach will still be there," Dae said.

She said the beach would be there, but he heard something different.

*She would be there.*

Jim and Dae visited Brax for the next couple of days and on the third, they came to bring him home. The catheter was uncomfortable and, as Brax waited for them, he felt conspicuous as if it were noticeable under his warm-up suit. He had come to grips with his condition, though, and he was anxious to leave the hospital.

When they arrived, they tried to get him to take a wheelchair, but he refused.

"Hospital policy," the male nurse insisted.

Brax slumped into the wheelchair with a sour look that stayed on his face until he was out the front door and on his feet.

Jim put the suitcase in the trunk while Brax moved into the passenger seat and Dae behind him.

On the trip home, the conversation was light and Brax said little about his stay at the hospital. Jim and Dae avoided it as well.

As they neared Seaside, Brax asked "Who's ready for a little walk?"

"Are you crazy?" asked Jim. "You need to take it easy for a while."

"I said a little walk—real little. I need to get some fresh air. The people at the hospital were nice but I feel like I've been cooped up in a test tube."

"I've already walked," Jim said. "I'm ready for my nap."

"I'll go with you," said Dae.

Jim dropped them off at Dae's house, but for the first time, they didn't walk the beach. Instead Brax asked Dae to drive him to the backside of the island and she drove to a secluded area tucked among trees and dense undergrowth.

Dae parked near a path that led toward the marshes. After a short stroll, they came to a clearing and stopped to rest, sitting at a picnic table. In the distance, a truck crossed the bridge headed to the mainland, but sitting under the moss-draped trees as egrets waded in the backwater nearby, it was as if they were disconnected from the rest of the world.

"This is so peaceful," Dae said.

Brax frowned. "Someday they'll clear this out and put up more … development."

"But that someday isn't here yet," she said. "We have it all to ourselves right now."

"You're right," Brax sighed. "Why am I worried about something that hasn't even happened? Sometimes I get carried away thinking about things that really don't matter a hill of beans or worrying about stuff I can't do a thing about. Jim will jerk me back to earth. He's more pragmatic that I am."

"You're a thinker. I am, too, but I try not to get caught up in negative thoughts."

"That's a good way to be. Maybe you can help me learn to think like you do."

"I'll try, but I've seen your positive side—your sense of humor. That's something a lot of people don't have, especially as they get older."

"That's the Jekyll and Hyde in me. Sometimes I feel like I'm a teenager again, with no cares in the world, and sometimes I feel like the world has gone crazy and I'm the only sane person left." He raised his hand and cupped his forehead. "See, here I go, just jabbering away again with this crap. From now on I'm going to be positive, like you."

"I didn't say I was always positive. I just said I tried."

"I guess that's all any of us can do, isn't it?"

"I think so."

They sat silently, each in their own thoughts, surrounded by the wildness of nature. A few minutes later, they started to leave the picnic table for the short walk back to her car.

When they stood up, he touched her arm and said, "I need to tell you something."

"What is it?" She looked at him with a gleam in her eye, as if it might be something she wanted to hear.

Brax gently led her to the bench seat and sat down beside her. He turned his head toward her but spoke without making direct eye contact. "I enjoy being with you, but I don't want to push myself on you. I know you have a life of your own and I don't want you to think you have to avoid me or feel sorry for me. We live in a little fishbowl community and I want you to feel comfortable doing whatever you want to do."

"I understand," she put her hand on his. Neither of them spoke for a minute until she added, "Brax, I like being with you, too. I thought I might be pushing myself on you by coming to the hospital with Jim every day. Maybe we should just … be ourselves."

"You mean, just let things happen?"

She nodded. "Yes."

"I've got this … health thing, you know." He stopped himself from saying "cancer." "I think I'll be all right, but I don't know for sure."

"No one has any guarantees for tomorrow."

"No we don't." He hesitated, searching for a way to tell her his most personal concern. Finally, he looked directly at her and said, "I'm different now. I mean, this operation takes something out of a man." He turned his face away. "I'm not as … complete … as I used to be."

"Brax, I know this changes a man physically." Her eyes were moist. "I've only known you for a short time, but I know you.

You're as complete as any man I've ever known." She put a hand in his. "And there's something I need to tell you."

He turned back to her and saw the look of pain on her face. But she didn't speak. Was she hiding the same thing from him that he had hidden from her?

"Is it about cancer?"

Dae sighed and wiped a tear. "No. It's …" She paused for several seconds. After a long exhale, she said, "Well, yes. I had breast cancer ten years ago and I had a mastectomy but I'm cancer free now."

He peered into her eyes as if he could see into her spirit. Then he pulled her to him and embraced her silently for a long time. When they separated, he said, "Maybe we're good for each other."

"I believe we are," she responded. "I really do."

On the drive back to Seaside, they barely spoke in the few minutes it took to get home. As the blacktop road disappeared behind them, Brax knew there was another road they were going down together and he was sure she knew it too.

Dae dropped him off at his unit and, before Brax got out of the car, he leaned over and gave her a hug. He pressed his face to hers, kissed her on the cheek, and said "Thank you." She turned her face to him and, unable to resist the temptation, he kissed her on the lips.

She smiled and said, "Thank you."

The smile on her face and those two words—*Thank you*—were more powerful than any of the drugs prescribed by Dr. Eisenberg. In that moment he forgot about cancer, memory loss, impending development, endangered turtles, and all the other real or imagined threats to his wellbeing.

All he could think of was the woman he'd only known for a week.

# *12*

Brax called his oldest son in Dallas and told him about the operation.

Mason's voice rang with frustration. "Dad, why didn't you tell me?"

"Everything will be okay. I feel good. They think they got it all."

"What do you mean—they think?"

"I'll go back in a couple of weeks to have my blood checked and I'll be as good as new. I just needed an oil change."

"I can't believe you didn't tell us."

Brax moved the conversation away from his operation and asked about Mason's wife and children. Then he mentioned that he was going to start playing his trumpet again.

"That's great. I haven't played my sax since I can't remember when. But you were always more into it than I was."

"Remember the last time we played together? We were Soul Men." Brax sang the last two words as if he were one of the Blues Brothers.

"That was fun." Mason laughed. "I remember you had a real good time that night."

"Yeah. I don't think Jane did, though. Ha!"

———❖———

Brax would never forget that night. It was twenty-five years ago at a club in Athens after the Homecoming game. Earlier in the day he had joined the motley assemblage of the alumni band on the field as they entertained the crowd before the kick-off. The atmosphere was electric and Brax felt like a kid again playing the fight song on his trumpet in front of the juiced-up fans who carried hidden flasks of liquid spirit in their pockets.

That evening he joined Mason's group, five guys from the Marching Redcoat Band who called themselves the Hot Dawgs. The small club was alive with a raucous crowd of young revelers and the live, brassy music amplified the high voltage atmosphere. From his vantage on the stage, Brax could see that Jane was uneasy among the crowd of college kids, but after a beer and a dance with one of Mason's friends, she seemed caught up in the spirit. For him, the energy in the room generated an adrenaline rush he hadn't experienced since the days when he had his own band.

After one of the breaks, Brax and Mason appeared on stage dressed as the Blues Brothers, complete with black suits, fedoras, dark glasses, and stick-on sideburns. Brax took center stage as Jake Blues with a trumpet and Mason stood in as Elwood with a saxophone. When the opening bars of "I'm a Soul Man" blasted into the room, the crowd stirred with excitement. Brax and Mason held their instruments aside as they sang the lyrics and moved in unison with side shuffle steps. The audience joined in the chorus and the ear-splitting sound filled the club. When the song was over, the room remained abuzz with energy. The crowd gave the Blues Brothers enthusiastic applause and cheered for more. Brax and Mason, both dripping with sweat, looked at each other, then prompted the band to play "Gimme Some Lovin'." They hadn't practiced the song a lot and played around with it before shedding their coats and hats to do some impromptu dance moves.

After the Blues Brothers act, Brax left the stage and joined Jane in the audience.

"That was wild," he said.

Jane gave him a hug. "You guys were great."

It was after one a.m. when the band closed the show. Brax, having felt the energy of the crowd and thrown himself completely into the music and the bourbon between breaks, was feeling no pain. The Hot Dawgs cooled down with more drinks before hooking up with their girlfriends and heading for places where young couples go in a college town after a football game.

Jane, slightly buzzed but still sober, took the keys from Brax and got behind the wheel as he poured himself into the passenger seat. On the way to the hotel, he rolled down the window and started blowing his trumpet. The notes came out as random noise, nothing close to a tune.

"Brax, quit!" she shouted. "The police will pull us over."

He blew the trumpet loudly again, then rolled up the window and slumped down in his seat, leaning against the door with his eyes closed.

Fifteen minutes later Jane pulled into the parking lot of the motel. There was no sign of life from Brax and he didn't respond when she tried to wake him. She walked around the car to open his door and tried to get him moving. She had barely cracked the door when the weight of his body pressed the door open and the trumpet fell from his lap onto her feet. She kicked the trumpet aside and tried to hold Brax, who had slumped headfirst halfway out of the car, but he was too heavy. Struggling to keep him from hitting his head on the pavement, she let him collapse completely out of the car. She grabbed an arm and shouted, "Brax, get up!"

Finally he roused from his stupor and rose to all fours. He tried to stand, leaning heavily against the car, then collapsed again onto the asphalt of the empty space beside them. They were on an incline and Brax began to roll downhill like a runaway log down a mountainside.

When he stopped rolling in the middle of the parking lot, he opened his eyes and looked up to see Jane standing over him.

"I'm a soul man," he said meekly.

Jane wasn't amused. "You're drunk. Get up, I'm ready for bed."

The free fall on the pavement stirred a little life in him and he was able to stand. He mumbled the "Soul Man" song to himself as they walked toward the motel. When he came to the trumpet on the pavement next to the car, he stopped to pick it up.

"Don't blow that thing again," she said.

He blew it again.

She tossed him the car keys, went to the room and slammed the door, locking him out.

Brax staggered to the car and fell face down in the back seat where he would spend the rest of the night.

He awoke the next morning with a hangover and little recollection of the night before. But Jane refreshed his memory in vivid detail.

———◆———

Brax chatted a little while longer with Mason and promised to keep him up to speed on his condition.

"Say hello to Sandy and the kids for me."

"I will. Keep on tootin' your horn."

"Okay, but I guess after this crotchectomy I can't be a horny old man anymore. Ha! Bye."

Brax hung up, feeling an odd satisfaction with the reference. He had used that one on Jane about a million times: the reference from her trumpet-playing husband as being a horny guy. She would casually dismiss his corny puns but she always seemed to appreciate his sense of humor. Except for that night in Athens.

*Damn, it was cold in that car.*

———◆———

In the quiet, lonely hours Dae couldn't rid her mind of thoughts about her relationship with Brax. She liked him, no doubt, and when she was with him she felt more alive than she had in a long time. Still, she had only known him for a week. What if he turned out to be different than he seemed? What if he tired of her? Living close to each other in a tight-knit community might be awkward if something came between them. She had yet to tell him about John and, the more she delayed, the harder she found the nerve to face up to it. It hung over her like an albatross, yet somehow she thought Brax would understand. And here was Brax, a cancer patient. She had given him the impression that it didn't matter, but was she ready to accept the possibility that he might have an extended illness, or even die? And what about her own health? Since the mastectomy ten years ago, there had been no further sign of cancer but there's always that fear in the back of one's mind. Maybe she was letting things happen too fast.

Those were the thoughts of her rational self, an educator trained to think logically. Thoughts of a serious person with the discipline and intellect to author a scholarly text. Those of a mature woman, settled into the unforgiving realities of life. But there was a part of her she had kept under control for years. It was her emotional self. John's depression had distanced her long ago and now that Julie and Justin were far away, she was left with a sense of emptiness. She felt differently when she was with Brax and she couldn't deny the attraction.

For the first time in a very long while, Dae was seriously attracted to a man and she knew he felt the same way. It was a good feeling but one that took some adjustment. Now, there was a new presence in her life, a presence that viewed her as more than just another lonely woman in her senior years. She had always taken pride in her appearance and had kept her wardrobe up to date and full of bright colors. People often told her she didn't look her age. She couldn't fool herself, though; she wasn't young anymore. When she looked in the mirror she studied the wrinkles beneath her eyes and the skin that was no longer tight around her neck.

There was a time when Dae looked in the mirror and staring back at her was the prettiest girl at St. Edwards High School. It said so right there in the year book. Above her picture the caption read in big letters "Best Looking." Her hair was longer then and swept back on the sides, with thin bangs in front like a brunette version of Sandra Dee. A tight sweater accentuated the full development of her femininity. Below the picture the caption read in bold, fancy print "Dae Spencer" and scribbled across it were the words "Love you forever, Tommy."

Tommy Reavis was Dae's first love and his picture in the yearbook was captioned "Best All-Around." He was the quarterback on the football team and she pranced on the sidelines in her cheerleader uniform as he led the team to a few more wins than losses. They went steady their senior year, and when he followed in his father's footsteps to study pre-med at Emory University she followed him to Atlanta and the nearby, female-only, environs of Agnes Scott College. She dreamed of being with Tommy forever and being near him and away from home couldn't have been more perfect. They were grownups now, free from the confines of their families, free to set their own boundaries, even sleep together.

But life in the big city was different and Tommy began drifting away in search of even more freedom.

"Do you still love me?" she asked.

"Sure I do, but we don't need to be together all the time. We need more ... experiences."

It was all she needed to hear. They remained friends, but forever didn't happen. In time she came to realize she wasn't ready for forever either. That would come later, after she had graduated and moved back home. There she would meet a young man from Brunswick named John Whitehead, but she never forgot Tommy Reavis. He didn't make it back to the high school reunions and she lost track of him. Even though things didn't work out for them, there was always a place in her heart for him. It was like a long, beautiful movie that finally ended, but the memory lingered on.

Twenty-five years later, after John had retreated into himself, she thought that seeing Tommy again might boost her spirits. In a weak moment, she even had guilty thoughts of trying to revive their relationship. She assumed he was probably married and the idea of adultery was shameful, but the temptation of reviving first love persisted.

Defying her conscience, she tracked him down through the Internet and learned that he was now Dr. Tom Reavis, Professor of Anatomy at Rutgers University. She waited months before placing the call to New Jersey then started to hang up when a woman answered. But she stayed with the call and nervously introduced herself as an old friend.

"Unfortunately, Tom passed away last year," the woman said.

"Oh, I'm so sorry." She felt a shock as if she had been hit by lightning and she stammered self-consciously. "My name is Dae Whitehead and I went to high school with Tommy ... uh, Tom ... in Savannah."

"Dae? Yes, I know about you. I'm sure there could only be one girl named Dae in his class. It's a pretty name. I know you were his girlfriend and he always spoke fondly of you. I've seen your picture in the yearbook and you were so pretty."

For a moment, Dae could see herself at eighteen. "Thank you. That was a long time ago."

There was an inviting tone to the woman's voice as if she had been expecting the call and it put Dae at ease. It surprised, yet comforted, her to know that the woman knew of her.

"Well, I'm sorry to bother you and, again, I'm sorry to hear about ... uh ... your husband. I don't mean to be insensitive, but do you mind telling me the circumstances of his death? Had he been ill?"

"No, I don't mind. And, in fact, he hadn't been ill. At least, not in the physical sense. It was an accident but in a way he took his own life. Drugs, you know."

"Oh."

"It's taken me a while but I've learned to live with it. I hope I haven't upset you."

"No. I mean, it's tragic but … I … I have fond memories of him as well. May I ask your name?"

"I'm Linda."

"You've been very gracious, Linda. I wish you the best"

"Thank you."

After Dae finished the conversation with Tommy's widow, she buried her face in her hands and cried. She was saddened to learn of Tommy's death, especially the sordid circumstances surrounding it. Wanting to preserve his memory as she knew him, she had no desire to know in detail what had happened.

But mostly she was ashamed of her motivation for calling.

The face in the mirror stared back at Dae and told her that within three months she would be sixty-seven. She figured Brax was even older. It didn't matter that they had only known each other for a week. It just felt good in a way she hadn't felt in a long time.

———◦———

When Brax went back to the hospital for his follow-up visit, he received a good report. He felt as much relieved for Dae as for himself. His biggest fear was leaving her with a sense of responsibility for someone she barely knew. Of course, he thought of his own mortality as well but he had come to grips with that.

"Looks like I've got some mileage still in me," he said, sitting in her living room. "Now, if I can just keep from losing my feeble mind, I'm as good as a used Honda with new tires."

"That's wonderful," she said.

He set his coffee cup on the end table and moved from his side of the sofa next to her. She leaned into him and he embraced her.

He kissed her and her lips tasted like the sweet fruit of a new beginning. They held the kiss for a moment. Then she put her head on his chest and he wrapped her in his arms, feeling as if she had become a part of him.

"That was nice," she said.

"Yeah, even better than that first time in the car. Remember that?"

"Of course." She smiled. "How could I forget?"

"Just checking."

———⊰⊱———

The new couple met in the clubhouse each morning. Brax was usually waiting for Dae, his crossword puzzle neatly completed. If he got hung up she would wait patiently until he filled in all the blank spaces. They walked the beach, or sometimes other parts of the island, with disciplined regularity. As the days passed they became more at ease with their conspicuousness. The other residents smiled cordially at the familiar pair and greeted them by their odd names.

Slowly they learned about each other, but Brax insisted they not dwell on the past.

"I think there is something attractive about not knowing everything about someone," she agreed. "It adds a bit of mystique that can whet your imagination. It's what's ahead of us that's important."

"I think so. I don't need a background check on you. But it would be nice to know if you are now, or ever have been, a member of al-Qaida."

"Oh, shut-up," she said through a grin. "You know what I mean."

"I'll take that as a no."

Yes, he knew what she meant. She didn't need to know everything about Jane and how much he loved her. And he didn't need to know everything about John. They would come to know each other for the persons they are now. The past would reveal itself as surely as the memories that lingered in their souls.

Every day Brax pulled his trumpet out and practiced intermittently for an hour or so. The instrument had rested quietly in its case for years, but now it seemed as vital to his wellbeing as his aortal artery. He sandwiched short practice sessions between listening to brassy tunes from his CD collection. His sound began to open up and hints of sparkle appeared in his tone. But fatigue soon set into his face muscles and after a few lines he would have to pause to let his chops recover. Normally he used his mute and, even though the garages on either side of his unit served as a buffer, he avoided playing too early or too late so as not to bother the neighbors.

The music was a way for him to wrap himself in a cocoon of serenity. Listening to the tunes, he felt as if he were in another world, one in which there was no ugliness, only beauty. And when he played his horn he felt like he was a part of that beauty. The melodies spoke to him in a way that stirred feelings well beyond the limitations of words. He often wondered what might have been had he devoted himself fully to his music and resisted the temptation to get a "regular" job. It might not have worked. Maybe a full dose of music would have dulled his appetite like the time he ate too much of his mother's German chocolate cake. Or the time he had spent selling insurance, a time that just happened to span most of his adult life.

Only a few weeks removed from the flat line existence of malaise, Brax now felt a quickening to the pace of his life. It was invigorating and he felt a new sense of purpose.

One night he couldn't sleep. Thoughts rolled around in his head as he tossed and turned. He looked at the clock on the nightstand and the time glowed back at him. It was twelve minutes past one in the morning. There was no use staying in bed; he had to release some of the pent up emotion welled inside of him. Turning on the night lamp, he got out of bed and pulled his horn from its case.

With the trumpet in one hand, he walked into the living room and stood motionless for a few seconds, resisting the urge to blow the horn. Surrounded by the quiet, he knew what he had to do.

He put on a sweat suit and sneakers, then took his trumpet with him to the garage and got into his car. Leaving the complex, he drove to a side road not far away and parked in an isolated palm thicket in the interior of the island. He got out of the car with his horn and leaned against the front fender. The night air was warm and the full moon bathed the brass trumpet in a soft glow as he began to play "When I Fall In Love." His lungs felt strong and the notes drifted cleanly into the calmness around him. After the first verse, he stopped and held the instrument at his side.

"I love you, Jane," he said to the stars. "I always will."

He knew what she would say. *It's okay.*

He played another verse and then was ready to go home. As he approached the entrance to Seaside, he got a glimpse of the whitecaps through the roadside foliage and heard the surf breaking through the open car window. He thought about the eggs of an endangered sea turtle buried in the sand dune near a warning sign. It wouldn't be long before the tiny hatchlings would break their shell and make the treacherous journey to the safety of the ocean. Some wouldn't have the strength to make it; others would be the victim of predators along the way. Those that made it to the water wouldn't just survive; they would live in natural abandon in their briny home.

That's what he would do: play music, walk beside the ocean, experience the joy of love once again. Not just survive, but live.

In a few hours he would go to the clubhouse, make some coffee, and open the paper to the crossword. Soon the night would be over, then Dae would come.

# 13

Dae walked into the clubhouse the next morning to find Brax sitting at his usual table with the newspaper in front of him.

"Good morning," she said. "Have you finished the crossword?"

"Yeah." There was sour look on his face and he didn't return her greeting. "Did you read yesterday's editorial page?"

"No, I—"

"Take a look at this," he said, handing her the paper folded to the page in question.

Dae sat down and read the article as Brax sat silently with his arms folded on his chest. The article was written by the leader of a group that advocated preserving the undeveloped parts of the island. In part, the article read:

> The plan for additional development on this island is unwanted, not only by local residents but others throughout the state. This island, as a state-owned property, has been spared large scale commercial development. Much of it has been operated as an inexpensive state park with modest amenities. While our neighboring islands have become densely populated with upscale residential communities and expensive resorts, we need to resist that path from which there is no going back. Immeasurable damage to the ecosystem of plant and wildlife is inevitable. And, there's no doubt that commercialization will create a hectic atmosphere, while, in the process, destroying the peaceful lifestyle valued by residents and visitors alike. Further, the affordable acces-

sibility to the island valued by many citizens of Georgia as well as others from around the country and, indeed, the world, would be greatly diminished.

But big money is hard for state officials to resist. New sources of tax revenues are inviting to bean-counting bureaucrats even in light of obvious environmental consequences. However, concerned citizens realize that the plan as currently proposed would bring scores of tourists, new residents and commercial businesses on a scale that would totally transform the nature of the island. This would completely violate the spirit of the law that sets aside a large portion of the island in its natural state.

At the end of the article was the notice of a public meeting to be held at the island conference center for state officials to discuss the plans for development.

"Do you want to go to the meeting with me and Jim?" Brax asked.

"Yes," Dae replied. "I'd like to know how we might be affected."

"I don't think it's a matter of might," replied Brax. "They're going to do whatever they want. They'll build their big hotels so that you can't even see the beach and they'll make everything expensive to keep out the riff-raff. People will swarm here like a plague of locusts and we might as well live in a Holiday Inn on Daytona Beach."

He paused and she didn't respond.

"It's all about the money," he continued. "The island is just another piece of real estate. They don't care about the wildlife, or the fragile nature of the land."

He stopped himself from continuing. "Hey, I'm just ranting. Sorry, it's too early for that."

She hesitated at first, but then said, "Why don't you say those things at the meeting?"

"Like I said, it won't do any good. I'm just a senile old bastard ranting away. Besides, it's hard to have any credibility when you have such an obvious vested interest. I like things the way they are and I don't want them messing up my little world."

"It's my little world too."

"I know, and it's a lot of other people's little world. Not just people here at Seaside or other people that live on the island but people who come here because of the way it is. It just seems that there should be one place that is not ... I don't know ... over commercialized."

"Maybe it won't be so bad."

Brax squeezed a grimace on his face and grunted. "Yeah, maybe not."

Dae set the paper aside and stood up. "Come on, let's go for our walk."

His mood shifted and he got up with a playful grin. "After you, old lady."

On the beach, the air was thick and warm in the soft light of early daybreak.

"Those clouds sure are dark," Dae said. "I think it's going to rain any minute."

"Not for a couple of hours," Brax said. "At least, that's what the weather lady said."

They walked for several minutes, speaking few words and keeping to the dry sand as the tide edged further ashore. The day slowly began to brighten, but the sun remained hidden. In a short while, they saw several people in the distance, talking excitedly and bent over to observe something near a cluster of sea grass in the dunes.

As they got closer to the commotion, Brax noticed a stream of small creatures crawling from the high bank of sand toward the beach. His eyes lit up and he began to walk faster. "Hey," he gushed, "I think they might be watching some baby turtles come out of a nest."

"Oh, that would be something," Dae said, keeping up with his pace.

When they arrived at the dune, an amazing scene was unfolding. Tiny sea turtles were scurrying from a hole in the sand and making their way in an unsteady crawl toward the water.

"I can't believe this," Brax said to a man he knew to be a long-time island resident, though not by name.

"Yeah," the islander said, "This is very unusual. I've never seen it happen in the daylight. We need to keep away the gulls as best we can. And those dogs that people walk without a leash every morning. These hatchlings are easy pickings."

Brax and Dae watched in fascination as newborn turtles continued to scramble from the hole and head for the beach.

"Geez," Brax said, "there must be at least a hundred of them."

"What an incredible sight," Dae said. She bent down, resting her knees in the sand, and picked up one of the stray hatchlings who appeared to be moving slower than most.

"No," the islander warned. "They need to make their own way. That gives them the strength they need in order to survive when they get to the water."

Dae complied and the baby turtle continued to struggle forward as others passed by. Brax helped her up and they stood on the dune until the last hatchling emerged from the hole. Then they joined others on the beach to help shoo away pesky seabirds.

The hatchings crawed into the mild surf without hesitation and floundered about furiously like a child learning to dog paddle.

"That was unbelievable," said Brax, as the last hatching disappeared from view. "I've never seen that. Like the man said, it always happens at night."

"I can't believe how lucky we were to see it," Dae said. "They were so cute with their little flippers and heads sticking out under their shell."

Brax stared out at the sea and visualized the infant turtles being drawn by instinct into their new watery world. "They're little now but they get huge—three or four hundred pounds. Even more, maybe. And some they say might live to be older than we are."

"How do you know so much about these turtles?"

"I went to the wildlife center a few months ago. They had several big loggerheads that had been rescued and I watched a video about them. They're fascinating creatures. That guy who told you to put the hatchling down was there. We talked a little bit but we never introduced ourselves."

The excitement of the event lingered and, as the other beach-goers continued to chat about what they had witnessed, Brax and Dae resumed their walk. But he couldn't clear his mind of the miraculous life cycle of the loggerhead and his thoughts returned to the newspaper article. Without looking at Dae, he said, "The more buildings they put on the beach, the less we will see of this. The females won't lay their eggs if there is light at night. And even if they do, the hatchlings get confused with artificial light and head away from the water. They die from exposure."

"That's a shame," she replied. "But we agreed in the clubhouse that we weren't going to dwell on that this morning. Even you said it might not be as bad as you think."

He turned to her and conceded, "Yeah, I guess I did."

After a few more steps, she added, "Let's enjoy our walk." Her tone was more that of a command than a suggestion.

Brax realized that he had gotten on his high horse again. Dae was more inclined to take things as they came. After all, that's what they had agreed to. Just let things happen. No, it couldn't be too bad, he thought. Not as long as she was there.

———

Brax made the short drive to the Island Convention Center with Dae beside him and Jim in the back seat. They arrived forty-five minutes early and took seats near the front of the big room. By the time the meeting began, the room was full and people stood in the side aisles. Most of the residents of Seaside were in attendance and, along with other locals, anxiously waited to hear what was promoted by State officials as a "proposal of scope."

The top state official was a portly man, well past middle age, with a round, pink face and dressed in a gray pinstriped suit that hung like a tent over his pear-shaped body. He spoke from behind a lectern, with talking points displayed on a large screen to one side. His presentation emphasized the positive impact of the proposed project and how it would bring a new vitality to the island.

"The economic impact will be significant to the whole area," the state official said. "This project will bring jobs and badly needed revenue in the form of taxes and tourism."

After a few minutes, the government man turned the presentation over to a representative from the developer's office. The speaker was a young man, early thirties at most, and presented a picture of corporate polish in a blue suit perfectly fitted to his tall, slender frame. He began his talk as images appeared on the screen showing the scope of the project and sketches of what it would look like when completed.

Ignoring his concession that the development might not be "too bad," Brax whispered to Dae, "This is a bunch of horse manure. They've already made a deal. They just got us here to grease the skids of progress."

"They're just showing how it *could* be," she said

Brax looked at Jim who shook his head and frowned.

The developer's presentation lasted more than an hour. After that, the government official returned to the lectern to answer questions.

Brax stood up and addressed the pink-faced government man. "So when does all this begin?"

"That has not been decided. It has to be approved by the State Legislature and then signed by the Governor."

"How many lobbyists have the developers hired to wine and dine the State Legislators?"

The developer stepped to the lectern and whispered something to the government man who nodded. Brax stood defiantly waiting for an answer.

"That is not relevant," the government man replied, raising his voice. "This project has been handled ethically and completely above board." He set his jaws and stared at Brax.

"Do you stand to gain anything personally from this project or represent anyone who does?" Brax asked, a sarcastic emphasis on the word project.

"Absolutely not, sir." The government man's face turned from pink to red. "I resent that question," he said with glaring eyes.

"Just asking," Brax said as he sat down. He turned to Dae and spoke in a low voice but loud enough for those around them to hear. "He's lying."

"How do you know?" she whispered.

"He's a politician."

The government man looked around the room. "Folks," he said, "this whole issue has been debated in the public forum."

Brax stood up again. "Is that what you call this—a debate?"

Soon others from the audience began to ask questions and the mood in the room became openly adversarial. Small conversations broke out in animated discussions aimed at stopping the development or, at the least, containing it to a more modest size.

The developer returned to the lectern to calm things down. "I understand your concerns. I take it that you're residents of Seaside. That property will remain as it is now. There are no plans to encroach on that facility."

Jim stood up and shouted, "What about the area around us? All the hotels and condos and restaurants. Nothing but noise and traffic and obnoxious weekenders. And what about the beach? There'll be people everywhere so you can't even enjoy it without listening to loud music and dodging Frisbees."

The developer gripped the lectern tightly as if to hold his temper, then leaned forward. "We can't keep these beaches empty. There is a limited amount of beachfront available and it needs to be made accessible and attractive to as many people as possible."

"It's accessible and attractive now!" Brax shouted, as he stood up again. "You don't want it to be available and attractive, you want to ruin it!"

The pink faced government man spoke up again. "That's not true. There will be plenty of beach property set aside for public use."

The comment shocked Brax. He had never considered the issue of the beach domain. "Public use?" he asked. "So how much of the beach will be private? What about the beach directly across the road from Seaside?"

The government man looked at the developer who responded to the question. "That's all a part of the master plan. There are several variations being considered."

"Being considered by who?" Brax asked, mockingly.

"Listen folks, don't you see?" the developer asked. "This project will increase the value of your property. Increase it dramatically."

Jim chimed in. "We don't care about that." He looked around the room and surveyed the large portion of the audience made up of his neighbors from Seaside. "We're more interested in the value of the time that we spend living out the rest of our lives." That drew approving comments from his elderly friends.

Another man rose from the audience. "Yeah, that's all y'all care about—that senior citizen place where y'all live. Well, you people have only been here a few years and I've lived here practically all my life. So I think I got a better idea of what's right for this island." The man was elderly himself, at least sixty. His head was bald on top with a rim of long gray hair that framed a leathery brown face and tied in a ponytail in back.

"What's right for one of us is right for all of us," Jim said.

"I ain't so sure about that," ponytail replied.

"Gentlemen," the politician said, "we can only have one person talk at a time."

Jim deferred to the native inhabitant and sat down.

"I got a house on this island that's worth a lot to me," said pony-tail. "But it ain't worth much to anybody else. The land, now that's different. If big money comes in here, they might just pay a right smart for the property rights to my little acre. Enough for me to come out on the good side. For the right price, I'll leave this pile of sand and never look back."

"Yeah, tell 'em J.D.," yelled a voice in the audience.

"Sir—sorry I didn't catch your name—that's the point I'm try-ing to make," said the politician.

"I'm J.D.," ponytail said. "They gonna buy us out?" he asked. His voice carried the cynical resonance of mistrust as he stood defiantly looking at the pink-faced politician and the young de-veloper in the blue suit.

"I can't make any promises—" the politician began to say.

"We have shown you the master plan," interjected the devel-oper. "That's the extent of what has been committed."

Brax rose from his chair again and addressed the local man he had never met. "J.D., I think I know the answer to that."

J.D. turned to look at Brax and waited for him to speak.

"Hold on," the developer interjected in an attempt to stifle Brax.

"No, you hold on," Brax said to the developer. Then he turned back to J.D. "You know you don't own that land, the state does. They might buy you out and give you a fair price. And they might not. They could just strong-arm you with that crap called immi-nent domain if they want it bad enough. None of us knows what's going to happen, but you can be sure of one thing—we'll be the last to know. And if nobody buys your lease, you might find your-self right next door to a convenience store or a bar or who knows what. You're right about us at Seaside being latecomers, but I think you'll agree we've been good neighbors. This whole development is designed for outsiders, people who don't live here and don't give a whit about those of us who do."

"Now that's not true," said the government man.

"No, it isn't," said the developer.

J.D. shook his head. "If you ain't buyin' us out, then it's true." He sat down and began a conversation with those around him, including a familiar face.

A man sitting next to J.D. shouted, "We'll lose the loggerheads," but remained seated.

Dae touched Brax's arm. "That's the man who was on the beach when the turtles hatched."

Brax nodded.

Another voice came from the back of the room. "You people don't understand," Howard Satterwhite said, as he rose to speak. A well-respected, middle-aged, local businessman, Satterwhite presented an impressive appearance with a trim, athletic physique. Neatly dressed in khaki pants and a starched shirt, his deep mellow voice flowed with the subdued drawl of Southern gentry, like aged bourbon.

"This island has to be improved," Satterwhite said. "It's deteriorated to the point where something has to be done. The thing is, we don't need to go from one extreme to the other. What worries me about this plan is that it's too big, too ambitious. We need to upgrade the facilities we have, but we don't need to turn it into a place that only the rich can afford. This island has always been a place where regular families can come and relax without having to worry about congestion and spending an arm and a leg. I'm concerned that this development goes against that whole concept. The plan needs to be completely rethought. This island is like an old Ford on its last legs that needs to be traded in for a new model. But we don't need a new Mercedes, just a new Ford."

The government man responded. "This plan was developed with a variety of facilities to appeal to a broad range of the public, from economy to luxury."

"That won't mix," Satterwhite said. "Economy don't work side-by-side with luxury. Pretty soon it becomes economy quality at luxury prices. Besides, it's not just the question of economy versus luxury. It's the size of the whole thing. That, in itself, brings problems—traffic, overcrowding on the beach, a drain on public services. It needs to be scaled down."

"All of that is being considered," said the developer, "but investors have to have a return. This project is very costly and the investors as well as the state are looking for a big boost in revenue. This island has been a drain on the state for many years."

"That's a damn lie," an old man shouted from the back of the room, creating a chorus of support.

"So if that's what it's come to," said Satterwhite, talking over the buzz, "just admit that all the State cares about is the money. And the bigger, the better. That's what has been decided, right?"

"For a project like this, the economy of scale is very important," the developer replied.

"Then I guess our input doesn't mean anything," Satterwhite countered.

Other people began to stand up and shout at the two speakers and the meeting quickly disintegrated into an angry confrontation.

Brax looked at Jim and said, "What a waste of time. This is a complete set-up."

"Yeah," Jim agreed. "It's bullshit with a little perfume sprayed on."

The government man tried to quell the boisterous audience, but people began leaving their seats and walking out. Others approached the two speakers around the lectern and began hurling questions at them as if they were attacking them with hand grenades.

As the audience made their way from the room, many Seaside residents approached Brax and Jim, shaking their hands and thanking them for defending their interests. Dae followed the two men to make their way outside and through the small groups that milled around in the parking lot. Several people stopped them to vent their opinions, but the trio discretely pulled themselves away to escape into Brax's car.

As soon as they were clear of the parking lot and on the road, Dae said, "I'm glad you guys spoke up."

"It didn't do any good," Brax said.

"Not a damn bit of good," Jim added from the back seat. "It's going to happen. We might as well get used to it."

The car became quiet, the sullen resolve in the men's voices hanging in the air.

Brax broke the silence. "To hell with it. I'm not going to worry about it."

"Well," Jim said, "if we're going to lie like that blood suckin' developer, I'm not going to worry about it either."

Dae continued to silently look out the window.

Brax looked at her. "So what do you think?" he asked.

She deliberated for a moment before replying. "To hell with it. I'm not going to worry about it either."

A smile crept over Brax's face and turned into a hearty laugh. He reached over and slapped her leg. "You're some kind of woman," he said. "I think, by God, I might just be glad I know you."

"I might be glad of that, too," she said, with a smile. Then she slapped his knee and added emphatically, "By God!"

From behind, Jim let out a loud, "Oh shit!"

# 14

Brax was a native Georgian, but the coastal area so familiar to Dae seemed a world away from the Appalachian foothills of his upbringing. On St. Simons Island, they visited the eighteenth-century British settlement of Fort Frederica. At the visitor's center, they watched the film of the Battle of Bloody Marsh, the pivotal conflict that drove the Spanish out of Georgia. Afterward, they lingered among the ruins of the settlement and Dae acted as personal guide for Brax.

"My family came here from England in 1750," she said, "not long after Oglethorpe settled in Savannah. It was only eight years after the Battle of Bloody Marsh. We've been here since Georgia was a colony."

He listened as Dae explained the history of the area as if he were one of her former students.

"I hope I don't bore you with all of this," she said.

"No, not at all. Places like this fascinate me," Brax said. "I could spend hours here, reading every plaque and just imagining what it was like to be in this place almost three hundred years ago. It's fascinating. I think I would have liked to be a history teacher like you, but I couldn't have put up with the little urchins."

"Most of them were good." She paused to reflect. "Well, honestly, it did get a little frustrating in the last few years. My ambition was to teach at the college level but universities expect you to have a doctorate and, after I got married and the family came along, I gave up on that. Eventually, I did get a Master's Degree."

"You would have been a great college professor."

"I guess it wasn't to be, but I can envision *you* in a dingy university classroom with a beard and a sport coat with leather elbow patches." She laughed at the image.

"Oh sure, I'd be a regular Mr. Chips." He gave her a look of self-parody, then stepped closer to read a plaque on the remains of a tabby structure. "Anyhow, my wife liked coming to places like this too, but she would get her fill of it pretty quickly."

Dae looked at him seriously. "Jane—you can say her name." Suddenly she shifted the conversation completely away from the historic ruins. "You loved her very much, didn't you?"

He nodded and stared at the ground. "Yes."

"I loved John, too," she said. "And he loved me—I never doubted that. I just wish he had loved himself as well."

Her comment hinted at a mystery, but Brax didn't pursue it. "That's the hardest thing to do sometimes—love yourself," he said. She would tell him about John when she was ready, he thought.

They continued to walk through the ruins, but now their minds were elsewhere.

In a short while she spoke again. "John was ill. Eventually he just faded away." She took a deep breath. "It was horrible. I …" She closed her eyes and put a hand to her mouth.

He put his arm around her shoulders and gently pulled her to him.

After a brief silence, she seemed to gather herself and moved from his side. She turned to face him directly and clutched his right hand with her left. "When we first met, you said that you never get over the loss of a loved one and that's true. When you lose someone, you don't stop loving them. But you don't have to follow them to the grave."

It was such a simple statement, yet it hit him in the gut. Jim had said the same thing, less eloquently—gotta keep spittin' and gettin'.

"No, you have to keep on living," he said, speaking to himself as much as to Dae.

"That's right," she said. "John would want it that way and I think Jane would, too."

"Good, we're in agreement."

Brax turned to a young couple nearby. He took his camera from his pocket and asked, "Excuse me, would you mind taking a picture of us?"

"Sure," the girl replied.

He handed the camera to the girl and led Dae to a spot a few feet away. A minute later, he admired the image of him and Dae standing beside an old cannon with the remains of a tabby and stone garrison in the background. They looked very much alive among the relics of the past.

---

Lunch was usually a light snack at Dae's place, but dinner was Brax's favorite time. Most evenings they left the island to sample restaurants on neighboring islands, in Brunswick, further inland, or all the way to Savannah. Some nights they ate at small diners with scruffy floors and well-worn tables, ignoring the fast food places. On week-ends, they often dressed less casually for dinner and splurged on upscale fare.

One afternoon they went to Savannah and Dae guided Brax to her old neighborhood. When they approached the house where she had lived for so many years, he started to pull onto the driveway but Dae stopped him.

"Park here on the curb," she said. Two cars visible through the open doors of the garage signaled that the new owners were at home.

"Do you want to ask them if we can go in and look around?" he asked. "They probably won't mind."

"No, I think not. I loved that house but I don't want to dwell on it."

"It's a good house," he said. "I can see you living there."

"It was time to leave," she stated coldly.

With a hand propped against her cheek, she stared at the hedges on one side of the house. She could see the rusty Jeep, the hose, and John's body slumped in the front seat. She had thought it would be nice to see her old home again, but now she wished she hadn't come.

"Do you see those holly bushes running beside the driveway?"

Brax looked toward the driveway, but before he could answer, she said, "I hated them."

He shifted in his seat and cleared his throat.. "Do you want to leave?"

"Yes."

Dae spoke haltingly as she guided Brax through streets unfamiliar to him. When he stopped at a red light, she said, "Thanks for taking me."

He looked at her as if he sensed her discomfort. "You're welcome."

She reached over, patted his leg and smiled.

When the light turned green, he urged the car forward and she felt her past slip further away.

Later they strolled through the historic district of the city and Dae filled Brax in on some of the lesser known local lore that escapes most of the tourist guides.

"You love this town, don't you?" he asked.

"It's not a perfect place. I suppose nowhere is. But it's a part of me and, I think, in some small way, I'm a part of it. I've traveled around the country and I know there aren't many cities that respect the past the way Savannah does. Charleston and Boston, and San Francisco and a few others, have kept a lot of their charm. But most cities in America have torn down the past and replaced it with a hodgepodge of random urban … clutter."

He sighed. "Like Atlanta."

"Yes, like Atlanta is now. When I went to Agnes Scott in the sixties, Decatur was a charming little town, and Atlanta was a young, vibrant city. Now, when I go back, it seems so busy, yet lifeless. Gosh, that's completely contradictory, isn't it?"

"No, I know what you mean. That's a good description—busy, but lifeless. That's why I left."

———

In the evening, Brax suggested they pass on the crowded bars and restaurants along the river front and chose instead to dine at the Hyatt Regency. They took the elevator to the restaurant on the top floor overlooking the Savannah River.

Relaxing with a glass of scotch before the meal, Brax was struck by how perfectly the setting complimented Dae's features. Though her skin had lost the tautness of youth, it still radiated under the low lights of the chandeliers. She had high cheek bones, blue eyes, and perfectly coiffed short hair with just a hint of gray. A simple diamond pendant rested gently on her sweater. She seemed to fit among the gilded china, the white linens, and the crystal goblets as if she had been placed there for a photograph. Beyond the big plate glass window, the street lamps and shop lights illuminated the river walk below, alive with activity. The river, bathed in the glow of an early moon, stretched before them, a calm reminder of the roots of commerce for the city.

Dae looked at the moonlight shimmering on the water and took a sip of wine. "Moon River," she said, singing the words softly.

"So are you that woman in *Breakfast at Tiffany's*? You know—what's her name?"

"Do you mean Holly Golightly or Audrey Hepburn?"

"Yeah, Holly Golightly."

"No, I didn't like that character. I just liked the song, 'Moon River.' Johnny Mercer wrote it. He's from Savannah."

"Yes, yes he was." He couldn't resist adding, "I know a few things about music."

"Really? You've never said anything. I want to hear more about this. I love music, too."

"Some other time. I promise. I'll bore you to tears about my taste, but I'll warn you, I'm pretty much old school."

"Me, too. In fact, I guess I'm just an old school teacher. Ha!"

He looked at her with a huge grin. "You're my kind of girl."

"A girl? Oh my, I haven't been called that in a long time." She grinned and then her face turned serious. "Thank you."

He knew what she meant. The wellspring of youth never completely dries up.

Soon after the main course was served, Brax impulsively brought up the subject of the development of the island. "It's going to happen, you know. And soon."

"It doesn't change anything," she said. "We'll still have the beach and our homes. All the things we have now."

"Yeah, I'm pretty settled in. I'm not happy about the development, but it's not just that. I want the world to stop spinning around at warp speed for a while. I used to feel like I was pretty much in control of my life but now everything has gone crazy. There's no common decency anymore. Politics, movies, sports—everywhere you turn, the lines of what's acceptable just keep being pushed further away. It bugs the hell out of me. The island was a place for me to get away from all that and live my last years in peace." He paused. "I'm sorry, there I go again. My senility kicking in."

"No, I know what you mean. Things are a lot different now than when we were younger. Life seemed a lot simpler then."

"Jim says I worry about things too much and he's right. They say you shouldn't worry about things you can't control and that's the way I need to look at it."

"I'm glad you feel that way. Everything will turn out okay. We'll be just fine."

Her words had a soothing effect, as if they were coated with aloe. *We'll be just fine*, she said. The two of them. It wasn't the first time she had said it and the thought made him realize what was really important to him and how trivial his other concerns were.

"Yeah, we'll be just fine," he said.

They looked at each other as if they had just agreed to become "we."

After dinner there was an hour and a half drive back to the island. When they got to the interstate he put a CD in the player and the mellow sounds of Nat King Cole oozed from the speakers.

"That's beautiful. Is that your kind of music?"

"It's one kind. Nobody sings like that anymore."

"Yes, you're right."

The track changed to "When I Fall in Love" and neither of them spoke as they lost themselves in reverie.

When the CD ended she said, "That was very nice. Everything about today was nice. Thank you."

"Hey, you had as much to do with it as I did. Thank you." It took him a second to realize how formal that sounded. "Gee, we sound like the Royal Family, or something."

"Well, whatever, it was the best date I've been on in a very long time," she said with a grin.

"Is that what you call it—a date?"

"Well, it's not business and we're not married. So what else would you call it?"

"Dinner," he said straight-faced.

She had said the word "married," a first for either of them. But she had dismissed the word flippantly. Or had she?

When they arrived back at Seaside it was almost ten o'clock. He pulled into her driveway and led her to the door.

"Would you like to join me for a nightcap?" she asked. "I have some good sherry."

"I never turn down an offer for a drink from a pretty woman."

She led him inside and poured each of them a glass of sherry and retrieved a CD from a rack on the bookcase.

"This is the kind of music I like." She put the disk in the player and the stirring sounds of the Percy Faith orchestra playing the "Theme from a Summer Place" began. The music continued with other memorable themes from classic movies of earlier days. The last track was "Love is a Many Splendored Thing."

"Those are great songs," he said. "Great music can make a movie. A lot of times I remember the tune more than the movie."

"Yes, these songs just lift your spirits. They're so inspiring."

She played more music and they listened with little talk as they nursed the sherry while listening to Anne Murray and Josh Groban.

"I can tell that you like good music. Do you sing or play an instrument?" he asked.

"I used to play piano, but I gave it up years ago. I gave mine to my daughter. And I used to be in the choir at church, but now I only sing in the shower—off key." She smiled and added, "How about you?"

"I played a little trumpet," he said modestly. He wasn't ready to tell her that he played solo in front of forty thousand people or that he played professionally part-time for years. "I guess that's why I'm just a big blowhard."

"You're not a blowhard."

"I used to be. But I try not to be that way anymore. I'm getting mellow in my old age."

They watched television for a while and soon it was eleven o'clock.

"I'd better be hitting the road," he said.

She walked with him to the door. He turned to her, put his arm around her waist and pulled her toward him. He kissed her gently. She held to his embrace and he closed his eyes, savoring the touch of her body against his.

"Stay here," she said.

He stayed.

He slept on the side of the bed that she never used.

# 15

Brax awoke and rolled over to see Dae facing him with her eyes closed. He lay motionless, studying her features as his eyes adjusted to the pre-dawn darkness. She half-opened her eyes and looked at him.

"Hi," she said.

"Good morning."

"What time is it?"

"A little after six," he replied.

"I'll get up in a minute. I always shower before I walk."

"We can sleep in."

"Really? Do you want to?" she asked.

"We've got all day to walk."

"Good, I'm sleepy."

He nudged against her and felt her soft warmth. They went back to sleep to the rhythm of separate heart beats.

When Brax woke again he put on his pants and went into the bathroom to freshen up. Dae was awake but still in bed. The pulsating wail of a siren stirred weakly in the distance, then became progressively louder as the vehicle got nearer.

"Sounds like it's coming here," he said. "I hope nobody's kicked the bucket. I'm going to take a look." He hastily finished dressing.

She sat up with the sheet pulled to her neck.

"Are you coming?" he asked, as he buttoned his shirt.

"No."

"Okay, I'll be back in a bit." He leaned over to kiss her on the cheek, then hustled away.

The siren was loud now and came from the direction of the front gate. Dae heard the front door close behind Brax. She sat paralyzed on the side of the bed, recalling the eerie sound of a siren years before.

---

Dae looked at the clock on the bedside table and it was after three o'clock in the morning. It had been a fitful night of little sleep and when she turned toward John he was gone. She rose and sat on the side of the bed to get her bearings and listened for him rattling around in the dark house. He had been acting very depressed and she wondered if he had taken his medication. She turned on the nightstand light, pulled herself from the comfort of the bed, and grabbed a robe from the closet before starting to search for him.

There was no sign of him in the other rooms upstairs, and no answer when she called his name. Downstairs, she walked through the kitchen and three other rooms, repeating his name louder. No response. She was beginning to get an ominous feeling. Through the windows she could see that the deck was empty. Checking the garage, both cars were in their normal spots. A surge of adrenaline rushed through her body as she grabbed the kitchen phone to call 911. She pressed one number, then placed the phone back in the cradle.

Collecting herself, she closed her eyes and yelled, "John, where are you?"

Maybe he was outside in the yard, or taking a walk. He had been unpredictable for the last several days and she wanted to do everything she could think of before calling for help. Grabbing a flashlight from the pantry, she walked from the front door into the yard. She heard a familiar noise coming from the side of the house. Almost hidden by the tall shrubs, she could see the old rusty Jeep he used for hunting and fishing. The engine was running and when she pushed through the shrubs she could see a large hose extended from the exhaust to a crack in a back window. The dark shadow of a figure was visible behind the steering wheel.

Her heart was jolted as if she had just touched a high voltage line. In full panic, she rushed over, pulled the hose from the window, and then tried to open the driver's door. It was locked. She tried the other doors with the same result.

Some landscaping rocks lay nearby and she wiggled one furiously to lift it from the dirt trench. The glass on the window was stronger than she expected and it took three tries to break it. Each time, she yelled "John! John!" A brief whiff of fumes hit her face as the window broke, then quickly dissipated. In a nightmarish daze, she reached through the broken window and unlocked the door, her head uncomfortably close to his motionless body. With the door open she reached past him to turn off the ignition, then shook his shoulder and yelled again, "John!" With the seat tilted back, his body leaned to the rear.

"John, John, wake up!" She continued to plead through her tears.

She put her mouth to his and breathed into it furiously. After a few seconds that seemed like hours, he let out a low grunt, tilted his head toward her and opened his eyes slightly. She rolled down the other windows and opened the doors before unbuckling the seat belt and grasping him by the shoulders. At well over two hundred pounds, he was too heavy for her to lift but she tugged at him as hard as she could to pull him from the vehicle.

As Dae grappled with him, John began to show signs of life. He let out a loud "Aaah," and gasped for air. "Medic … medic … men down," he said as he lifted himself from the seat and fell halfway out of the door.

Dae pulled and shoved, wrestling awkwardly with his big frame until he was free of the Jeep and on the ground.

"Get down, Charlie's out there," he said.

She ran inside, called 911 from the kitchen phone and hurried back outside. Sitting beside him, she took his hand and tried to comfort him as he muttered words that made no sense.

"Mother, tell Daddy I'll be back in a little while," he said.

She pressed her face to his and kissed him repeatedly, then buried her sobbing face in his chest until she heard the distant shriek of a siren. In minutes, the front yard glowed in the light of the strobe on the emergency truck and three men in blue uniforms approached. One carried a bag, another a small metal cylinder.

Dae stood and spoke excitedly. "He was unconscious when I found him but he's awake now."

The men knelt down beside John and one began to check his pulse while the one in charge spoke to him.

"How do you feel?" the paramedic asked.

"Where's Jerome?" John said.

"He's not thinking straight," Dae said to the men in blue.

The man with the oxygen tank moved in, placed the cover over John's nose and mouth, and told him to breathe deeply. John's eye's opened wide in a trance-like gaze as he breathed heavily, his chest heaving with the effort.

"How long was he in the vehicle with the engine running?" one of the men asked.

"I don't know," Dae replied. "The motor was still on when I got here."

"We need to get him to the hospital," the man said.

John was quiet and calm as the EMT crew lifted him onto a gurney and rolled it through the back doors of the emergency truck. "We're taking him to St. Joseph's," the leader said.

Dae gathered herself as the mind-blasting shock of suddenness drifted away and the pall of reality began to set in. Still in her robe and nightclothes, she stepped into the back of the vehicle.

John lay motionless, staring vacantly at the roof. Then he

turned his head and looked at Dae. "Mama, don't let Charlotte have my rifle."

She could almost read the muddled thoughts in her husband's mind. Jerome, whom he had asked for earlier, was his best buddy, killed long ago in a war that never ended. Charlotte was his sister. She was dead, too, as were his mother and father.

Dae had a feeling that, in a way, John had passed on as well.

She looked away from her husband and into the knowing eyes of the paramedic. The siren started again as the big white truck pulled out of the driveway.

———◆———

Brax arrived at the front gate as the ambulance wailed by. He followed it for no more than a quarter of a mile before it pulled off the oceanside road with lights still flashing. Beyond the dunes, he could see several people gathered around something on the beach. As the rescue team scrambled from the vehicle, Brax got out of his car and headed for a nearby footpath. In a matter of seconds, three EMT's passed him at a run carrying bags of gear, an oxygen tank, and a gurney.

Approaching the beach, Brax realized that the onlookers were standing near a body lying on the sand just beyond the tide line. Even from a distance he recognized the familiar pair of tropical design shorts and the large, pale figure sprawled out like a beached whale. The squatty, brown figure of Mamadou Jawara was bent over the body of Jim Hawkins, pumping his chest.

A twinge of panic hit Brax. *Be alive, big guy.*

The EMT's hustled to the scene and urged everyone back. Brax followed and joined the growing number of onlookers, feeling conspicuous in the loafers, slacks, and button shirt he had re-trieved from Dae's bedside. One of the crew took over from Mo-madou and continued to apply CPR. Slowly, Jim's labored breath-ing improved.

"What happened?" Brax asked Momadou.

"A cardiac seizure, I think," Momadou answered. "I think he's okay now, but he needs to get checked out."

Within a few minutes, Jim appeared to be on the way to revival. After the medics lifted Jim onto the gurney, Momadou helped them carry it over the soft sand to the ambulance.

Brax leaned to Jim before he was placed in the vehicle. "How do you feel?"

Jim looked up from his supine position. "I'll live." He spoke in a low voice, almost a whisper. "You can't kill an old drunk that easy." He reached into his pocket and handed Brax his cell phone. "Call my daughter. She's on the list as Kathy with a "K." She's coming to see me tomorrow. Tell her not to worry."

Brax took the phone and wondered what he was going to say to Jim's daughter without alarming her.

As they lifted Jim into the ambulance he motioned toward Momadou and spoke to Brax. "He kissed me."

Brax turned to Momadou with a questioning look.

"CPR." Momadou smiled.

Brax reached out to shake Momadou's hand as the ambulance drove away. "Thanks, Jaws. Have you ever done this before?"

"A few times, but only as practice. I worked as a Nursing Assistant before I got into hospital administration."

"You may have saved his life."

"I just happened to be there." Momadou let out a long breath. "Just lucky."

———

Dae was dressed and standing outside of her front door when Brax returned.

"Is anyone hurt?" she asked.

"It was Jim. Apparently he collapsed on the beach and Jaws gave him CPR. He was conscious and seemed to be feeling okay by the time the medics arrived. They took him to the hospital to check him out."

"Oh dear."

"I'm going to the hospital now. Do you want to come?"

"Yes, of course."

"I've got to go inside to get my billfold and keys."

She followed him inside, and while he was gathering his things in the bedroom, she poured herself a glass of water in the kitchen.

Returning from the bedroom, he said, "I'm going to run home for a minute and change clothes. I'll drop by and pick you up."

She stood at the counter with her back to him, but he could see that she was trembling. The water sloshed around in the glass from her shaking hands. He moved beside her and she was crying.

"Dae, what's wrong? Is it about Jim?"

"No." She stopped shaking and brushed the tears from her face with her hands. "Of course, I care for him, but I guess I'm just having an anxiety attack. I'll be fine, but—I'm sorry—I'd better stay here. You go on without me."

He hesitated, torn between trying to help her deal with her emotions and going to the hospital to be with his friend. A sense of urgency pulled him toward the hospital.

"I'll be back as soon as I can." He kissed her on the cheek. "Love you."

When he opened the door to leave, she forced a prune-faced smile as a new set of tears rolled down her cheeks. "Love you," she said.

The last words, *Love you*, echoed in her mind as she went into the living room to sit in the big easy chair and collect her thoughts. She pulled a tissue from the dispenser on the side table and dried her face. The echo continued.

*Love you. Love you.*

———

It all happened so fast. One day she was alone in a big dark house that harbored ghosts of the past. The next day it seemed as if she were in a different world with a heart full of mixed-up feelings. Her life had brought her to a totally unexpected place. Dae needed someone to talk to, someone to just listen. There was only one person for that—Julie.

It would be at least six o'clock before her daughter got home from work. She would have all day to sort through things before Julie called her back.

"Julie," she said to the recorder, "call me tonight, please, when you have a little quiet time. I'd like to chat for a minute."

That should get her daughter's curiosity working overtime. She wasn't exactly sure what she wanted to say. She had to think about that.

It was almost eight-thirty when Julie retuned the call.

"Sorry I couldn't call sooner. I had to work late and grab a bite of dinner before we put the kids to bed."

"It's nothing urgent. But it's been almost a week since we last talked."

They spoke briefly about the children, Ben's travels, and Julie's work.

"How are things with you?" Julie asked.

"Just fine. Everything is so different. It's different in a good way, but … I've been caught a little off guard." She didn't intend to get into it right off the bat, but she couldn't keep the words from spilling out.

"Off guard?"

"Yes. I've been out of the social circle for a long time."

"You mean like dating and going out with men?"

"Yes. Being with the opposite sex. Especially as an old woman."

"Oh, you're not old. You're just full of life. And you're still beautiful. So … you have some men friends?"

"Just one."

"It's the man that you told me about, isn't it? The one you asked to your place for dinner when you first moved in."

"Gosh, you remember that?"

"Of course, I remember. I was happy to see you settle in so quickly."

"Well, yes, it's the same man." She felt strange talking to her daughter about affairs of the heart. It's supposed to be the other way around, she thought.

"What's his name?"

"Braxton. Everyone calls him Brax. He's maybe a few years older than me, but he's fairly attractive and fun to be with."

"Brax? As in B-R-A-X?"

"Yes."

"I like that. It's a nice name. How serious is this?"

"I don't know. We see each other every day and we do a lot of things together." Dae sighed. "Julie, I feel so guilty. He doesn't know."

"Mom, you'll have to tell him. He'll understand."

"Maybe, but I don't know how. I've let it go too far."

"Well, you don't have to answer this question, but I have to ask. Has he used the 'L' word?"

"It's not like that. We're not kids, and we don't sit around making goo-goo talk." She hedged the question. Brax had used the word casually, almost like a throw-away line as he walked out the door. Was he serious?

"So he hasn't made his intentions known?"

"Kind of, but not in so many words. Julie, here's why I called—I want you to know that I'm dating a man, or I'm seeing a man, or whatever you call it. But I'll always love your father."

"You don't have to tell me that, Mom. I've never doubted it. You've stayed true to him all these years. I told you before, it's time for you to think of yourself. No one can blame you for that."

"I have to feel good about it myself."

"If you feel good when you are with … uh … Brax, that's all that matters. Whatever you do, do it on your own terms. You're still a very pretty woman and there are a lot of older men who would be attracted to a classy lady like you."

"Maybe, but he hasn't pushed me. It's a mutual thing. I know him well enough to be convinced he's not some lothario." As she spoke, Dae realized that she didn't *know* as much about Brax as she *felt* about him.

"I think you recognize where you're heading. If it makes you feel good, even if it doesn't work out in the long run, it's a good thing. But you can't let him get too involved before you tell him."

"You're right. I'm going to."

"I'm glad you called and, by the way, that answers my question about the 'L' word. Carpe diem, Mom."

"Love you."

"Love you, too. Bye."

*Love you.* The words wouldn't go away. Brax had said them first, but she didn't hesitate to return them. It felt as good to say the words as it did to hear them.

# 16

Brax arrived at the hospital shortly after Jim was taken into the emergency room. He had been encouraged when he saw Jim on the beach, awake and able to speak, but now felt anxious as he awaited the diagnosis.

Using Jim's phone, he called his daughter, Kathy, in Warner Robins and told her what had happened. He tried to reassure her, but there was no way to make the incident sound harmless, especially for a man of Jim's age and physical condition. Brax gave her the address of the hospital and she said she would be there in about three hours. A few minutes later a doctor entered the waiting room.

"He's had a heart attack and there's arterial blockage," the doctor said. "He needs to go into surgery right away."

"So is he in immediate danger?" asked Brax.

"He's in good hands," the doctor said. "We're getting set-up for the prep work now."

"Can I see him?"

"Just for a minute, no more. We need to sedate him right away."

"Sure."

Brax went into the room where Jim lay on a bed in a hospital gown. "How're you feeling?"

"Fit as a fiddle—with a broken string. Never understood that saying."

"They're going to fix your string."

"Oh, hell, I'm beyond fixing. They can just patch me up and

I'll be back pounding the sand with all the other old geezers in no time."

"That's right, just like I did."

"Yeah, you had a good incentive."

Brax looked at him quizzically.

"Dae. You didn't waste any time going after her."

Brax smiled and made a slight closed-mouth laugh.

"Don't blame you either."

"Okay, that's enough about me. I just wanted to see you for a minute and let you know I'm pulling for you. I can't stay long. The doc says they need to put you into dreamland."

"Thanks. Appreciate you being here."

"I'll see you after the surgery." Brax turned to leave.

"Did you call Kathy?"

Brax stopped and looked back. "Yeah, she'll be here by the time you wake up."

"Don't let her get upset. I'll come out of this spittin' and gettin'."

"I'm sure." Brax nodded. "I'll be with her." He left the room, knowing that Jim was not as calm as he let on. He could see it in his friend's face.

Now the roles were reversed, and it was Brax's turn to be with Jim in the hospital. He walked outside to get some fresh air and called Dae on his cell phone.

"It was a heart attack and he's going into surgery now. They're putting in a stent."

"Gosh, that happened fast," she said. "I'm glad they got to him so quickly."

"The doctor said Jaws saved his life."

"That's wonderful. I can't leave right now, but I can be there in about an hour."

"There's no need. I don't know how long he'll be in surgery and after that he'll be out of it for a while. I'll call you when I know something."

Brax moved from his seat beside Dae in the waiting room and moved closer to Jim's grandson, Ethan. He held open a Sports Illustrated magazine to a full page action shot and pointed to a baseball player making a tag at second base. "Wonder who that is."

"That's Derek Jeter," Ethan said. The young boy wore shorts, sneakers, and a blue T-shirt with Calvary Baptist in script on the front and the number three on the back.

"Derek Jeter? He plays for the Braves, doesn't he?" Brax grinned.

"No! The Yankees," Ethan screamed.

"Oh yeah, he plays catcher for the Yankees." Brax faked a serious look.

"No! Shortstop." Ethan's face morphed into a smile, in obvious recognition that Brax was playing a little game.

"Boy, you're smart," said Momadou, from across the room. "You play baseball?"

"Sometimes," Ethan said. "Baseball season is over. I play soccer now."

"How old are you?" asked Brax.

"I'm six."

"He's so cute," said Dae.

Brax set the magazine aside and stood to face Jim's daughter, Kathy, as she entered the room. Momadou and Dae rose from their chairs as well. They looked at Kathy and waited for her to speak.

"He's awake," Kathy said. She was red-eyed and sniffley, but calm. "Thanks for giving me a few minutes alone." She looked at Brax. "You can go in now."

"And you," Dae said, looking at Momadou. "We can't all go at once." She turned to Kathy. "I'm sure they won't mind if you're in there, too. I'll stay with Ethan."

"Thank you." Kathy leaned down to speak to her son. "She'll

take care of you. I'll be back in a little while."

Ethan looked at Dae and then back to his mother. "Okay. Did Granddaddy get hurt?"

"Just a little bit," Kathy said. "But he said that when he gets well he'll take you fishing."

"I like going fishing with Granddaddy."

Kathy kissed her son. "I won't be gone long."

Brax joined Kathy and Momadou for the short walk to Jim's room.

Jim was sitting up and appeared to be alert. A smile came across his face when he saw his buddies.

"Hello, old man," Brax said. "You doing all right?"

"I'm not exactly full of piss and vinegar right now, but I guess heaven's not ready for me yet." Jim's voice was lower than normal and he spoke deliberately, as if it were an effort.

"Maybe not," said Brax, "but there's an angel here." He tilted his head at Momadou.

"Yeah, I think you're right." Jim looked at the black man and raised his voice a notch. "How are you, Jaws?"

"I'm good," Momadou said. "I hope you're feeling better."

"Ah, I'll be spittin' and getting' in no time." He took a labored breath. "I owe you my thanks for that. I don't remember falling down, but I remember looking up and there you were. Boy, you were there all right—right in my face."

"You couldn't breathe." Momadou sounded apologetic. "I had to get some air into you and get your lungs working again."

"You did the right thing." Jim paused and took a deep breath. "I'm grateful, to say the least."

"And I am as well," said Kathy, looking at Momadou. "Thank you very much."

"I was lucky to be there at the right time. I just did what had to be done."

"Maybe so," Jim said, "but that's not the way I look at it. The way

I see it, you're my hero. Like Brax said, my angel. A black angel for an old redneck. How about that?" He smiled broadly as the others had a laugh.

Kathy moved to Momadou and gave him a hug. "Thank you, again," she said. Then she turned to Brax and hugged him. "And thank you, too, for calling me and being here with us."

"I'm just doing what he did for me. I was in the same boat not along ago."

"Oh?" said Kathy.

"He didn't have a heart attack," said Jim.

"No," said Brax. "But I had surgery and I didn't know what might happen. Jim was here with me. Anyhow, if there's anything I can do for you, let me know."

"That's really nice of you. I'm glad Dad has friends like you."

In a few minutes, Momadou excused himself and Dae came in to pay her respects. She leaned over and touched a cheek to Jim. Stepping back, she smiled at him and said, "You look good."

"You're a nice woman, Dae, but a bad liar. I know I look like a loggerhead that's been run over by one of those dune buggies. It's good to see you, though."

"You have such a strong spirit. I know you're going to do well."

"Yeah, they've got their work cut out for them with me, but they know what they're doing. It's probably a good thing it happened. They got me rerouted now. It could have been a lot worse."

Jim's voice began to fade again and he looked tired.

"We better leave now," said Brax. "We'll be back after you get some rest."

"You don't have to leave," Jim said. "I feel alright."

"No, Dad," Kathy said. "The doctor told us not to stay long. We'll be back."

Jim looked at his daughter, then Brax, and Dae. "Thanks for coming. Good to see all of y'all." As they were leaving the room, he closed his eyes.

After leaving the hospital, Brax spoke to Dae in the parking lot as she approached her car. "Jim's daughter wants to take him home with her when he gets out."

"Really? Did she tell you that?"

"Yes. She doesn't like him living down here by himself. She's tried to get him to come live with her before and this makes her more determined."

"What does he think?"

"I haven't had a chance to talk to him about it, but I know him, and he won't agree to it. We've hashed it out before and he doesn't want to be a burden on anyone. I know how he feels and I feel the same way."

"Brax, when people are family and they love you, you're not a burden."

"We are family. You, me, him, Jaws."

Dae stared at Brax for a second. Then she said, "You have three sons, and grandkids, and daughters-in-law. That's your family."

"And I love them all. That's why I don't want them to be tied down to me."

"That doesn't make sense."

"I know it doesn't to you but it does to me. And to Jim. Kathy won't understand it either, but I have to explain it to her as best I can. She can't make him go against his will and I don't want them to have a falling out because of it."

Dae shook her head. "He could have another heart attack and die here with no one around. That would be tragic."

"He could've died yesterday, or the day before, or he could die tomorrow. Or he might outlive both of us." Brax paused seeming to collect the words to fit his thoughts. "Look, there's one thing you've taught me and that is to hold on to today and then start all over again tomorrow."

Dae gazed at Brax, absorbing his words. Then she stepped to him and they embraced. "I like being a part of this family," she said.

In her car, she thought about what she had said. *Have I forsaken my own family?*

––•––

Jim was released from the hospital four days later. Brax did his magic and convinced Kathy to give Jim time to fully recover from his operation before bugging him about moving.

A couple of weeks after he returned to Seaside, Jim was back on the beach, but he no longer walked alone. He and Momadou became an oddly familiar sight as they walked side-by-side, the big, bulky white man next to the short, stocky black man.

"We're like a big ice cream sundae," Jim said one day. "Two scoops of vanilla and one scoop of chocolate."

Momadou didn't respond and Jim realized that, in an effort to be cute, he had made a comment that implied inequality. "I just meant size-wise, not quality. Sometimes one scoop is better than two."

Momadou recognized the mea culpa and a smile broke out on his face. He stuck out a fist and Jim bumped it with his.

"We bros now?" Jim asked.

"Yeah, we bros," Momadou replied.

A little further down the beach Jim turned the conversation to a serious tone. "Way out there somewhere," he said, looking at the ocean, "beyond all of that water is Africa."

Momadu assumed an anxious look, not knowing what Jim was getting at.

"I guess your ancestors, sometime way back when, came from there."

Before Jim could continue, Momadou said, "My great-great-great grandfather was a slave. We don't know any further back than that." He stopped in his tracks, his body tensed, and there was anger in his voice.

"Don't get mad, Jaws. That's what I'm getting at. I'm not sure I know how to say this, but I feel like I need to." Jim hesitated to gather his thoughts. "I know a lot of things were not right in the past. And I can't say that I wanted things to change so maybe, in a way, I was part of the problem."

Jim looked at Momadou who had turned stone-faced and he wasn't sure how his words were being received.

"When I had my little episode right here on this beach, you saved me with your own breath. I hate to say it, but I'm not sure that if the situation had been reversed I would have done the same thing. But now I would. At least I'd try. Not just for you, but for anyone. You know, no matter what they looked like."

Momadou seemed to ponder Jim's comment for a moment. Then he said, "I understand," and resumed walking.

"Good," replied Jim. "Don't go so damn fast," he said, as he shuffled to catch up.

# 17

It all started the day they saw the first sign go up. Brax had taken Jim back to the doctor for a follow-up visit, and Dae went with them. On the way back, about a mile and a half from the entrance to Seaside, they saw the flatbeds unloading grading equipment and workers beginning to unroll the chain link fencing. Two men held up a large sign while two others worked on setting it in the ground. **ABERNATHY CONSTRUCTION**, the sign read, along with permit numbers and encroachment warnings.

"There goes the neighborhood," Jim said.

"I knew that meeting was a waste of time," Brax added. "The sign says construction but it should say destruction. That's what they're really doing."

"It's a little way from us," Dae said, looking at the sign. Then she turned to Brax. "Besides, remember what we said after the meeting? We said we weren't going to worry about it. I thought we had agreed not to let this spoil our lives."

Jim faked a cough and Brax looked him with one raised eyebrow, acknowledging that his friend hadn't made any such agreement.

"Hey," Jim said, "this is just the beginning. The plans that politician showed us at the meeting indicated a lot of space shown as future potential. They'll be working on this thing for years. No telling how big it'll get. The bastards won't be happy 'til you can't walk the beach without stepping on some lard ass Yankee fiddling with his pod phone, or whatever you call those things."

"Oh, Jim, don't be so dramatic," Dae said.

Brax didn't say a word. As much as he wanted to agree with Dae, he was beginning to feel like an endangered species again.

It didn't take long for the activity level to ramp up. The flow of trucks of all shapes and sizes and vans shuttling workers back and forth was virtually non-stop from early morning until after dark. Other vehicles traveling on the road near the construction site were required to slow down and often come to a complete stop. Using the main road that circled the island, the residents of Seaside usually avoided the area by taking the long way around. Still, there was only one way on and off the island. Traffic often backed up on the six mile stretch of causeway leading to the high-span bridge that connected the island to the mainland.

Brax and Jim went to the construction site every day. Usually, they walked down the beach and watched the activity beyond the barriers that extended to the high tide line. Some days they drove a car, parked on the side of the road, and peered through the chain link fence.

Soon the foundation of a large building became evident beyond the office trailers, construction vehicles, and piles of materials. One morning, Brax and Jim watched as a new, more impressive sign was erected:

**THE BREAKWATER**
**At Serenity Shores**
**Your Escape to the Golden Isles**
**A Wainwright- Haskins Development**

"Serenity Shores?" Jim said. "Who came up with that crap?

"I guess they can call it whatever they want," said Brax.

"Maybe we need to name our beach."

"Yeah, something like … Geriatric Shores," Brax deadpanned.

"Too corny," Jim countered. "How about ... Dead Dauber Dunes?" He grinned.

"A little too descriptive," Brax replied. "I don't think Dae would go for that."

They tossed around a few more names until the stream of ridiculous ideas petered out and they stood mumbling to themselves, poking around in the corners of their mind for a clever thought.

Finally, Brax threw out a name that had a serious ring to it. "How about Sunrise Beach? That's when we're there a lot of times—at sunrise."

Jim pondered the thought. "Yeah, that's not bad." He nodded approvingly. "Sunrise Beach—that fits." A scowl formed on his face and he blurted out loudly, "Screw 'em and their damn Serenity Shores!"

"Yeah."

*Sunrise Beach.* Brax figured Dae would like that name.

———◦———

Brax lay on the sofa in a pair of sweat pants and a T-shirt trying to take a nap when the doorbell rang. Opening the door, he was greeted by two men. He recognized one of them as the young developer's representative from the rancorous meeting at the Conference Center a couple of months earlier. He couldn't remember the man's name, but the blue suit he was wearing appeared to be the same one he wore at the meeting. The other man appeared athletically fit and militarily neat in a white short-sleeve dress shirt and black tie.

"That's him," the man in the blue suit said softly to the other one.

"Good afternoon," the man in short sleeves said. "I'm Special Agent Jameson of the Georgia Bureau of Investigation." He displayed his badge. "Are you Braxton Donovan?"

"Yes." A rush of anxiety knocked the drowsiness from Brax.

"Could we have a few words with you? This is Mr. Templeton. He represents Wainwright-Haskins, the developers of Serenity Shores. I believe you gentlemen have met."

"Yes, we have," Brax said. He acknowledged Templeton with a look of disdain.

Templeton responded with a placid, "Hello."

Brax ushered the two men inside, wondering how it was that his opposition to the development could have reached the level of the GBI. "Have a seat." He extended a hand and the two men sat down on the sofa. Brax settled in the recliner directly in front of them.

"Mr. Donovan," Jameson began, "there was an incident at the Serenity Shores work site recently, and I'd like to ask you a few questions that might help us in our investigation of that incident."

Jameson leaned forward. With a solidly built body, muscular arms, thick neck, and close-cropped dark hair, he looked like a linebacker out of uniform. His sharply chiseled face and assured tone in his voice added to the demeanor of authority.

"Incident?" Brax asked.

"A shooting," Jameson replied.

"One of our men was almost killed," Templeton interjected.

Jameson turned to Templeton and raised his hand in a quieting gesture. "No one was injured," he said, returning his eyes to Brax. "But someone could have been. A little after seven o'clock last Friday night a shot was fired and nearly hit one of the foreman as he walked out of his trailer."

"Really?"

"The shot came from behind one of the other trailers and, in the panic, no one saw the shooter get away. We've seen some shoe prints in the sand leading to the road and tire tracks on the side of the road. That's how we think the shooter got away, but honestly, there is so much activity in that area that there are tracks all over the place. We did, however, recover the bullet from the trailer."

"Hmm," Brax mumbled.

"Now, Mr. Donovan, we are not implying that you had anything to do with this, or that you were even aware of it. But we know that some people are not in favor of the development and we thought you might have some insight that could be helpful."

Despite Jameson's circumspection, Brax felt on the spot. "You're right about a couple of things," he said. "I was not aware of any shooting. And you're also right about a lot of people being against … the development, as you call it, myself included. But you're wrong about me having any insight. I don't have a clue as to who might be stupid enough to shoot a gun at the workers."

As he spoke, Brax could still hear the anger in Jim's voice when he had said, "Screw 'em and their damn Serenity Shores," but he dismissed the possibility that Jim would resort to violence.

"Sometimes smart people do stupid things," Jameson said.

"I might shoot off my mouth," Brax said, "but I don't own a gun and I don't know anyone who is that crazy."

"My job is to check out everything," Jameson said. "I don't take anything for granted. Just go where the facts lead me."

"Why is the GBI involved in this?" Brax asked. "This seems like something the local police should be investigating."

"First of all," Jameson said, "I'm a friend of the county Chief of Police and he has requested my assistance. Secondly, this development is a high profile story around the state and the Governor is concerned about the possibility for unlawful acts of protest. We're not going to allow any disruption of the development to escalate further."

Brax looked at Jameson sternly. "You came here just because I spoke up at the meeting last month, didn't you? How did you know where I live?" As soon as the words left his mouth, he knew it was a foolish question.

"We knew from your comments that you're a resident of Seaside. Disregarding that, finding out where someone lives is not difficult. As I said, I'm not accusing you of anything. You're not the only person we'll be talking to, of course. The fact that you spoke up in front of a lot of witnesses might actually be in your favor. It could indicate that you would be the least likely person to bring suspicion upon yourself." Jameson gripped his hands together with the fingers laced and his eyes narrowed. "But it also tells me that you are a leader of opposition to Serenity Shores and, as such, you might know the person we're looking for."

"So you think I may have encouraged this?" Brax turned his eyes from Jameson to Templeton and back again.

"No, you're free to have your own opinion and speak your mind. The purpose of my visit is solely to seek information. I want you to know, however, this is serious business. We won't tolerate any acts of violence."

Brax returned Templeton's icy stare. Then he said, "Why is he here?"

"Mr. Templeton is simply an interested party. This is not an official interrogation. I can ask him to leave if you like."

"No, that's okay. I don't have anything to hide."

"Good. I hope his presence didn't make you feel uncomfortable. I'll not make that mistake if we meet again."

"I doubt we will."

Jameson continued to keep his eyes glued on Brax. "I hope not." Then he leaned back and seemed to relax. "Mr. Donovan, this may be an isolated incident and maybe it was intended just to scare people or draw attention. But if something else like this happens or if we perceive a threat, the island will be crawling with agents and I guarantee you we will find whoever is responsible."

Brax nodded. "I'm sure you will."

"The shot was fired from a thirty-two caliber pistol. We've got the bullet and if we can find the gun we can match it. You said you don't own a gun, but would you happen to know anyone who owns such a gun?"

"No," Brax said, obviously irritated. "Would you like to search my house?"

Jameson shook his head. "No."

"Look," Brax said. "I don't like this development—you know that—but I would never resort to violence or condone it."

"Good," said Jameson. "I would just ask you to keep your eyes and ears open and let me know if you become aware of anything that might raise a flag. I assure you any information you provide will be handled in strictest confidence." Jameson stood up and reached into his shirt pocket, retrieved a business card, and handed it to Brax. "You can leave a message if I don't answer."

Templeton rose from the sofa and also handed a business card to Brax. "Mr. Donovan, I would like to invite you to my office for a one-on-one chat about Serenity Shores. I think I could allay some of your concerns if you would allow me to show you what our vision is. We really want to create a partnership with the people who live on the island. I will call you once this incident is resolved and, hopefully, we can get together."

Brax took Templeton's card, which showed him as a partner in a law firm. He looked at the young man without responding.

As the two men began to leave, Jameson stopped in the doorway. "Thanks for your cooperation. Have a nice day."

"You, too."

Brax closed the door behind them and ripped Templeton's card into four pieces and threw it in the trashcan. Then he thought about Jameson's comment. He had never owned a gun and didn't know anything about the caliber of bullets they used. But there was one thing he knew for sure.

Jim had a gun.

# 18

After Lt. Jameson left, Brax couldn't get the thought of Jim's gun out of his mind. What if it is a thirty-two caliber? Had Jim fallen off the wagon again and done something stupid in a drunken rage? No, Jim wouldn't do a thing like that. There are plenty of people upset about the development and maybe one dumb enough to fire a shot. Or maybe it didn't have anything to do with the development, just some crazy nut causing trouble.

An hour after Lt. Jameson left, Brax called Jim. "I had an interesting visitor a while ago."

"Yeah, I know. The GBI agent just left my place. I guess there was a little excitement at the destruction site."

"Was the young guy in the blue suit—the developer's rep from the big meeting—with him?"

"No." Quickly, Jim backed up. "Well, wait a minute. Now that you mention it, maybe so. I saw another guy, but he stayed in the car and I couldn't see him very well."

"I'm sure it was him," said Brax.

"Hey, come on over, we can compare alibis. Ha!"

On the way to Jim's place, Brax was hopeful he would clear up any questions about the gun. He didn't like the idea of having even the slightest suspicion about his friend. When he arrived, Jim greeted him cheerfully. The house was neater than he had ever seen it. It wasn't the picture of a man gone off the deep end.

"I guess they think we might be a couple of crazy old codgers,"

Jim said. "Nutty enough to shoot one of the sorry bastards work-ing for them."

"That's insane," Brax said. "They're looking at us just because we opened our big mouths at the meeting. Hell, it's a free country. They can't arrest us for speaking our minds. It pisses me off that they even questioned us, especially with that asshole developer along."

"Like I told you," Jim said, "he didn't come in my house. It was just that fellow with the GBI ... uh ... Jameson. He thinks he can intimidate us. It's all bullshit. I guess he asked you, like he did me, if you knew anybody that might be mad enough to take a shot at one of them."

As soon as he heard the words "take a shot," Brax recalled the vision of Jim's loaded revolver in his hand. He leaned back on the sofa with his arms across his chest and muttered, "Uh huh." He stared at Jim with piercing eyes, as if he could read his mind.

Jim returned the stare and the two men sat frozen in silence. Finally, Jim said, "I have a pistol."

Brax nodded. "I know."

"It's the kind they said fired the shot, a thirty-two caliber."

"Really?" Brax raised his brows. "I mean, I know that's the kind they're looking for. I didn't know what kind yours is. I don't know anything about guns."

"I didn't shoot anybody."

"I didn't think you did."

"I didn't tell them I had a gun, especially not a thirty-two."

"I didn't tell them either," Brax said.

"Thanks." Jim paused and seemed to measure his next words. "Did they give you the crap about being able to match the bullet to a particular gun?"

"Yeah."

"That's all Hollywood horseshit. Bullets don't have DNA. They're just trying to bluff somebody. That Jameson is sharp—the

GBI doesn't hire dummies. But he didn't ask me if I had a gun and I didn't tell him that I did. I didn't lie, I just didn't tell him. You're the only one around here that knows."

The implication was clear to Brax. He was Jim's cover. He rose from the sofa, and looked at Jim solemnly. "Jim, if you're not involved, don't play games. If they find out you're holding back information, they'll be on you like stink on a pig."

"I'm a big boy," said Jim.

Brax nodded. "Yes, you are," he said as he started to leave. When he reached the door, he turned and added, "We can't stop them. It's a losing battle."

Brax wasn't sure who was telling the truth about matching the bullet to a specific gun. If Jameson was right, Jim could clear himself by having his gun tested. On the other hand, if the test was inconclusive, Jim could be implicated by circumstantial evidence. He still believed that Jim didn't shoot at anyone, but he couldn't help wonder if there was more to it than Jim was admitting. It made him dread the possibility of seeing Lt. Jameson again. If he didn't tell Jameson about Jim's gun, not only might he implicate himself, but the act of complicity would weigh on his conscience as well. If he did tell him, it would be a violation of Jim's confidence and their inferred agreement of silence.

Conscience was a simple, straightforward thing to Brax, but it sometimes complicated the hell out of his life.

---

The warm days began to taper off as the daylight hours got shorter and nightfall put a chill in the air, casting a nippy spell in the early morning hours. Brax and Dae wrapped themselves in warm clothes and steadfastly made their walk each morning.

"We must be crazy," Brax said, as they left the clubhouse to begin their trek in the foggy grayness of dawn. "For my whole life I wished that I didn't have to get up so damn early to beat the traffic

*Michael K. Brown*

and get to work. I would have given anything to sleep a couple of more hours. Now, I don't have anywhere to go and here I am heading out for a stupid walk at the crack of dawn."

"It feels great," Dae said. "You don't have to do it. I can go by myself."

"Just try it." He turned his head to talk as they walked abreast.

"You just like to complain," she said, looking straight ahead. "You can take a nap when we get back."

"Don't worry, that's number two on my to-do list."

"Oh. What's number three? Or is that none of my business?"

"Well, you're right, it is none of your business. But for your information, there is no number three. I don't want to over schedule myself."

"No, that wouldn't be good."

As they walked from the dunes and onto the beach, they noticed a crude wooden sign affixed to a stake stuck in the sand. "Sunrise Beach" was painted in block letters on the sign.

Brax grinned and shook his head in amusement.

"Where did that come from?" asked Dae.

"That's Jim's handiwork. We agreed on the name after we saw that big sign proclaiming the development as Serenity Shores. We're staking our claim on this stretch. You like the name?"

"Oh, yes. It's a nice name." Then she added in a mocking voice, "And such a lovely sign."

"I told Jim you would like it."

They had been walking on the beach for a few minutes when Brax mentioned his meeting with Agent Jameson. "I had an interesting visitor yesterday—actually two," he said.

"Really?"

"Yeah. A GBI agent came to see me and wanted to talk to me about a shooting at the Serenity Shores work site. That developer guy from the meeting at the Conference Center was with him. You know, the young guy in the blue suit."

"A shooting? I haven't heard about that. What happened?"

"I don't know exactly. They said a shot was fired but nobody was hit. I guess that's why it hasn't been in the news. It may have been someone just sending a message. Who knows?"

"Why did they come to your house? They didn't think you had anything to do with it did they?"

"Maybe. I opened my big mouth at that meeting and I guess they looked at me as the kind of crazy old coot that would fly off the handle. They didn't accuse me, but they thought I might know who did it. The GBI guy was very professional—I don't know why the scumbag developer was there. Anyhow, he asked me to let him know if I pick up any wind of who might have done it."

"I haven't heard a thing about it. I can't imagine anyone getting that upset over this. Can you?"

"Hell no. Dae, I hope you don't think for a minute that I would do something like that."

"No, I don't. I didn't mean it like that." She grabbed his arm and leaned her head affectionately into him as they slowed the pace. "I hope we don't have any trouble around here. I moved here to get away from that."

"Yeah, me, too."

Brax had decided he would not tell anyone about Jim's gun, but he had become so close to Dae that he felt he should be totally honest with her. On the other hand, it might be in her best interest if she didn't know anything about it. Then if questioned, she could honestly deny any knowledge of a gun. He was torn about which way to go before finally echoing the words of Lt. Jameson. "Sometimes smart people do stupid things."

"What does that mean?" she asked.

"It's what the GBI man said to me and it's true." Forethought aside, he blurted out impulsively, "I'm going to share something with you and it might not mean anything—it might be totally co-incidental—but I want you to know. Jim has a gun and it's the same caliber as the one that fired the shot."

"How do you know that?" Dae looked surprised.

"I've seen the gun. I don't know anything about guns, but he told me it was a thirty-two."

"Did you ask him about the shooting?"

"Yeah. He said he didn't know anything about it and I believe him."

"I do, too," she said.

"Good. But Jim and I are both being looked at as the enemy by the developers. We put the spotlight on ourselves at the meeting in the Convention Center. Anything we do now will make it look like we're encouraging violence."

"Brax, please don't do anything to stir things up. It's not worth all the trouble. I know that what's happening to the island really bothers you, but changes are going to happen and we'll be all right. It's not the end of the world."

Brax paused to think. "This is my world, right here on this island. I feel like I belong here and I like it the way it is. Now everything is changing and that's been hard for me to accept. I guess that's the way life is. Every time you think things are sailing along smoothly a damn storm comes along. But you're right—I'm too entrenched in my ways. Like you said, we'll be all right."

He liked the sound of that. *We'll be all right.* No matter what happened, the two of them would be just fine. Even as he spoke, it dawned on him how differently he saw things since he had met her. And he realized that the island wasn't his world. He looked at this woman who made him feel like a man again and he knew where his real world was.

He said, "I need to talk to Jim again. We've got to put this to rest."

"Yes," she agreed, edging slightly ahead of him.

The conversation went dry for a minute as they continued the walk. Then Brax spoke again. "Thanks," he said.

"I don't know for what, but you're welcome. And pick up the pace."

He grinned like a possum and quickened his step.

———————

That evening at Jim's house, Brax sprawled on one end of the sofa while Jim leaned back in his recliner as they watched the local news on television. The lead story was about the status of development on the island. The story included a mention of the shooting incident at the work site and Special Agent Jameson appeared with a reporter interviewing him.

"Do you have any leads as to who might have been involved?" the reporter asked.

"Not at this time," Jameson replied. "We ask that if anyone has any knowledge about this incident to call the GBI and we will assure them that their identity will be protected. As you know, there has been opposition to this project expressed by some citizen groups but at this time, we have no evidence to suggest a connection. Hopefully, this is an isolated incident and won't happen again. We've increased security at the site and work will continue on schedule."

When the news segment ended, Jim reached for the remote and turned off the television. "They'll stay on schedule," Jim said. "A little thing like a shooting won't stop them."

"It makes no sense," said Brax. "Who would be foolish enough to do something like that when it's such a public issue?"

Jim picked up his glass from the side table and took a sip of iced tea. He gazed down and swirled the cubes in the glass, then looked up. "You said you didn't know anything about guns, so I told you about mine, an old Smith and Wesson thirty-two. It's not a common weapon."

Brax didn't respond, sensing that Jim was letting go piece-by-piece.

"Do you think I'm the one they're looking for?"

"Jim, you told me you didn't shoot at anyone." Brax tried to sound as if he was convinced.

Jim hesitated a long time, staring away from Brax, before turning to face him. "Well, the answer is yes and no. It was my gun, but I didn't fire the shot."

Brax grimaced and sat up straight. "Jim, how did you get involved with something like this?"

"Stupidity." Jim sighed. "You asked who would be dumb enough to do something like this and you're looking at him. I didn't mean for it to happen, but I guess thinking about it is about as bad as doing it. One of the guys at the VFW said he would give 'em a scare. You know how some of these old vets are when they get liquored up. Well, I was sober—I swear—but I let the idea get away from me. He came by the house and I gave him my gun."

Brax leaned back and continued to listen.

"It's bothered the hell out of me. I don't want to get the guy in trouble 'cause I know he didn't mean to hit anybody, but it was my fault and it was wrong."

"I'm glad you see it that way, and I appreciate you telling me."

"You can handle it however you see fit."

"It's over. I trust that it won't happen again, at least not with your gun."

"Well, I got the gun back. It's a family keepsake. But no, it won't happen again. I talked to the guy and he feels as bad as I do. I swore to him that I would never tell anybody and he swore the same to me. Now, I've broken that promise, haven't I?"

"You think enough of me to tell me the truth. You have to trust me with that truth."

Jim nodded his assent and took another sip of tea.

"Like I told Jameson," Brax said, "I can't imagine anyone who would do a thing like that." He spoke matter-of-factly as if his words didn't contradict his knowledge.

Jim's shoulders sagged and he exhaled a long puff through his nostrils that seemed to release the burden of secrecy from him. Then he reached into the drawer of the table beside him, pulled out the gun, and stood up.

Brax tensed up and said, "What are you doing?"

"Don't worry, it's not loaded." Jim flipped the cylinder to show the empty chambers. "Let's go."

"Go where?" Brax said as he rose from his chair.

"To get rid of this thing."

Jim led Brax to his car and drove to a spot not far away where he parked on the shoulder of the road near the beach. The shore gleamed in the moonlight and they could see that the pier was empty. As he got out of the car, Jim stuffed the pistol in his pants and covered it with his shirt.

The two men walked through the dunes, the soft sand almost swallowing their shoes, then across the breadth of the firmly packed beach and onto the pier. The stillness of the night was broken by the sound of the low white-capped breakers beating gently against the pylons. When they reached about halfway the length of the pier, the sea settled with an inviting calmness. The end of the pier was at a right angle, forming the head of a large letter T. They passed the remnants of fishing scattered about—bait, blood, some lines and hooks—and the strong smell accentuated the salty lure of the ocean that stretched into the darkness.

Jim walked to the railing on the edge of the pier, removed the pistol from his pants, and dropped it into the water.

"I guess it's been in the family long enough," he said. It was the first words either of them had spoken since leaving the car.

"That's good", Brax said.

They began to walk back, quietly again, as if they had been to a funeral.

When they reached the vehicle, Jim sat silently behind the wheel for a moment without starting the engine. "It seems like you're always with me when I'm getting rid of something I shouldn't have."

"Yeah." Brax knew Jim was referring to the time he watched him throw the liquor in the dumpster. "Kind of like my mother when she made me get rid of those girlie magazines." He hoped the humor would bring Jim back to earth.

Jim turned the ignition. "You're so full of bullshit," he said, as he eased onto the road. "But you're right about one thing—you're like a mother all right, but not the kind you're talking about."

Brax brushed aside the comment with a grin Jim couldn't see. "I'm glad you got rid of that thing and I'm glad you told me the truth."

"I'm glad, too."

A few minutes later, Jim pulled into his garage. "You know, I've decided that maybe it's not such a good idea for an old drunk to hang around the bar at the VFW."

Jim sounded childishly remorseful and Brax was struck with the folly of the whole episode.

"You're such a dumb ass," Brax said in mock seriousness.

Jim smiled and then began to laugh. Soon, both men were laughing hysterically in the way that sometimes serves as an antidote for seriousness.

Brax wiped the tears of laughter from his eyes as he got out of the car. The two men parted and Brax headed for his house. His mood turned sober when he remembered the definition of a word that often appears in crossword puzzles.

Abet: Assist, as in a crime.

# *19*

Brax continued to practice his trumpet. He was beginning to get the feeling back, but he knew he would never be able to play like he did as a young man. Still, he was encouraged that he hadn't lost his ear and when he hit a good lick he felt the same stir in his heart he had fifty years before. He was ready for a trial run and when he asked Jim to come over one afternoon, he looked upon it as an audition of sorts.

"Do you like big band music?" he asked Jim.

"Uh … you mean like Glenn Miller and Tommy Dorsey? That kind of stuff?"

"Yeah, and Louis Armstrong and Duke Ellington. Oldies from the thirties and forties."

"I like that sometimes, I guess. I've kind of given up on music. Country's not country anymore and rock and roll died a long time ago. And that crap they call hip-hop is just an excuse to cuss and grab your crotch in public. I used to listen to Bing Crosby and Dean Martin and guys like that, but that was back when we had records. You know—those big vinyl seventy-eights. I don't guess they sell those anymore."

"No, I don't think so." Brax walked over to the wall unit, pulled out a CD, and placed it in the player. "Listen to this. It should get your juices flowing."

The pulsating sound seemed to jump from the speakers, the full effect of the big orchestra punctuated with long solos from different instruments. Brax couldn't contain himself from slapping his legs with his hands, bobbing his head, and tapping his feet to the up-tempo beat of the music. He smiled like a chimpanzee at Jim who was moving his head to the music as well.

"That's good music," said Jim. "I haven't heard that in a long time. What song is that?"

"It's called "Sing, Sing, Sing," although I don't know why since nobody ever sings. That's the Benny Goodman Band, with him playing the clarinet. Gene Krupa was the drummer. The guy on the trumpet was Harry James. He was married to Betty Grable at one time."

"Betty Grable," Jim said, wide-eyed. "Haven't heard that name in a coon's age. I was still in diapers when she was popular, but I remember she was a real blonde bombshell. Had a pair of knockers on her, too. I couldn't forget that even if I was too young to know what they were good for. I'll bet ole' Harry had fun tootin' on those."

"Probably so, but she was more known for her legs. A famous pin-up girl. Anyhow, I used to play the trumpet and I was married to a pretty woman, too."

"Really? You never told me about that. I mean I've seen pictures of that babe you married, but I don't know about a trumpet."

"Yeah. I played in the band at Georgia and I used to play in small bands and combos on the side. It was a lot of fun. I've been practicing a little lately. I'm not that good anymore, but it's a way to get connected again. It's hard to be quiet with a horn though. It's not like a piano or an acoustic guitar. I try not to disturb the neighbors."

"Has anyone complained?"

"Not yet."

"So don't worry about it until they do. I want to hear you play."

"Okay, but don't expect Harry James."

Brax went into the bedroom and came back with the trumpet.

He spent a couple of minutes warming up with lip slurs. Then he began to play "Stardust." It was a song he had played countless times before, but it still touched him personally as if he had written the song instead of Hoagy Carmichael. Even when the words weren't sung, they were inseparable from the tune and he could hear them in his head as they floated out of the horn with the notes.

He played the whole song slowly, feeling the tenderness of the plaintive lyrics recalling lonely nights and a haunting melody that drifted through his mind like a heavenly nimbus. When he finished, he was drained, emotionally as well as physically. It was his best rendition of the song since he had started practicing again.

"That was great," Jim said.

"Thanks," Brax responded, with labored breath. His face was red and his hands twitched as he set the instrument aside. "I've got a ways to go, but I'm getting better."

"It sounded good to me. Looks like it took some effort."

"Yeah, I'm not exactly in my prime. I missed a few notes, but it wasn't terrible." Brax got another CD and put it in the player. "This is how it's supposed to sound."

The strands of a trumpet playing "Stardust" began again.

Jim squinted his eyes and tilted his head. "Who's that playing?"

Brax raised a wait-a-minute finger in the air and closed his eyes, lost in the music. When the first track ended, he said, "That was me. My son made the CD from some old tapes that I recorded in a studio about thirty years ago."

The CD continued to the next song and Jim didn't speak as Brax hummed along with "When I Fall in Love." Those were the only two songs. The quality of the recording was not great, but the beauty of the music was unmistakable.

"Damn, you could blow that horn."

"I liked to play but it was hard to make a living at it."

"All you hear now on the radio is noise," Jim said.

"I know. Speaking of noise, listen to this one. This is from an old tape we recorded live at a New Year's Eve Party one year."

Brax put a different CD in the player. Then the infectious sound of "When the Saints Go Marching In" filled the room and they both became stoked with energy. They sang the words and bobbed their heads up and down as they marched around the little room like a couple of kids. Brax played the trumpet in sporadic bursts and Jim moved the slide back and forth on an imaginary trombone. When it was over, they collapsed into separate chairs to catch their breath.

"Whew," Jim said, with a big exhale. "The last time I heard that song I was walking with my buddy, Jack Daniels, down Government Street during Mardi Gras in Mobile. I better not push the old ticker any further," he added, between gasps.

A guilty shock hit Brax. He had gotten carried away with the music and didn't account for Jim's heart condition. "I'm sorry," he said. "I forgot."

"Oh, hell, don't be sorry. If I can't do something like this I had just as soon go ahead and die."

"Well, I don't want you to die in my house and I don't want to be accused of killing you."

"Don't worry, the only way you could kill me with that horn is if you beat me over the head with it."

"I sure as hell won't do that. I wouldn't want to ruin the trumpet."

They traded a few more verbal jabs before Jim turned the conversation.

"Are you going to be around here for Christmas?"

"No," said Brax. "All of my family is meeting at my oldest son's house in Dallas. How about you?"

"I'll be at my daughter's house in Warner Robins."

Christmas? It was only a few weeks away and the usual commercialization of the season was all over the television and in the stores. He had decorated his house with a small tree and a wreath on the door. Yet it didn't dawn on Brax until that moment that he hadn't bought Dae a Christmas present.

After Jim left, he began thinking about his trip to Dallas. He had made his plans long ago and it would mean being away for more than a week. He had bought a few gifts and had sent Mason money to get things for the young kids. There would be five children altogether, ranging from nine to seventeen years old. Logan would fly in from Seattle. Dylan and his wife and daughter would drive from the outskirts of Atlanta. It would be the first time they had been together in five years and some of them had never met each other.

He had looked forward to being with his whole family for a long time, but now he couldn't deny that he would miss being with Dae. It was crazy to feel that way, he told himself, and it made him feel childish. But the more he thought about it, the more he felt that maybe it was a good thing to be away from her for a while. It might be good for her as well. It would give them a little breathing time to think about things. So he decided he would buy her a nice present and they would enjoy their last night together for that year at the community Christmas party. If things worked out like he hoped, it would be different next Christmas.

His thoughts returned to Dae's present. He racked his brain to think of something tasteful and personal, but not too personal. For years he had bought gifts for Jane, usually clothes that she liked, or at least pretended to. But he didn't know Dae like he knew Jane, so this was a first time effort. The next day, after their morning walk, he headed to Savannah for the mall to complete the gift buying mission without the vaguest idea of what he was looking for.

At the mall he ambled around aimlessly from one store to another, feeling frustrated and claustrophobic among the throng of shoppers. The place was abuzz with activity and he felt like he lived in a world apart from people carrying shopping bags and pushing strollers and groups of strangely dressed young people jabbering away on electronic gizmos.

A nice sweater; that would be it. All women like clothes, he reasoned, and he had noted what Dae wore when she wasn't beach casual. She was about Jane's size, maybe a little smaller, so a medium should fit. In Macy's he found his way to the pricier section of women's attire. He looked at every sweater in the department and went back and forth, trying to make up his mind. Finally, he selected an off-white, long sleeve cashmere with a prestige label and corresponding price tag. As he waited patiently in line at the register, he couldn't take his eyes off the girl behind the counter. Her flaming red hair and lipstick stood out as a splash of color against her porcelain white skin and the all black attire that the store apparently required. He looked at her and he saw Trish.

Redheads were his Achilles heel, even after all those years. It must have been more than thirty years ago, though he couldn't remember the exact year. But he knew that Jane never forgot. He hated that. Like a bad memory that holds on as tight as a good one, it didn't seem like that long ago.

---

Trish was a lot younger than Brax—she in her twenties, he in his forties—and she had the same beautiful red hair and delicate white skin as the girl at the counter. He had taken her along on a few calls as part of her training as a new sales rep. She was sharp and had a way of connecting with the customers. He encouraged her and she took a liking to him. There was an off-site retreat for two days at Lake Lanier with a few meetings interspersed with golf and tennis. After the dinner at the hotel, he joined a group of company people congregated in the bar.

When Trish joined the group, Brax made a seat for her next to him and they spent the next two hours drinking and socializing. The more he drank, the more attractive she appeared and he sensed encouragement from her when they made eye contact. It all kicked in: the lure of forbidden fruit, the macho challenge of conquest, the brain-numbing effect of alcohol. Before he got up to leave he slipped a business card to her under the table. He had written his room number on the card, and what followed was a night that he would live to regret.

She came to his room and soon their clothes were strewn on the floor. Afterward, they fell asleep and when he awoke he had a hangover, a naked girl in the bed beside him, and only thirty minutes to get to his first meeting. He spent the day in a fog of guilt with a throbbing head. The minutes seemed to drag by in slow motion until the presentations finally concluded just before five o'clock. Brax left the hotel as quickly as he could, sneaking past the covey of fellow managers lingering in the lobby.

On his way home, he dreaded the thought of pulling into his driveway, knowing he had violated the trust of the woman he loved so much. He felt dirty and unworthy, as if he had gotten away with a crime. Yet he would soon learn that, to some degree, he had been caught.

On Monday morning he was approached by one of the administrative assistants. "Brax, you need to be more careful," she said.

"What do you mean?" He could almost feel the guilty look creep upon his face.

"People talk. You know what I mean."

He knew what she meant, but he didn't know what she knew. Worse, she not only worked with him but also lived in his neighborhood and was a friend of Jane's. He never confronted Trish to accuse her of a loose tongue and, to his knowledge, no one else ever said anything. Still, he knew how the word of a juicy affair spreads in circles. All he could do was limit the damage.

He and Trish remained cordial in their professional roles, but Brax made it clear that there would be no more escapades. They went their own ways and she left the company six months later.

It was several days before his conscience won the battle and lead him to talk to Jane.

"At the retreat last Friday night, I had too much to drink."

"That's what y'all do at the meetings, isn't it?" she asked.

"Sometimes. But this time I really made a fool of myself."

"You mean with the young red-headed girl?" Jane looked at him casually.

Her words stunned him, as if she had hit him in the head with a brick.

"Yeah."

"I'm glad you're telling me."

"I'm sorry that I have to. I mean I'm sorry it happened. It's never happened before and it won't happen again. I promise."

"It still hurts."

"I know it sounds stupid, but it hurts me too. I let it go too far."

"I don't want to know how far it went."

Jane was aloof for a couple of weeks, but eventually the iciness melted away. Brax never knew the extent of her knowledge and that uncertainty was part of the price he had to pay. There were other temptations over the years, but he kept his promise. He hoped that the pain he caused her was less than the humiliation he felt for letting her down. Their marriage survived the episode and he never doubted that she loved him. The incident was branded in his memory, but like a deep gash in the skin, the pain went away after a while and, though the scar never disappeared, it became less noticeable over time.

It had been a long time since he had thought about Trish and it reminded him of his base instincts. When the girl behind the counter spoke to him, he was still in a trance-like state.

"May I help you," she said.

"Oh, yes," he said as he handed her the sweater and began fumbling for his credit card. With the sale completed he turned to walk away with the sweater in a bag. Then he turned back and said, "I love your red hair."

"Thank you very much," she said, with a big smile.

He couldn't change what had happened a long time ago, but he was still a sucker for a pretty woman with red hair.

———◆———

Dae had plans for Christmas as well. She would be traveling to Charlotte to be with Julie and Ben and her two grand-daughters. Jenny was nine and Emma was almost seven and they thought that the sun rose and set on Gramma. Later Justin would arrive from Korea on New Year's Eve along with his wife, Seon, and daughter, Snow. Dae didn't want to drive by herself so she arranged for a ride with Julie's in-laws. Ben's parents lived near the Florida state line in St. Marys, about an hour to the south. They would pick up Dae on the way and the three of them would ride together to Charlotte. Dae was looking forward to being with her family so much that the excitement was causing her to sleep restlessly.

She bought Brax a button-up shirt as a Christmas present. It was a safe choice, light blue with the logo of a polo player stitched where the pocket should be. John had always complained about that missing pocket—no place for a pen or cigarettes—but she had seen Brax wear the same kind. She didn't understand why that shirt cost twice as much as the others, but it was on sale and she knew that some men were just as fussy about their clothes as she was. So she plunked down a hundred dollar bill and got less than a third of it back. *Some sale,* she thought.

The weather was still balmy and the landscape in South Georgia looked nothing like the snow-covered scenery in the Christmas cards. At midday people were in short sleeves. Still, like most other people, it was Dae's favorite time of year. Scattered tastefully throughout her new home were holiday pillows, miniature Santa Clauses and elves, scented candles and potpourri, and other reminders of the season. A small artificial tree stood in one corner of the main room. The atmosphere looked bright and cheery, but one thing was missing: family. It was the first time that the White-head clan wouldn't gather at her house for Christmas. Even after John was gone, Julie and Justin and their families would return to Savannah for the holidays and gather at the place they all considered home. Dae and Julie would prepare big meals and the house was always full of pleasant smells and happy voices.

This year was different. No one would come to her house. She would spend Christmas with Julie's family and, even though it was at her own daughter's house, she would be a guest. It was a strange feeling, as if she were going to Christmas instead of it coming to her.

Brax was the closest thing she knew to the kind of family she was used to. A lot of things were different about this Christmas and he was a big part of that. She felt comforted to have him near, to share at least a part of the season, and she thought he felt the same way. They would only be apart for a week or so and knowing that he would be there when she got back gave her something to look forward to. As the time approached, she began to feel a little guilty that, as much as she was looking forward to being with her family, she would miss being with Brax.

*That's silly. It's only for a few days.*

# *20*

Brax rapped on Jim's front door a couple of times and walked inside. He had been invited over for grilled burgers and figured Jim was tending to his cooking duties on the patio. From the kitchen, he saw Jim and Momadou talking outside. Their backs were turned and they didn't notice him before he stepped into the bathroom to relieve himself. He didn't bother to close the door and the muffled sound of their conversation seeped inside. Momadou was doing most of the talking. When Brax heard the word "gun," he quickly finished his business, withheld the flush, and remained silent to eavesdrop. He strained to pick up occasional words.

"Scared the ... hell out of that ..." Momadou said with a laugh.

"Well ... it's gone ..." Jim said.

From fragments of the conversation, Brax pieced together references to developers and the GBI. His mind flashed back to Jim's account of the incident with the gun and he had an uneasy feeling that Momadou had been involved. Stirred with suspicion, he flushed the toilet and went outside to join his friends.

"How's it going?" asked Brax.

Momadou turned and flashed a toothy smile. "If it was any better I couldn't stand it."

"Hey, Captain Hornblower," said Jim. "Grab a plate, the burgers are ready."

The three men chatted about sports and politics for almost an hour while enjoying their food.

Afterward, Brax leaned back in his chair, and took a swig of tea. "That was good, Jim."

"Yeah," said Momadou. "Real good."

"Thanks. It must have been okay—I see y'all ate everything but the plates."

"That's dessert," chuckled Momadou.

"Nice evening, too," said Brax. Then he looked at Jim. "Not nearly as dark as that night we tossed your gun in the ocean."

Jim looked stunned and didn't say a word. Momadou's smile disappeared and his eyes turned to Jim, then back to Brax.

"You know about that don't you, Jaws?" He kept his eyes trained on Momadou, who didn't reply.

"Why should he?" asked Jim.

Brax shifted his eyes back to Jim. "Let's cut the crap, Jim. I told you not to lie to me." He paused to let the words sink in. "You said the GBI agent never asked you about a gun. I knew that wasn't true. He's too sharp not to question you about that. So you must have lied to him like you lied to me."

"What the hell difference does it make? It's gone."

"Yeah, it's gone. Just like that guy from the VFW that you say you gave it to." He looked at Momadou. "That wouldn't be you, would it, Jaws?"

Momadou remained unresponsive.

Jim shoved his chair back and stood up. "None of this matters. I told you it wouldn't happen again. Drop it." He began to clear the table.

"Yes," Brax said, "it does matter. I helped you get rid of the gun which makes me a party to a cover-up. More importantly, I expect you to tell me the truth. That's what friendship is all about."

Jim's face became red and he set the empty plates back down on the table. "Listen, damn it!—"

Momadou interrupted. "I fired the shot."

Brax nodded, confirming his suspicion.

All three men paused in silence for a moment.

Jim picked up the plates again. "Okay, Perry Mason, what are you going to do now? Turn us in as terrorists?"

"We didn't know anyone was there," said Momadou. "Nobody was around and it was late. The lights were on inside the trailer, but they always keep them on at night. We didn't see anyone moving inside. I was just shooting at the sign on the side of the trailer. Then all of a sudden, a guy walked out. I didn't come within twenty feet of him."

"What the hell were y'all thinking?" asked Brax with his voice raised. "What was that supposed to accomplish?"

Momadou shook his head and Jim frowned. Brax waited for an answer.

Finally, Jim spoke. "It's not like we killed somebody like they're killing this island." He paused and took a deep breath. "But it was wrong. We were thinking through our asses."

"We didn't mean any harm," said Momadou. "We were just mad."

"You were mad all right. Mad as in crazy. But now we have to decide how to deal with it. We could forget about it and maybe it will blow away. I don't see how they can ever trace it back to you guys, but you've put me in a tough position. I can't lie or hold back information from the GBI."

"So tell them what you know if that's what you want to do," Jim said.

"Yeah," Momadou concurred.

"It's not what I want to do and you know it."

"I'm sorry I got you into this mess," Jim said.

"He was trying to cover for me," said Momadou.

"No, I started it," Jim protested. "And it was my gun."

Brax put a hand to his chin and shook his head in disgust. "We need to come clean." He looked at both of his friends. "Will you talk to Jameson? That's the GBI agent that questioned us."

Momadou looked at Jim, then turned to Brax. "Yeah." The tone of resignation in his voice matched the slump of his body.

"Okay," agreed Jim, equally downcast.

"Thanks," said Brax.

Jim seemed to come alive and bellowed the familiar phrase that, for years, blared from television on Monday nights. "Are you ready for some football?"

The men cleared the table and went inside to watch the game.

Brax was confident that he finally knew the truth. He didn't know how the authorities would look at things, but he was convinced his friends had simply made a foolish error in judgment.

Retrieving the business card from his desk, Brax made the call to Jameson. Afterward, he began to wonder if he had done the right thing. Why not just let the incident fade away? No one was harmed and the chances of anyone finding out what happened were remote. But the wheels were in motion and Jameson would be there in a few hours. Too late to turn back now.

He walked into the living room, wrestling with his thoughts, and picked up the trumpet from the sofa. After blowing a few weak notes, he laid the horn down. Then he pulled the cell phone from his pocket and made two more calls.

Jim and Momadou both agreed to be there when Jameson arrived. It was encouraging to know they were sticking by their commitments. Still, he felt uncomfortable in the position of providing testimony incriminating his friends and, to a lesser degree, himself. Worse yet, was the realization that he had started something over which he had no control. Had he put his friends in jeopardy of going to jail? He needed to make one more call.

"I need to tell you something," he said, when Dae answered. "Let's go for a walk."

"Right now?"

"Yeah. Can you go?'

"Uh ... okay. I'll be ready in ten minutes."

Being with her would ease his mind. What the heck? Everything will be fine.

Brax carried Dae's big umbrella beside him as they walked along the beach under dark clouds that threatened to burst open at any minute. A strong wind blew from the sea and the crescendo of waves crashing down before rolling peacefully to shore was a calming backdrop.

"I found out what happened with the shooting last week," Brax began. "Jaws fired the shot and Jim was with him. They told me last night right before we watched the football game."

"Oh, for God's sake! What possessed them to do that?"

"Just being knuckleheads. They said they didn't know anyone was around and Jaws said he wasn't shooting at anyone. I believe him."

"I do, too. I don't think either of them would harm anyone."

"No, but they could have, accidentally."

"Thank goodness they didn't."

"Yeah."

He let it drop for a minute and they stopped at the edge of the water to bask in the scene around them. The stiff ocean breeze was invigorating and the high-pitched squawks of gulls overhead blended in harmony with the deep roar of the surf.

"I reported them," he said.

"To whom?"

"The GBI agent that questioned me. I'm involved to some extent, myself. I told you about going with Jim to get rid of the gun."

"You didn't do anything."

"No, that's the extent of my involvement, but I guess I'm what they call an accessory. Anyhow, all three of us are meeting with the GBI agent at my house at four o'clock today. I'm not sure what will happen, but I feel like I've put Jim and Jaws in a bad position.

I should have just kept my big mouth shut."

"No, you couldn't do that." She reached for his hand. "Don't worry. Everything will be fine. C'mon, I'll make some chili for lunch."

A light rain began to fall and he opened the umbrella. The rain became harder and they huddled to keep their heads dry but the blustery wind blew the drops sideways, soaking their clothes as they made their way home.

*Everything will be fine.* He knew she would say that.

———

At quarter of four, the three men sat in Brax's living room awaiting Special Agent Jameson.

"Couldn't this wait 'til after Christmas?" asked Jim

"Yeah," Momadou echoed.

"You know how these guys are," said Brax. "Once they smell blood, they're like piranhas." He realized instantly he had fumbled his thoughts. "No, that's a bad analogy. What I mean is—it's their job." He studied the serious faces of his two friends. "It's not a capital offense. We just need to take our medicine and get on with it."

"I've got the most to lose," said Momadou. "I fired the shot and … I'm a black man with a name that sounds threatening. That's two strikes."

Brax and Jim exchanged glances and the room became quiet.

Jim broke the silence. "No, I fired it."

Brax felt that Jim was covering for his friend but at this point, he wasn't sure of anything. "Okay, y'all said you'd tell the truth, so don't play games. Jaws, we've got your back. We won't let them go after you unfairly."

Momadou nodded. "I didn't mean to say that. I'm responsible for what I did."

A few minutes later, Brax looked through the sidelights of the door to see Agent Jameson pull into the driveway.

"Ah, hell," said Jim, rising from the sofa. "I've changed my mind. I'm taking the Fifth and going home."

"Me , too," Momadou said, as he stood.

Brax's eyes widened like saucers. "Guys!"

# 21

Brax kept an eye on the sidelights as Jameson approached the door. He shot from his chair in panic and looked at his friends in disbelief. Both men were about to renege on their promised confession. Standing speechless, his mind raced with one thought. *I should have kept my big mouth shut.*

When the doorbell rang, Jim and Momadou sat down.

"We're just kidding," Jim said, with a big grin. Momadou laughed.

"Damn!" Brax exclaimed. His anxiety quickly disappeared and a smile burst upon his face as he opened the door. "Mr. Jameson," he said calmly as he reached to shake the agent's hand.

"Good afternoon, Mr. Donovan." The agent stepped inside and looked at the other two. "This is Jim Hawkins," Brax said. "I believe you two have met. And this is Momadou Jawara. We call him Jaws. He's one of our neighbors here at Seaside."

"Gentlemen," Jameson said.

Handshakes were exchanged, Brax offered a chair to Jameson, and everyone sat down.

"Mr. Jameson," Brax began, "thanks for meeting with us. I'll get right to the point. We were responsible for the gun shot at the construction site last week. There was no harm meant and we didn't know there were any people around."

"He's covering for us," Jim said. "He didn't have anything to do with it. It was me and Jaws here that did it."

"That's right," Momadou agreed.

Jameson leaned back and put a hand to his chin. Looking at Jim, he said, "Why?"

"It wasn't him, it was me," said Momadou. "I wasn't shooting at anybody, just the sign on the trailer."

"It was stupid," said Brax. "Childish mischief. Frustration."

"That's no excuse," said Jameson. "A gun is a deadly weapon. It's not something to be used as a prank." He sounded like a father scolding a child and the others didn't respond. "But you gentlemen know that. And whether you meant to or not, you endangered someone's life. The question now is—what do we do about it?"

"Yeah," said Brax, "that's why I asked you here."

"Normal procedure is for me to report it to the construction company and see if they want to press charges."

"What would the charges be?" asked Momadou.

"Depends. The most severe would be reckless endangerment, which could be a felony."

"Felony?" said Brax. "Look, this was an accident. We're reporting this out of good faith. We're not a bunch of criminals."

"Ah, for crying out loud," said Jim.

Momadou leaned forward and shook his head.

"I said could be," said Jameson. "It's usually judged as a misdemeanor. Depends on the circumstances and the background of those involved." He looked at Momadou. "Let me ask you—have you ever been convicted of anything that would show up on police records."

"No," said Momadou. "Just a few speeding tickets. Nothing in the last few years."

"How about you, Mr. Hawkins?"

Jim took a deep breath and looked very uncomfortable. "A few DUI's. Public drunkenness. Disturbing the peace, I think." He shifted in his seat. "I've never been violent or hurt anybody." His face turned red and he added, "At least, not since I got out of the

Marine Corps."

"Nothing for me," said Brax. "Just traffic violations, like Jaws. But let's back up a minute. We voluntarily reported this incident. If you're going to make a federal case out of it, we can just deny it. You don't have any evidence or any other witnesses and if it goes to court, you can't make us testify against ourselves. And you haven't given us our Miranda Rights."

"You're not in custody, Mr. Donovan. Are you a lawyer?"

"No, but I've been on a couple of juries." Brax suppressed an embarrassed grin, realizing how silly his response sounded.

"Then let me understand. You gentlemen asked me here to confess to the shooting, but you don't want to accept the consequences. Is that what you're saying?"

"No," Jim said. "We're saying there was no intent to harm anyone. If anything, it was simple vandalism."

"It sounds like that was what you were expecting before Mr. Donovan arranged the meeting. You don't view it very seriously, do you?"

"Sure we do," said Jim. He leaned to Momadou and they spoke in whispers. Turning back, he said, "Go ahead and tell us what the damn penalty is."

"It's not my decision to make, but I can tell you what my recommendation would be." He stopped for a moment as the others kept their eyes glued to him. "A misdemeanor with a fine. Maybe a thousand dollars. We need to send a message that this kind of stuff won't be tolerated."

Brax looked at Jim who shrugged, then Momadou who nodded. "That sounds reasonable.'

Momadou spoke up. "I'll pay it."

"No," Jim said. "We'll split it."

"Hold on, I can't guarantee any outcome," Jameson responded. "This has to be reviewed before any decision is reached. But I can tell you my recommendation carries a lot of weight. Are you willing to go with that?"

The men exchanged glances for a moment.

Momadou was the first to speak. "Yeah," he said.

"All right by me," Jim seconded.

Jameson looked at Brax who shrugged and said, "Do it."

"Then I'll make my report and get back to you." Jameson rose from his chair and the others also stood. "So you're a Marine, Mr. Hawkins?" he asked Jim.

"Yeah," Jim answered. "1960 to '63."

"You get in on the fun in Vietnam?"

"I was there in '61 and part of '62. What a damn fiasco that whole war was!"

"I got out in '92, right after Desert Storm" Jameson said. "We kicked ass, then things got all screwed-up like in Nam."

"Yeah," Jim said, "another damn waste of lives."

Jameson shook his head and reached to shake Jim's hand. The two exchanged Semper Fi's. Then he shook hands with Momadou and Brax and left.

The three men remained standing in silence, gazing at the front door as if reflecting on what they had just agreed to.

"I think he'll do right by us," Momadou said.

"I trust him," Jim agreed. "He's a tight-ass jarhead."

"You guys did the right thing," Brax added. He felt relieved it was over and confident there wouldn't be strong repercussions. With a sly grin, he said, "I don't think you'll be in jail too long."

Momadou grimaced. "Man!"

"I outta shoot you," said Jim.

They broke out in laughter like a pack of hyenas.

———◆———

Three days later, Brax rode with Jim and Momadou to the GBI office in Kingsland. Momadou handed over the check to cover the fine and they each signed papers admitting to their actions. Before they left, Jameson had a parting word for them.

"If I hear one more peep out of you guys, I'll be all over you. No more interference with the construction. Is that clear?"

They all agreed.

Jim settled behind the steering wheel of his big Buick on the drive back to Seaside with Momadou in the passenger seat. "Well, Jaws, I guess they've got us by the gonads now."

"They can kiss my shiny butt," said Momadou. "I don't have to like what those sonsabitches are doing to the island."

Brax chimed in from the back seat. "You know what I just heard?"

"What?" asked Momadou.

"I heard a peep."

"Ah," Momadou groaned.

"Well, don't go turning us in again," Jim said to Brax.

"Don't worry, Al Capone," Brax said. A minute later he added, "Faster, James, faster. Paradise is just ahead."

An ironic thought came to Brax as they headed back to the island. It was as if they were returning to their nesting place, just like the loggerhead turtles do from instinct. The cycle of life would go on.

Dae was right. Everything will be fine.

# 22

A week after leaving the GBI office, Jim stood among a group of vets sharing off-color jokes at the VFW. Across the main hall, he recognized a familiar face among two men coming from another room. He walked over and approached Special Agent Jameson.

"Hello, I think we've met before," Jim said.

The agent stared at him for a second. "Yes, we sure have." He stuck his hand out, and the two men shook. "How've you been, Mr … uh … Hawkins, I believe?"

"That's right. I've been staying out of trouble. You haven't heard a peep out of me." Jim smiled like a Cheshire cat.

Jameson nodded with a grin. "Very good." He looked at the other man without introducing him, then turned back to Jim. "Well, sorry, but we've got to run and meet our wives for a movie. Give my regards to your friends."

"Will do. Semper Fi."

Jameson returned the greeting and hustled away.

Jim shook his head. Meeting the GBI agent was an embarrassing reminder of his foolish involvement in the shooting at the development site. He couldn't help but see the irony of encountering the agent at the VFW post, considering the absurd story he had told Brax about hatching the plot there. The post was his refuge and he felt bad about implying a sinister influence. He felt a strong connection with veterans of his age, especially those who, like himself, had outlived their wives. The bond of brotherhood was his safety net, wound tightly with endless conversations of cursing politicians, modern society, and the general state of the world. When the inevitable round of anecdotal war tales began, he felt a surge of something that filled a blank space in his life. A sense of belonging.

An hour later, Jim sat at a table as the last game of Bingo wound down. He took a swig of coffee and set the cup down beside his card.

The man up front turned the crank on the tumbler and pulled out a number. "B-thirteen," he yelled.

"Bingo!" yelled a voice from the crowd. A white-bearded man in a plaid shirt, suspenders, and cap inscribed with Navy Retired pumped his fist in the air.

The room buzzed with small conversations as people began leaving their tables to mill around inside the room. The deep moan of Johnny Cash singing "Ring of Fire" escaped from the lounge, drifting over the din of voices.

Jim turned to his friend, Charlie Wainwright, and said, "Another dry hump."

"Me, too," replied Charlie. "I'm going out for a smoke. Want to come?"

"I guess so. I'll stand by and watch you kill yourself."

"At least I'll be in the U.S. of A. when I go. That's more than I can say for some of my buddies."

Jim nodded and followed Charlie outside to join a small group on the smoking patio. A man sat at a picnic table with a large photo album spread in front of him with three onlookers huddled around. Jim sauntered over to the table as Charlie lit a cigarette and struck up a conversation with another Vet on the far side of the patio.

"That's Tommy Jernigan," the man said, pointing to a picture of a young man in camouflage fatigues, combat gear, and black face paint. "He was killed in a firefight near Dak To." After pausing for a second, he added, "Twenty years old." The others were silent. The man turned the next page which was labeled at the top with Vietnam Veterans Reunion. "That was in Savannah in 1992, twenty-five years after I got back."

Jim looked over the man's shoulders at a double page spread of photos, some of people in groups, others standing together with their wives. He looked intently at the picture of an attractive couple without admitting he recognized the woman. "Who's that?"

"That's John Whitehead and his wife. Everybody called him Whitey but I called him Day-O."

"Day-O?" Jim asked, privately connecting the dots.

"Yeah. His wife's first name is Dae—short for something else. I forget what. Anyhow, she was his girlfriend at the time. He was always talking about her, so whenever I wanted to get under his skin, I'd start singing that Harry Belafonte song—'Day-O, Day-a-a-a-O.'" The man grinned as he made a feeble attempt at the tune.

"I'll be a son-of-a-gun," Jim said. "I know Dae. She lives out at Seaside where I do."

"Really?"

"Yeah, she's the lady friend of my best buddy."

The man turned to look at Jim directly. "Lady friend? You sure it's her?"

"Yeah, how many women are named Dae? Besides, she still looks a lot like that picture. She's well preserved."

Jim looked on and listened to a running commentary as the man rifled through the remaining pages of the photo album. After the other onlookers drifted away, Jim remained and asked the man to turn back to the photograph that piqued his interest. "Do you know Dae?"

"I used to. Haven't seen her in several years."

"How did her husband die?"

The man reared his head back and looked puzzled. "Die?"

After their morning walk, Brax accompanied Dae to her house before heading to his. He had barely opened the front door when the phone rang.

"I need to talk to you," Jim said. "Are you by yourself?"

"Yeah. What's up?" Brax screwed his face at the urgency in Jim's voice. "Are you okay?"

"I'm as good as grits. It's not about me."

"Hmm, so I guess you didn't win the lottery. Well, don't keep me hanging. Come on over right now if you want to."

"I'm on my way."

Brax grabbed a Diet Coke from the refrigerator and plopped down in the living room recliner. His curiosity cranked into overdrive, trying to imagine what had his friend so pumped up.

A few minutes later, after a quick knock on the door, Jim entered just as Brax yelled, "Come on in."

"Did you just get back from your walk with Dae?"

"You know I did. You saw us leave."

"Y'all are getting along pretty well these days, aren't you?"

Brax eyed Jim suspiciously. "Okay, quit screwing around. What's on your mind?"

"Well … I consider you a good friend and I consider Dae a friend, too." Jim squirmed on the sofa cushions, looked away for a moment, then looked back at Brax. "And I'm guessing you look at her as more than just a friend."

A twitch of anxiety hit Brax but he didn't say a thing and his expression didn't change. He suspected Jim was about to spit something out that wasn't pleasant for either of them and he braced himself.

"But there's something I think you ought to check out."

"I'm listening."

Jim took a deep breath. "I don't think Dae's actually a widow."

Brax let the words sink in. He arched his back with a pained look on his face. "What do you mean?"

"I mean … apparently her husband is still alive."

"Her husband's dead," Brax said emphatically. "She told me."

"Did she say when he died? And how?"

"What brought all of this up?"

"Last night I met a guy at the VFW and he was in Nam with an Army grunt named John Whitehead. He showed me a picture of him and Dae at a Vietnam Vet's reunion. Said the guy was still alive in an assisted living place in Savannah. I think he knows what he's talking about. He wouldn't have any reason to b.s. me."

Brax shook his head. "Damn it, here you go again with this stuff from the VFW. You haven't been drinking again, have you?"

"No, hell no." Jim rose from the sofa with a scowl on his face. He raised his voice and spoke faster. "Look, don't blame me, I'm just trying to be a friend. The man told me he keeps track of the guys who were in his outfit in Nam. He updates it whenever somebody passes. He checked on this guy with the nursing home just a couple of months ago. So I think he knows what he's talking about!"

Brax's heart sank as he tried to digest the thought of being lied to by Dae. "Aah," he moaned. "Okay, I believe you. Sit back down."

The ruddy scowl disappeared from Jim's face but he remained standing with his arms folded on his chest.

Brax set his Coke on the side table and stood, facing Jim. "Maybe I misunderstood her. Maybe they're divorced."

"Yeah. Maybe pigs fly, too. You don't misunderstand something like that."

Brax grunted in frustration. "Have you told anyone else?"

"No, of course not. This is between you and Dae."

"Not even Jaws?"

Jim looked at Brax with a face of disgust. "I just said I didn't tell anyone. Don't keep giving me the third degree. This is really none of my business. I wasn't looking for this crap. I just stumbled across it, and I'm telling you because I thought you needed to know."

Brax closed his eyes briefly and rubbed his forehead. "I'm sorry

... thanks. I believe you." He lowered his hand and looked aside with his eyes in a glassy fog, and his mind stirring with confusion. He turned and stared out the window in silence. "I appreciate you letting me know, but I trust Dae." Turning back to Jim, he added, "There's got to be more to this."

"Probably so." Jim nodded but there was a lack of conviction in his voice. "I like her, too."

"It's not that big a deal," Brax said with a complete lack of conviction in his voice.

"Good," Jim said. He walked to the door, then stopped and turned. "Do whatever you want to but I'm telling you this in confidence, so don't get me involved."

"Don't worry, I won't."

After Jim left, Brax stood in the living room for a moment, numb with the anesthetic of doubt. There had to be an explanation. Dae wouldn't lie to him.

Then he remembered what she had said about her husband at Fort Frederica. *He eventually just faded away.* How damn clever! He never questioned what she meant and now it was obvious she had carefully avoided a lie and the truth at the same time. He felt betrayed by something worse than a lie: deception.

———•◦•———

"Ooh, that was delicious." Dae took the napkin from her lap, laid it on the table, and pushed her chair back.

"Yeah," Brax agreed, his face expressionless. Placing the money beside the check, he drained the last drop of decaf from his cup, and stood up.

They left the restaurant and stepped into the thick, brackish air of the nearby marshes. She took his hand and they left The Crow's Nest for the short drive home. Outside, a lily-edged pond glistened under a full moon and a water spout created a calming patter of water. Seashells crunched under their feet as they made their way across the unpaved parking area without speaking.

Brax looked straight ahead in silence as he eased his car onto the shadowy road near the beach.

"You've been awfully quiet tonight," Dae said. "You sure you feel all right?"

"I'm fine."

"No, you're not. You're holding something from me."

"I guess so. I'm not as good at that as some people I know."

Dae felt the tension in his voice and a pained look flashed on her face. "What does that mean?"

"Nothing."

"Yes, it means something."

"We'll talk about it when we get home."

A knot twisted in her stomach as her intuition kicked in. *He knows.*

A few minutes later, he pulled into her driveway but made no move to get out of the car.

"Are you coming in?"

"No. I want to talk here."

Her heart sank. "Let's go inside, it's—"

"Hush! Just tell me the truth. Is your husband still alive?" His stern look, backlit by a street light, was intimidating.

"Brax ..."

"You're still married, aren't you?"

She closed her eyes. "It's not what you think."

"Just tell me the damn truth for once! That's all I want to hear." He turned from her and stared into the windshield with a firm jaw and tight lips.

She opened her eyes and a tear ran down her cheek. "The John that I married is gone. He doesn't remember who I am."

"I thought you were a widow. Why didn't you tell me your husband was still alive? You deceived me, damn it!"

"I didn't do it on purpose." She sighed and wiped her eyes as more tears welled on her face. "It's weighed on my conscience but I couldn't bring myself to tell you. I enjoyed being with you and you made me feel … special. I haven't had that feeling in a long time and I was afraid of losing it. It was wrong. I'm sorry."

"So you let me sleep in your bed and get all wrapped around you knowing that it couldn't go anywhere? All for you to feel special. What the hell about me? Did you ever consider how I might feel once I found out? "

"You don't understand everything, and I can't explain it while you're angry."

"I understand everything perfectly. I understand you've taken me for a stupid old fool."

"No, that's not true. Please don't make me out as a conniving witch. I feel awful about not being truthful, but I never for once thought of you as gullible. And you're right … I should have thought more about your feelings."

He didn't respond and the silence felt like a stone pressing against her.

Taking a tissue from her purse, she dabbed her eyes and nose. "Do you hate me?"

Again silence. In a sullen voice, he finally said, "No."

"What do we do now?"

"We say goodnight."

That was not what Dae wanted to hear. Brax got out of the car and before he reached her door, she was halfway out. She stood and looked at him firmly. "Don't be so judgmental."

"I'm not judging you," he said, "just the situation."

"I've already said I'm sorry for not being forthright, but the situation, as you call it, is not of my making. Goodnight." She moved past him and turned for her front door.

"Goodnight," she heard him say from behind.

Dae walked into her house, turned off the living room lamp and collapsed on the sofa, sobbing in the dark.

The tears soon dried up, but the heartache wouldn't go away. She knew it was bound to happen. Her whole world was crashing down and it was her own fault. Though she had denied it, the situation was of her own making. It wasn't her fault that John was sick, but to hide that fact to pursue her own desires was a heavy burden.

*I am a conniving witch.*

———✦———

When Brax got home, he sat in his car for a moment, reflecting on what had just happened.

"What a crock of bullshit!" he shouted at the windshield. Then he got out, slamming the car door behind him. Inside, he went directly to the bedroom and retrieved the trumpet from under the bed. Lying down, he raised the instrument to his lips, but there was no will in his lungs. He couldn't blow.

Lowering the horn to his chest, his mind wandered into the darkness of cynicism.

*You're always setting yourself up for a letdown when you want something too much. That's the way life is but you never learn. An old fool just keeps on being an old fool.*

His adrenaline began to ebb and anger turned to disappointment. He still had feelings for Dae and that's what hurt the most. Maybe he could have accepted her marital situation had he known earlier, but after being misled, that seemed impossible. It's hard, he thought, to put something back together when one of the pieces is broken.

Brax closed his eyes and his mind went blank. He laid there for a long time with no energy and no desire to move. Finally, he set the trumpet aside and got off the bed. He headed for the kitchen where a bottle of good scotch awaited in the pantry. Maybe he would sleep in and skip the walk on the beach in the morning.

He guessed Dae wouldn't be there either.

Brax stayed in bed until almost nine a.m. His head buzzed from two glasses of almost straight scotch from the night before. He trudged into the kitchen, started the coffee maker and stuck a bagel in the toaster. For the first time in more than a year, he skipped his morning routine at the clubhouse. Two cups of coffee, half a bagel, and three ibuprofen tablets settled him down.

Whiling away the early hours at home, he worked a crossword puzzle, played solitaire on the computer, and watched television with a complete lack of interest. He needed privacy but he felt oddly trapped as if everyone in the tight-knit community were waiting for him to walk out the front door. At mid-morning he got in his car and drove from the complex using the service road in the rear, avoiding the clubhouse and Dae's street.

He drove across the bridge and headed for the mainland with no particular destination in mind. Leaving the main highway, he drove aimlessly along lonely back roads he'd never traveled, occasionally stopping at a small store for a soft drink or coffee. Once, he parked near a desolate farmhouse and walked around, imagining what it might feel like to live apart from the rest of the world. Back on the road, the miles rolled by and the hours passed slowly as he tried to clear his mind but his thoughts kept coming back to Dae. What to do?

After a while, the refreshing effect of the private time took hold and he began to feel the lifeblood flowing back into his mind and body. After a few false turns, he wound his way out of the remote maze of blacktop roads and onto the highway. Before he reached the bridge to the island, he called Jim on his cell phone.

"I had a little business to take care of this morning. I'm on my way back and I thought I might stop by if you're not busy."

"That'll be fine," Jim replied. "I was just about to put on my jogging shoes and go for a ten mile run, but that can wait."

"I'll bet. See you in about fifteen minutes."

Brax walked into Jim's house and sat in a side chair. Jim lay on the sofa in shorts and a sweatshirt.

"I talked to Dae last night," Brax began.

"I know. I met her walking on the beach by herself this morning."

"What did she say?

"Just that y'all had a little disagreement and you didn't show up at the clubhouse."

"Did she say what we disagreed about?"

"No, and I didn't ask. 'Course, I knew."

Brax pinched his lips with his fingers. "It's true," he blurted. "She's married."

"Well, we're all adults. We can deal with that."

"It's not that simple—I have to live with myself. Besides, I see her in a different light now. She hasn't been straight with me. "

"Listen, dumbass, don't be so high and mighty," Jim said, sitting up. "You're not fooling me. I know you like her and she likes you. At our age, that's all that matters. Don't you realize what a lucky bastard you are?"

Brax grimaced. "I don't know. It doesn't feel right. I can't get involved with another man's wife."

"So tell me this—how would you get along without her? Would you be okay or would you be miserable?"

"I got along just fine by myself before I met her," Brax said defiantly. He leaned down and gazed at the floor for a good while. Then he looked up. "You know better than that."

"Yeah, I do."

"I could ask her to consider a divorce, but I don't want to be the cause of breaking up a marriage, especially since the guy is sick."

"It appears to me that it was broken up before she ever met you. It's your life but if I was you, I'd do what I wanted to and not worry about what anybody else thought." Jim smugly raised an eyebrow. "Look, remember that story you told me about getting sick on German chocolate cake?" He didn't pause for Brax to respond. "Well, it was bullshit. You said you ate too much of that cake and it taught you that sometimes things aren't as good as they seem. That's just your screwed up way of looking at things. What you've got to realize is that some things are actually as good as they seem if you don't screw 'em up. That was a good cake but you kept at it 'til you ruined it. It seems to me that Dae's the best thing to happen to you since your wife died."

Brax sighed, "You're right." Then he stood from the chair. "I'll figure it out."

"Yeah," Jim replied. "Yeah, you will."

As he left Jim's place, Brax wasn't sure what his next move was but he was confident in his words. He *would* figure it out.

—————

Brax sat on a stool at the kitchen bar, hovered over a crossword puzzle. He forced down a cup of coffee and bran muffin without the faintest sense of smell or taste. After a few minutes he put the pen down, unable to concentrate.

Two days had gone by since his last contact with Dae and, removed from the sting of disillusionment, he began to see things more clearly. He realized he hardly knew her and didn't discount that she might have purposefully lured him on, but he trusted his instinct. From the first time he met her, he had felt differently about himself. More alive. It was a good feeling and he desperately wanted to find a way to hang onto it. Still, the situation was messy and he didn't see an easy way to make it feel right.

Sometimes he did his best thinking with a hot shower. In the bathroom, he looked at himself in the mirror and all seventy-one years looked back at him. As he stared at himself, everything came into focus: the white hair, the puffy eyes, the creased face. He saw someone who, before meeting Dae, felt helpless as the grains of sand slipped through the hourglass of his life. But now he saw a man who wanted to hold onto those grains, no matter how many or how few there might still be.

He shaved, showered, and put on a fresh set of clothes. Then he went outside and started toward Dae's house. If she had taken her usual walk, she would be back by now.

—————

# 23

As he approached Dae's house, Brax recalled the first time she invited him to her place. He had a giddy-up in his step that evening and a seed of expectation in the back of his mind. This time, it was different. He rang the doorbell tentatively, not knowing what to expect.

The door opened and Dae stood in the entrance, clutching the handle. "Hi," she said with a smile that appeared to be forced.

"Good morning," he replied without a smile. "Mind if I come in?"

"Sure." She stepped back, closed the door, walked a few steps into the living room, and remained standing.

"Can we talk about what happened the other night?"

"Yes, I'd like to. Please sit down." Dae motioned Brax to the sofa and she sat in a chair facing him.

"I'm sorry if I was mean to you," he said, "but this was quite a kick in the gut to me and I worked myself into a knot about it."

"I understand, it's all my fault. I should have been more open with you up front." She paused and they looked at each other for a moment. "How did you find out?"

"I'd rather not say. It doesn't matter."

"I bought this house in my name and I haven't told anyone else here about my marriage. I wish you would tell me if anyone in Seaside knows."

"Jim knows, but don't drag him into this. He found out accidentally when he was at the VFW. He saw a picture of you and your husband at some kind of veterans' get-together and one thing led to another. Don't worry though, Jim won't say anything to anyone, not even Jaws. I trust him on that"

"So someone told him John was still alive?"

"Yeah. He said some guy keeps track of the Vietnam Vets."

"Did he tell Jim where John was?"

Brax hesitated, uncomfortable with going into all the details. "He said he was in a nursing home in Savannah."

"It's an assisted living facility."

"Look, I don't know what happened and I don't need to know any more than what you want me to. But I came to talk about us."

"I'm glad you did. I was afraid you might never speak to me again."

"I had to give myself some time to think."

He kneaded the arm of the sofa with his hand and inhaled deeply. "We need to talk about us. Where we go from here."

"Where do you want to go?" she asked.

Brax looked directly into her eyes. "I'd like to work something out so that we can stay friends."

"Friends?"

Brax squirmed uncomfortably. "No, more than that." He swallowed and pursed his lips, feeling the burden of taking the first step. "Dae, you know how I feel about you. That hasn't changed."

She rose from the chair and moved beside him on the sofa. "And I still feel the same way about you. I'm sorry I put you in such a terrible spot."

Brax felt his heart race and he spoke with a pleading voice. "I want us to be together."

"I want that, too." She sighed and leaned into him.

He put his arm around her, and pulled her to him. "Good," he whispered. "I need you."

"And I need you," she affirmed. She rested her chin on his shoulder with her cheek next to his and spoke softly. "I'll get a divorce."

Shocked by her boldness, he pulled his head back. "I can't let you do that. It wouldn't be right."

"Yes, yes it would. It's something I should have already done."

It seemed like a logical solution, but it didn't feel right to Brax. He didn't like the idea of taking advantage of a sick man.

"You said your husband just faded away. What did you mean by that?"

She sighed heavily and looked away with vacant eyes.

"Tell me everything," Brax said. "We can deal with it."

"We've been married for forty-five years," she began. "When I met John, he was kind and fun to be around and very passionate. I was madly in love with him and we were married right after he got home from Vietnam. I could tell the war had changed him. He was more serious, less outgoing, but he was still very good to me. We only quarreled over little things. Typical husband and wife spats. But as time went on, he lost his temper more often and the arguments became more heated. I tried to shield Julie and Justin, but they saw what was happening."

"Did he hit you?"

Dae was silent for a moment, as if studying her response. "It was mostly verbal. He didn't mean to hurt me. He was angry at the world, I suppose. Things he couldn't control or understand. He sometimes cursed about the death and destruction of innocent people and the senselessness of the war."

"You didn't answer my question."

There was another long silence.

"Just a shove or a slap, nothing brutal," she finally admitted. "It only happened two or three times and he always apologized. I think it hurt him more than it did me."

Brax gave his head a quick shake. He couldn't believe what he was hearing: victim's guilt. "How long did this go on?"

"Off and on for a few years. It didn't happen often. Most of the time he was not aggressive or argumentative. He was quiet and kept to himself a lot. By then the children were out of the house and that basically left me alone. After I retired I stayed as busy as I could away from home—bridge parties, book clubs, volunteering at the library, going to the gym." She looked down for a moment. "Then one night, he tried to kill himself."

"How?"

"He ran the exhaust pipe into his truck and sat inside with the engine running. I found him and called 911. He survived, but the carbon monoxide had a long term effect."

"When did that happen?"

"Eight years ago. After that, he was never the same. He began to lose touch with reality. He couldn't remember things and became very docile. It was a complete turn-around and, the odd thing is, he knew it was happening. Once he told me, 'I'm losing it.' The doctors said he had early stage dementia and it got progressively worse. He's a smart man—at least he was before—and very self-sufficient. It was heart breaking to see him become almost child-like."

"So he turned from a monster into a child?"

"I know it sounds bizarre and it was. It took a lot to take care of him. You can't imagine what it's like to tend to someone twenty-four hours a day for years. Especially when they don't really understand what's happening and they can't appreciate your sacrifice." Tears welled in Dae's eyes. "You're trapped and you don't have a life of your own. For me, it became a burden of duty and there was no reward, no love or thanks in return."

Her hands shook as she wiped her eyes with the tissue. "Things just got worse. Sometimes he called me Mama but most of the time he acted as if he had never met me."

Brax pulled her head to his chest and held her tightly. "You don't have to talk about it anymore," he whispered.

She raised her head. "Yes, you should know. Someone should

know. I didn't abandon John."

"I believe you."

"But you can't understand how difficult it was. I was physically and mentally exhausted and I knew I couldn't take care of him anymore. I agonized over it for months before I convinced myself to find a place for him. The doctors weren't sure if he had Alzheimer's or another form of dementia but the symptoms were the same. He's in an assisted living facility in Savannah. There's a special wing for late term dementia patients."

Brax shook his head in sympathy while privately fearing the possibility of someday succumbing to the same cruel fate. "I know that had to be hard for you."

"How can you let go of someone you love?" she said. "When I married John, I promised to be faithful, to love, honor and obey, for better or for worse, until death do us part. And I intended to do that, but after he became so removed, I felt abandoned. "

"This was after he totally lost it mentally?"

"Yes. My children actually encouraged me to be more social and not be tied down. They knew their father was troubled and they were always closer to me than they were to him. They said they would support me if there was another man in my life."

"Good. I guess they won't hate me."

"Brax, you've got to believe me when I tell you that I didn't plan this out. Yes, I was frustrated, but I never intended to get seriously involved with another man. When I met you, though, it just happened. It was like a void in my life had been filled and I didn't know how to deal with it. I met with my pastor and told him of my desires. Someone to talk to … to share things with … someone to touch.

"I'll bet that was an interesting conversation."

"Oh, it was. I was very nervous. I was afraid he would pen a scarlet letter on me right then and there and I'd be branded another Hester Prynne in his eyes. But he surprised me. He was very sympathetic and said I was not the first person to come to him in a similar position."

"Really?"

"Yes. He said he'd given a lot of consideration to the moral implication of companionship outside of marriage in a situation like mine. He said I'd been faithful to my vows, but now John had moved into God's house and wasn't able to fulfill his own vows. He was no longer the man I had married. 'The Lord knows what's in your heart,' he said, and he thought I should continue to be loyal to John's memory and provide for his care but be free to live my life in a way that was fulfilling. I don't remember his exact words, but that's pretty much the essence of it. We prayed about it. Having his understanding made me feel better, but I couldn't completely get rid of my guilt."

"I know it must have torn you up. Sometimes there's no right answer. "

"I visit John once a week and it's never pleasant, but I have to. Not for him—he doesn't know me anymore—but for my own conscience. I can't just forget about him."

"Of course you can't." As he listened to the story, Brax saw Dae in a new light and he mentally kicked himself for doubting her good intentions. Yet he couldn't help but wonder about the best way to deal with the situation.

"I respect your personal feelings," he said. "You know how I feel about you, but we don't have to go any further. As long as we can see each other, I'll be happy."

She closed her eyes for a second and then opened them. "Brax, I've thought about it a long time and I've made peace with the idea of divorce. My pastor was right—the John I married is no longer alive. And I know he would want me to go on just as Jane would want you to. In my mind, our situations are the same. I once told you that when you lose someone, you don't stop loving them, but you don't follow them to the grave. Do you remember my saying that?"

"Yeah. It was at Fort Fredericka, the first time we ever talked about our spouses. That's when you told me that John eventually just faded away."

"It wasn't my intention to deceive you. I wanted to tell you all of this, but that wasn't the time or place. I never found the nerve to bring it up and the closer we became, the more difficult it was. I'm sorry."

"I'm not mad at you. I was at first because it was a shock and I thought it meant I would lose you."

"You won't lose me."

"Are you sure you want a divorce? It might seem like a cruel thing to others."

"My children will understand." She raised her eyebrows. "Do you?"

It still didn't seem right to him, but he thought her feelings to be more important. "Yes, I understand. But it's your decision and I'm not pushing you to do this."

"I think it's the only way that we'll feel completely together." She arched her brows as if to beg a response.

He nodded.

"I'll have to be John's guardian," she said. "And I'll have to make sure he's looked after."

"*We'll* have to be his guardian. I'll do whatever I can."

"Thanks. It's a strain emotionally and it wears on me. It would be a big help to have someone to lean on."

"I guess it's decided then," he said.

"Yes, it is."

"There's something I want to do, though."

She looked at him curiously.

"I want to meet him."

She took a deep breath, closed her eyes for a second and then opened them. "I'm glad. It'll be hard for both of us, but I want you to meet John. I visit him every Thursday when I told you I was visiting a friend. But we can go any time."

"Let's go this Thursday."

"Okay," she said, then exhaled. "Oh-h-h," she sighed, "this is so difficult but I know it's the right thing." She put her cheek to his, pecked a kiss on his lips, and looked at him with a glimmer of hope in her eyes. "I feel like I have my life back."

They had only spoken for a few minutes but it felt like hours to Brax. A relationship that began by simple chance had become complicated, but the thought of spending his last years with Dae was like a jolt of new life. He had almost forgotten what it felt like to really love someone. Then he realized that he had only said the word "love" to Dae once, then in a comforting way after a peck on her cheek. Had never told her properly.

Nor had he ever thought he could feel that way about anyone other than Jane.

# 24

Brax cut the eight-ball into the side pocket, the cue ball banking safely off the rail. "Good game," he said. "You're getting better."

"Thanks, Minnesota Fats," Jim replied. "I'll beat your ass one of these days."

Momadou laughed as he stepped down from his stool against a near wall. "I'll see you, guys. I'm picking up my grandson after school and we're going fishing."

"Catch one for me," Brax said.

"See you later, Jaws," Jim added.

They gathered the balls from the pockets and nested them in the rack. Brax pushed it tightly to the break spot on the table and they returned their cue sticks to the wall frame. Leaving the clubhouse, they settled into deck chairs on the edge of the pool which had been covered for the season.

"So Dae's getting a divorce, eh?" Jim asked.

"That's the game plan. It's her decision, not mine."

"Hmm. And her old man's in a loony bin?"

"Don't start that. You know it's a bad situation and I don't need you to make light of it."

"I'm not making light." Jim frowned and shook his head. "Forget it."

"No, I can tell something's on your mind, so tell me what it is."

"Look, I told you before to do what you want to." Jim slouched heavily in his chair. "I don't know anything about this guy. He may be a complete jerk, but I know what he went through."

Brax narrowed his eyes. "You're having second thoughts, aren't you? It's about him being a Vietnam vet, isn't it?"

"Yeah," Jim answered with nod. "The guy at the VFW who showed me the pictures said he was in the same outfit as Dae's husband. He said they got caught in the Tet Offensive and it was hell. A lot of their buddies died. That'll change a man."

"I realize that and I know you feel strongly about it." Brax's voice softened. "I'm a little older than you and I was almost thirty when things really heated up. So I didn't serve. I have nothing but respect for you guys who did, but I don't think Vietnam has anything to do with what we're talking about here."

Jim maintained an icy stare.

"Dae's husband has dementia," Brax continued, "and no one knows exactly what caused it. It may have had nothing to do with the war. You and a lot of other guys that were there didn't go off the deep end."

Jim didn't respond and it dawned on Brax that he was speaking to an alcoholic who, until recently, kept a loaded pistol stashed in his living room.

"Regardless," Brax continued, "nothing can be done about it. Whatever happened fifty years ago is history and we can't change that."

"You're right," Jim said, but the words didn't match the look on his face.

"Jim," Brax said, slowly, "I've thought about this a lot and it's not a decision that came easily. As I said, it's what Dae wants. And it's not that we're being callous or disregarding her husband's feelings. We're going to see him Thursday but from what she tells me, he won't know her or understand anything we say."

"I guess you're going to marry her."

"We haven't gotten that far."

Jim looked puzzled. "I thought that was the whole idea, but that's your business, not mine." Then his expression turned serious. "I've got something I'd like you to look at. Can you come to my place?"

"Right now? What the heck is it?"

"You'll see. Let's go."

The men rose from their chairs and headed for Jim's house, only three blocks away.

Arriving home, Jim walked directly to a shelf next to the television. Brax watched curiously as his friend sorted through a stack of DVD's.

Jim turned around holding a single disk in a plastic cover. "I want you to watch this." He handed Brax the DVD. "Not here—take it to your place."

Brax read the label on the disk: Vietnam, The Red Horse. With a curious look, he asked, "The red horse?"

"You'll know what it means after you watch it."

"You're trying to make this hard on me, aren't you?"

"No, I want you and Dae to be together. It's a good thing. I'm just trying to give you a little ... perspective." Jim turned his gaze to the DVD in Brax's hands and then back. "When you meet the man on Thursday, he might not know you but you'll know him."

Brax could see the earnestness in Jim's face. "I'll watch it." He stepped away and opened the front door, then turned around with the DVD raised in his hand. "I know I owe the man my respect."

"You might've made a half-assed decent jarhead." Jim grinned slyly. "Semper Fi."

Brax shook his head and snorted in jest. "Hmmph."

He stepped outside, anxious to get home and view the DVD. Maybe, as Jim assured, it would help him understand the man whose shadow hung over him.

In the dark room with his chair only a few feet from the television, Brax sat spellbound. For forty-five minutes he had watched Vietnam vets recall their experiences in the war. Continually, images appeared on the screen with scenes from the long-ago conflict, then returned to the haunting face of the narrator. Many were reduced to tears as they spoke of friends who had been killed. Most wondered how, even why, they survived in the face of heavy casualties.

Now, the man on the DVD seemed to be speaking personally to him and Brax felt a profound sense of sadness.

Ray Hatfield of Bartlesville, Oklahoma, spoke directly into the camera, his voice flavored with a deep western drawl. His straw-colored hair was short and thin on top but long on the sides and hung like a curtain around his neck. A thick mustache covered his top lip and the years had etched lines around his deep-set eyes as if he were perpetually looking into the sun. Sharp cheekbones jutted from his gaunt face and a western-style shirt hung straight from thin, coat hanger shoulders.

"When I joined the Army," Hatfield began, "I was eighteen years old, barely out of high school. I'd never been far from home and was still wet behind the ears. Going through basic training and wearing that uniform made me feel like a real man. The first time I had ever been on a plane was when I went to Vietnam. Most of us tried to act gung ho, like we weren't afraid. But a few weeks after we arrived, we quickly found out what war was all about. We were in camp outside Saigon when all hell broke loose. Later we learned it was the start of the Tet Offensive." Newsreel footage appeared of initial assaults of the Tet Offensive on the Tan Son Nhut Air Base.

"We were hit by mortar fire and a guy I'd met on the plane coming over was killed in the first few minutes. A big piece of shrapnel hit him and tore his head right off. We lost two more guys that had just arrived that day and lots of others were wounded. It was total chaos and everything was happening so fast I was just running on adrenaline. The fear came later. You never knew when the next attack would come.

"After repelling the first assault, we were sent in a day later to help defend the city. Fighting was going on everywhere and we were under fire almost all the time. I'd never seen a dead person before, except at a funeral, but I saw plenty in those next few weeks. A lot of them were civilians—women, children, old people, even monks. The Viet Cong were killing their own people. And sometimes I guess we did, too. You couldn't always tell the enemy from the friendlies. The city was being destroyed at the same time. The military calls it collateral damage, which sounds better than what it really is—unnecessary death and destruction."

Scenes flashed of American soldiers and tanks firing at unseen enemies in urban fighting.

"We were scrambling down an alley when a buddy of mine I had met in boot camp was killed by a sniper. His name was Jesus Rodriguez and he was from Puerto Rico, a wiry little guy with hopes of being a professional boxer. He was hit in the back and the bullet went right through him, tearing his guts out. I helped load his body on the back of the deuce-and-a-half and it tore me up. I'll never forget the look on his face—calm as if he never knew what hit him. Jesus always carried a Bible with him and said that we were in the middle of the Apocalypse. He talked about the book of Revelation a lot and told me to watch out for the red horse, the one whose rider carried the sword of death."

Grainy images of the Four Horsemen from an old movie appeared. The movie was in black and white but the second horse was highlighted in fiery red. Words scrolled across the screen:

"And there went out another horse that was red: and power was given to him that sat thereon to take peace from the earth, and that they should kill one another: and there was given unto him a great sword." Revelation 6:4.

"For the rest of my tour, I lived in fear of the red horse.

"One day we met up with some Marines who'd withstood a siege from a large force of Viet Cong. There was a big hole in the ground that had been dug by a bulldozer, and as we got closer, I could see there were bodies of dead gooks piled in the hole. A couple of Marines stood on the side of the hole eating their C-rations. It sounds crazy that they could eat anything while standing over those bloody, stinking bodies, but that's how you get after a while. One of them yelled at me and said, 'Two hundred and fourteen Charlies FUBAR.' That means Fucked Up Beyond All Recognition. Then he took the rifle off his shoulder and fired a burst into the hole. 'The little Slope was moving,' he said.

"We didn't take many prisoners," Hatfield stated, the implication obvious.

"The scene I remember the most is when we came upon a spot in the jungle that had been cleared by napalm for a landing zone. There were a dozen or so charred bodies scattered around the area like burnt chunks of meat that had fallen off a barbeque spit. None of them were armed."

A brief clip was shown of a plane dropping napalm in a jungle, creating a huge ball with a trail of intense fire.

"They were innocent people who were cooked to a crisp like fried chicken just because they happened to be there." With a distant look in his eyes, Hatfield added, "I don't know where God was." He took a deep breath. "The capacity we had for killing was awesome and scary at the same time. That's when I realized I was riding the red horse.

"I drank my first beer and hard liquor when I was in Nam. Smoked a lot of weed, too. Most of the guys did. That's how we tried to forget about what was going on around us." A picture of U.S. troops smoking outside a makeshift bunker appeared. "A couple of times I tried the harder stuff—opium, heroin. When I got back home, most everybody wanted us out of the war and didn't appreciate those of us who had served. Everything seemed different than before and I didn't know how to deal with the everyday crap of civilian life. I kept drinking and doping, trying to forget the war and all the insane things I'd seen.

"When the politicians gave up and let the Commies have the country, it was a stab in the back."

Newsreel footage appeared of the final evacuation of the U.S. Embassy in Saigon.

"Although I never suffered more'n a few cuts and bruises, I personally knew thirteen guys that lost their lives. I felt like they all died for nothing, and thousands more like 'em. It bothered me a lot. I got deeper into alcohol and drugs, lost my wife and kids, and hit rock bottom. Finally, I'd had enough and got into a rehab program. I've been sober for over two years now and I've got a maintenance job at an apartment complex. Every day is a new beginning, and I'm trying to get back on my feet. But sometimes I still see that red horse in my nightmares."

The man's voice faded and a picture of a younger version of him appeared on the screen. His head was sheared to fine bristles with a GI cut and he held a cigarette in one corner of his mouth with a smile. He was thick-shouldered and a dog tag dangled on his bare chest. An automatic rifle rested in his hands just above his waist. A caption read:

Ray Hatfield died of a self-inflicted gunshot at the age
of fifty-eight.
His death occurred on January 31, 2008.
It was exactly forty years after the start of the Tet Offensive.

Brax pressed the remote and turned off the DVD. Sitting motionless in the chair, he stared at the blank screen for a long time. He wished he had known Ray Hatfield and had been able to help him. Then he thought of Dae's husband.

"He won't know you," Jim had said, "but you'll know him." Now he understood what Jim meant.

# 25

Brax followed the interstate north toward Savannah, unsettled by the prospect of meeting John Whitehead. He knew it was the right thing to do, yet it was unnerving to know he was heading for a meeting in which Dae would tell her husband she was divorcing him.

"You told me John is normally pretty calm, right?"

"Yes, he has been lately, but you never know."

"Has he ever been violent? I mean since he's been at this place."

"No, not violent. At least, not with me. He raised a hand to me one time. I shouted at him and called a male attendant. That was probably … two years ago, maybe longer. He used to raise his voice and curse a lot, saying people were stealing from him, but I'm told he hasn't done that in a good while."

"How do you think he'll take it when we tell him about us? We need to be honest about the divorce."

"Yes, I know." She paused. "I'm not sure how he'll react. He probably won't comprehend it but in case he gets angry, I'll ask Albert to stand by. He's one of the men who works there. John doesn't have good muscle control and he loses his balance easily but I don't want you and him to get into a confrontation."

"No, that's the last thing I want. But I will be straight with him, whether he understands what I'm saying or not. That's the main reason I want to meet him—to let him know I respect him and to satisfy my own conscience about making my intentions known."

"I'm glad you feel that way and I do, too. I would never start a divorce without telling him first. I think after you meet him, you'll know we've done the right thing."

"Is his health good, other than his mind?"

"For the most part. He has high blood pressure and he's on heart medication, but he gets a check-up a couple of times a year and he's doing okay." She took a long breath. "Oh God, it's sad. Once he told me he wished he would just go ahead and die. And, honestly—I know this is horrible to say—but he would be better off."

Brax glanced at her with a pained look. Turning his eyes back to the road, he asked, "And he doesn't know who you are?"

"Not really. I tell him my name but sometimes he forgets. He knows I'm kin to him or, at least a friend of the family, but he gets confused about our relationship. It seems so strange, hurtful really, since we were together for so long. Somehow, he has blocked me out of his memory. Sometimes he thinks I'm his mother. Other times he's called me Sis. One time he told me that he liked me. 'We ought'a get married,' he said."

Brax shook his head.

During the ninety-minute drive, Dae reminded Brax of some things to be aware of when he met John. "He might ask the same question over and over, even if you answer him the first time ... he might say some outrageous things—things that are only true in his mind. Whatever he says, just go along with it ... he sleeps a lot, so he might not be awake when we get there. We'll need to wait for him to wake up, or come back later ... he sometimes gets upset with loud noises or people who seem threatening ... Make sure you don't mention Vietnam or say anything about the Army. He gets very agitated when he thinks he's back in the war and it's hard to calm him down."

Nearing downtown Savannah, Brax pulled off the interstate and followed Dae's directions through a part of town unfamiliar to him. As they neared their destination, she asked, "How do you feel?"

"I'm not sure. A little anxious, maybe, not knowing what to

expect. But I'm ready to get it over." The words didn't sound right. "I mean I'll be glad to get through this meeting. I realize we'll have to deal with this situation beyond that."

"I know what you mean."

Approaching an intersection, he asked, "Turn left here?"

"Yes. It's just a little way down on the right. You'll see the sign."

A minute later, Brax turned into the driveway of Oakview. The attractive building looked fairly new and the grounds were well groomed. Moss-draped live oaks surrounded the low, brick structure and the front entrance was framed by a palm tree on each side. The setting presented a serene image in the glow of a cool, but sunny day.

He parked in the visitors section and turned to Dae, forcing an uneasy smile, before getting out to open her door.

"His wing is on the right," she said. "It's called the Beacon Community."

"I'll follow you."

They entered the main lobby, stopping at an office behind a big glass window. A woman sitting at a desk greeted them.

"Good afternoon, Miz Whitehead."

"Hi, Shirley. This is Mr. Donovan. He'll be visiting John with me."

"That's nice. Welcome Mr. Donovan."

"Thank you," Brax replied.

"Shirley," Dae said, "would you please call Albert and see if he could meet us in Beacon?"

"I sure will." The woman picked up the desk phone and dialed a number. A brief conversation ensued and she looked up. "Albert will be over there in a few minutes."

"Thanks."

They left the office and beyond the lobby was a sitting area where three elderly ladies sat quietly, one with a small dog tethered at her feet. Dae greeted them as if she knew their faces if not their names. Brax followed suit. Beyond the sitting area, Dae pointed out a well-manicured courtyard through the windows.

Across the lobby was a good-sized dining room, empty at the time, and adjacent smaller rooms, one in which card players gathered around a table. Dae commented, "This is where the regular residents eat and have their activities. There's something going on all the time."

As Dae showed him around, Brax noted the pleasant décor throughout the interior of the facility. Rich wood floors joined areas covered in pale green carpet and white chair rail lined the wall with subtly patterned wallpaper below. He followed her to the other side of the lobby and down an L-shaped hall that led to a secured door.

She pressed a large button to activate the automatic opener. "This is the Beacon Neighborhood."

Inside, they walked into a big, open room with several different seating areas. A large television, flanked by three sofas in a U-shape, was tuned to a "Bonanza" rerun. The sofas were empty. One corner of the room contained a kitchen and dining area. Four women sat at tables having their nails done. Nearby, a man slouched asleep in an overstuffed chair while a woman dozed on another sofa in a far corner.

Two sides of the main room were lined by twelve resident rooms, their doors opening directly into the common space. Some of the doors were open, exposing a direct view into the room.

Brax felt uncomfortable in the environment, feeling as if he were invading the privacy of those who lived there. He also wasn't sure how to interact with the residents nor could he immediately distinguish them from visitors and staff. Dae was obviously more at ease and he hung at her side, reluctant to say any more than necessary.

A black man in khakis and a blue shirt with an Oakview monogram appeared from another door. "Hello, Miz Whitehead."

"Hi, Albert. This is Mr. Donovan. Would you mind standing by for a few minutes while we visit John? We'll be speaking to him about something personal and I don't want Mr. Donovan to have to deal with John if he gets angry. I don't think he will, but just in case."

"No ma'am, I'll be glad to."

Brax stepped forward to shake Albert's hand. "Nice to meet you." Feeling self-conscious about asking for the man's help, he added, "We'll be okay."

Albert nodded. "I'll be right here if you need me."

They moved to John's room and Brax stood behind as Dae opened the door.

"Yoo-hoo," she said. "It's me."

Brax followed her in and his discomfort edged up a notch, knowing he was about to confront his lover's husband. The fact that his presence might be upsetting pulled the knot in his gut a little tighter.

John sat up on his bed as they entered.

Dae moved to her husband and gave him a quick hug. She stepped back and asked, "How have you been doing?"

Appearing dumfounded by the question, John replied, "Yeah."

Dae extended an arm toward Brax. "John, this is Brax Donovan."

Brax stepped forward and extended his right hand. "Hi, John. Nice to meet you."

John moved to sit on the side of the bed and shook hands with a limp grip. He stared at Brax and said, "What's your name?"

"I'm Brax Donovan."

"Brax lives near me on the island," Dae said. "We wanted to talk to you for a few minutes. Why don't we sit over here?"

She took John's arm and led him to a sitting area. They sat down on a loveseat and Brax settled in a recliner facing them.

In addition to the bed, loveseat and recliner, the room contained a wardrobe and a couple of nightstands with lamps. No television. There was a private bath with a sliding door. A double window opened the view to a woody expanse behind the complex, a reminder of the world beyond the confines of the four walls.

The setting was depressing to Brax, almost claustrophobic. Though the room was large enough, it felt restrictive, more like a cage than a place to live. He imagined being confined to this tiny part of the world and thought it might feel like being in a minimum security prison. He wondered if John felt the same way, or if he thought anything at all.

"You look good," Dae began. "Tell me what you've been doing since I saw you last."

"I got in my truck and bought some corn liquor."

"Why'd you do that?"

"Somebody stole mine. I drove out to Tybee and the cops on the beach tried to get my liquor. But I threw it in the ocean and they didn't get it. You know, those damn cops won't let you drink liquor on the beach."

"Well, I don't think so. You don't need to be drinking anyhow."

"You won't tell Mama will ya'?"

"No, I won't tell."

Brax kept his eyes on John as he exchanged nonsensical talk with Dae for another fifteen minutes. Dressed in a gray T-shirt and warm-up pants, John looked sickly, like a plant in need of sun and water. His complexion was ghostly and his face looked tired, or maybe just sad. A thin layer of hair covered his head, mostly dark with streaks of gray, combed flat to one side and slightly matted. Even so, his features were well-proportioned and it was easy to visualize him as a once handsome man.

"John, we need to talk to you about something," Dae said. She looked at Brax as if giving a signal. "It's about Brax and me."

Brax moved from the recliner and stood near the bed, closer to the other two.

John turned to Brax with a suspicious look. "What's your name?"

"I'm Brax."

"John," Dae said. "Brax and I have become good friends." She reached and took John's hand. "But you know I love you."

John looked at Brax again. "What's your name?"

"His name is Brax," Dae said. "Look at me, John. Brax and I are going to be together."

Brax spoke up. "Dae and I have become close." He waited for John's reaction.

John stared at Brax. "Do you like Georgia Tech?" he asked.

"Sure," Brax replied. "I like Georgia Tech. John, I want you to understand my feelings. I have nothing but respect for you and I know Dae loves you very much. But she needs someone to be with her when she can't be with you. I'd like to be that person."

"Julie goes to Georgia Tech," John said. "She's real smart."

Brax realized his words meant nothing to John but he had to say them. "We want to live together." He kept his eyes on John as he let the words sink in. "I'll take care of her just like you always have and we'll come see you often."

John's eyes opened wide and the glower on his face seemed a confusion of anger and fright. He stood up and shouted, "No! Julie has to go to Georgia Tech! Dammit, she has to!"

Dae rose beside John and Brax stood straight, tense for a possible confrontation. Alerted by the shout, Albert rushed through the door, but stopped short as the room became quiet.

Dae took John's arm. "It's okay," she said calmly. "It's okay. Sit down."

John stood motionless for a moment. The fire slowly cooled from his eyes and Dae gently eased him back onto the loveseat.

"Julie is already going to Georgia Tech," Dae said. She patted John's hand. "She's doing great."

Turning to the attendant, Dae said, "We're okay, Albert." As he turned to leave, she said, "Close the door, please."

Dae kneeled in front of John and put each of her hands in one of his. "John, I'm Dae—your wife. I love you, but I must leave you." She stood and kissed his cheek. "I'll be with Brax now." She moved to Brax and put a hand in his. "I have to get a divorce to make it right."

When she said the word "divorce," it hit Brax like a bucket of cold water. It was what they had agreed to say, but now it seemed so cruel.

"What's your name?" John asked, looking at Brax.

"Brax Donovan."

"Do you like Georgia Tech?"

"Yeah." Brax squeezed Dae's hand a little tighter. Then, determined to make sure he had said his part, he returned to the subject at hand. "We walk on the beach every day out on the island. We'll be living together there."

"Don't drink liquor on the beach. Those cops'll get your ass."

"We won't," Brax said.

"We have to go now," Dae said. She took her hand from Brax and stepped to John. "Give me a hug."

John rose from his chair and Dae embraced him. "You hug real good," he said.

Brax shook John's hand again. "See ya' buddy."

Brax opened the door for Dae and, as they left, John said, "Don't drink liquor on the beach."

In the main room, Dae spoke to Albert. "Thanks, Albert. Everything's fine. I'll see you next time."

"Yes, ma'am."

Brax followed Dae to the door leading from the Beacon Community. She entered a code on the pad and the door locked behind them as they entered the hallway.

He stopped and pulled her to him. Emotionally drained, he felt weak, but knowing she needed him, he wrapped her tightly in his arms. Though they didn't speak, he knew what she was feeling. Her body trembled, then began to shake as the tears finally came. With her head pressed against his chest, she sobbed into his shirt.

The midday sun blazed through a window that looked out to the small courtyard and Brax felt the fog of gloom begin to clear. Dae became still and the sound of her crying faded away. She raised her head and looked at Brax with wet, puffy eyes and mascara on her cheeks.

He kissed her on her forehead and she smiled weakly. "Are you ready to go?" he asked.

"Yes, but I need to step in the ladies room for a minute."

Dae returned with a dry face, clear of mascara streaks. She held some tissues in her hand and dabbed at the tear stains on Brax's shirt.

"Come on, it'll dry," he said.

---

After leaving Oakview, Dae stared out the car window, barely speaking. Brax kept his focus on driving, leaving her to her private thoughts. He knew there would be aftershocks from their meeting with John and he was feeling them, too.

When he stopped at a traffic light, she turned from the window and gazed straight ahead as if transfixed by something beyond the windshield. "I have an appointment with the lawyer tomorrow."

He looked at her and mumbled, "Good." He didn't know what else to say and he didn't want to start a conversation about it.

As he followed stop-and-go traffic on the way to the interstate, Brax spied a coffee shop. "How about a cappuccino?" he asked.

"Okay." Dae's voice carried a "why not?" tone.

He turned into the parking lot of a small, upscale shopping village. They went into the corner coffee shop and he bought two steaming cups of cappuccino.

"Is it too cold to sit outside?" he asked.

"No," she answered. "The air feels good and I'm warm in this sweater."

Styrofoam cups in hand, they strolled outside and sat down on a concrete bench. In front of them, a small fountain bubbled over a mushroom-shaped metal sculpture.

Brax took a big swallow of his drink and peered at the water feature. He turned his head, speaking to her obliquely. "I'm glad we went to see John."

She blew the steam from the top of her drink, took a sip, and looked straight ahead. "Me, too."

The words drifted from her lips with a sadness that told him exactly how she felt. He let the moment breathe and then said what he knew was the only thing to say. "I can't let you divorce him."

She pursed her lips with the start of a smile and, for the first time since leaving John's room, her face reflected the beam he had become accustomed to. She set her cup aside and leaned into him, burying her head in his shoulder.

"Thank you," she murmured.

"Can we still stay together?" he asked.

"Always."

That was all he needed to hear. Nothing else mattered.

# 26

Brax, spruced up for the Christmas party in a white dress shirt and green sweater vest, walked to Dae's house with an anxious pace to his steps. Carrying the neatly wrapped present in his hand, he felt like a teenager going to pick up his prom date. Lost in a lighthearted mood, he had completely freed his mind of the inconvenient fact that his date was another man's wife.

"Merry Christmas," said Dae, as she opened the door. She looked like the season's greeting in cherry red lipstick and a bright red sweater with embroidered reindeer that appeared to be flying above snow-covered ground atop her white slacks.

Brax's eyes widened. "Wow, you look stunning, Mrs. Claus."

"Thank you." She beamed. "I know it's warm but I wanted to look Christmas-y."

"You look Christmas-y, all right," Brax said. "You'll be the prettiest package around the tree." He kissed her on the cheek, inhaling a hint of perfume with the fragrance of jasmine.

"Umm, you look handsome, yourself."

The spirit of the season rose in Brax as he stepped into the living room. The mantel was draped with a string of garland and a small Christmas tree, dusted with artificial snow and sparkling white lights, rested on a table in one corner. Red and green throw pillows on the sofa were embroidered with snow scenes. A whiff of cinnamon drifted from a straw broom propped against the fireplace.

"Merry Christmas to you." He handed her a box with shiny silver wrapping.

"Thank you. I have something for you, too. But why don't we wait until later to open them? We can come back here after the party."

"That's fine with me. Ready to go?"

"Yes, let me get the casserole." She placed his gift under the Christmas tree and went into the kitchen. A moment later, she returned with a covered dish.

"Oh hell," he said. "I forgot the bread." The admission irritated him and he instantly remembered where he had left his contribution to the dinner party. "We'll have to go by my house on our way."

"Sometimes I'm kind of absent minded," he added.

"We all are, it's part of aging."

"I like the way you say that—aging. It sounds better than getting old. Anyhow, I hope that's all it is. I don't mind aging, I just don't—." He stopped cold, recalling the painful scene with Dae's dementia-stricken husband.

She put a hand on his arm.

———

"I'll Be Home for Christmas" wafted from two large speakers as Brax and Dae walked into the clubhouse. They gave the casserole and bread to the serving help and he poured each of them a cup of punch. Brax joined Dae to move about the room, mingling with other residents.

Brax noticed Jim enter the room escorting a heavyset woman whom he had never seen before. "Wonder who that beauty is," he commented.

"Brax, be nice," Dae said.

Jim walked over and introduced his friend. "Hi folks, I'd like you to meet Wanda."

As they exchanged greetings, Brax looked at Jim with an inquisitive squint of his eyes.

Jim made a slight gesture with open palms as if to say, "What?" Then he pumped a fist at a man across the room and yelled a Marine greeting. "Oorah, Colonel!"

Brax turned to see Wallace Kilmartin return Jim's greeting with two fingers in a Vee shape and a hearty Army "Hooah!"

Kilmartin, a retired Army officer, was known to everyone as "The Colonel." A distinguished looking man with a full head of dark hair that faded to gray at the temples, he was dressed in a blue blazer and a tie with an American flag design.

But instead of the spiffy Colonel, Brax could only see a young version of John Whitehead dressed in Army fatigues. He took a swig of punch, closed his eyes, and tried to swallow the vision.

"Doesn't everything look great?" asked Dae.

Her voice captured his attention and the apparition disappeared. "Yeah, it does."

For several minutes, the foursome exchanged small talk and then joined the crowd that had begun to form the serving line. After filling their plates, they found a spot at a table near the big Christmas tree. They were joined by Momadou and a female companion, both dressed in bright African garb.

"Everybody, this is Brenda," Momadou said. "She's an old friend from South Carolina." He looked at his lady friend and quickly backtracked. "Well, not old … you know what I mean."

The others laughed and introduced themselves to Brenda, a slender woman with tawny skin. She was taller than Momadou and appeared to be considerably younger.

"That's for Kwanzaa," Momadou said. He extended his hand toward the table with a candelabra and a display of fruits and vegetables. "The candle holder is called a kinara and the candles represent the seven principles we live by. I'll tell you about them and what the other stuff means later."

"I can't wait," Jim said, dryly.

"It's interesting," said Dae. Turning to Brenda, she added, "I'm glad you could join us for our party tonight."

"Thank you. Everything looks so beautiful."

"Yes, this is very nice," chimed in Wanda. "Thanks for inviting me," she said to Jim. "And the buffet is wonderful. I couldn't decide what not to take." She snickered and then looked at Dae. "I heard Brax say you made the squash casserole. It's delicious. I would've brought something if Jim had told me about this."

"Don't worry," said Dae. "You're our guest. Besides we have plenty to eat."

"Yeah, I think we'll have more than enough. Especially bread," said Brax. "You can't forget the bread." He looked at Dae straight-faced and she rolled her eyes.

"Well, I got in the spirit myself. I made a cake," said Jim.

"Really?" asked Dae.

"Yeah," Jim answered.

"He did," added Wanda with a moon-faced grin.

"I know you're lying," said Brax.

"Yeah, I gotta see this," chimed in Momadou.

"You'll see," Jim said, looking serious.

Christmas music continued in the background and the room buzzed with conversation as the crowd set upon the food and drink. Brax and Jim went back to the serving table to refill their plates.

"Where did you meet that woman?" asked Brax.

"At Kroger."

"What—you picked her up while you were cruising the aisles?"

"No, she works there. We got to talking and I guess she took a liking to me and one thing led to another. You know how that is. Kind of like you and Dae."

"Yeah, I can see the similarity." Brax squeezed his face into a fake grin and Jim smiled back.

Brax dished some food onto his plate and said, "I want to see this cake you baked." He moved to the end of the serving line where a big selection of desserts was displayed. Among them was a small cake inside a plastic container.

"So you made this yourself, huh?" he said to Jim. "Funny it has a Kroger sticker on the lid."

"Maybe I had a little help."

"Yeah, I think so. Would Wanda work in the bakery section by any chance?"

Jim arched his brows and shrugged.

"German chocolate, too," Brax continued. "That's real nice."

"I thought you might like it."

Later at the table, Brax told Dae about the time he had gotten sick from eating his mother's entire German chocolate cake. "I told Jim the cake made me sick as a dog and tried to make it sound like some profound message about life. In his usual response to deep thoughts, he said it wasn't the cake's fault. This is his little joke."

"That's funny." She took another bite of Jim's cake. "It's delicious," she said, with a laugh.

"Ugh, thanks."

There was a lull in the background music and Momadou walked to the CD player with Brenda at his side.

"Uh oh, no telling what Jaws is up to," said Jim.

Suddenly, the rhythmic beat of African drums and tambourines accompanied by a chanting chorus erupted from the speakers. Momadou and Brenda moved to the small space in front of the Kwanzaa display and began shaking their shoulders and swaying to the music. They were joined by another black couple and soon Jim got up from the table, pulling Wanda along with him to join the dancers. Jim shook his big body as if having a spasm and Wanda moved side-to-side with the grace of a pregnant hippopotamus. Most among the audience of seniors appeared taken aback by the abrupt interruption to the mood in the room. When the music ended, the dancers returned to their tables with a mixture of curious stares and polite applause from the onlookers.

As Jim and Wanda made their way back to their seats, he said to a man at another table, "Where the devil is Tarzan when you need him?" That got a big laugh from several people nearby.

Jim plopped down in his chair, still breathing heavily from the wild dance. "Leave it to Jaws to come up with a Black Christmas," he said, panting.

"Y'all looked like real natives out there," Brax said.

The room quieted down after the Kwanzaa music and a silver-haired lady moved to the front of the room. She made a brief speech thanking everyone for their attendance and help with the preparations. Then she passed out sheets to each table with the lyrics of traditional Christmas carols. When she began singing "The First Noel," everyone joined in.

Brax was struck by the beauty of Dae's voice as she sang along with the crowd. He had never heard her sing before and he listened closely with the ear of a musician. He recalled her saying that she once sang in the choir and admitting to full throated arias while soaking in the bathtub. He imagined her singing "When I Fall in Love" with the same conviction in her voice that Jane had fifty years before.

When the last carol ended, the party began to break up. Someone started the CD player again and Christmas music filled the room as people gathered their things and started clearing the tables. The sentimental sound of Bing Crosby singing "I'll Be Home for Christmas" stirred the air with nostalgia.

Brax rose from his chair, looked at Dae, and said, "May I have this dance?"

The surprised look on her face turned into a smile. Without answering, she got up and took his hand. They walked to the open area in the front of the room and began swaying to the music. Shortly, Jim and Wanda joined them on the impromptu dance floor.

"You have a beautiful voice," Brax said. "My guess is you were the lead soprano in the choir. Am I right?"

"Thank you for the compliment. And, yes, sometimes I sang the solo, but I'm really out of practice."

"I think you're being modest. You should start singing again. The world needs to hear that voice."

"Oh gosh, you're embarrassing me. But honestly, I have to admit it gives me a warm feeling coming from you." She pressed tighter to him. "You have a nice voice, too. It has a deep richness."

"Hmm, a deep richness. Is that a good fit for your high richness?"

Dae put her head on his shoulder. "Yes, I think so. We fit together perfectly."

Brax closed his eyes and they continued to dance as the music changed to Mel Torme singing "The Christmas Song." They were left alone as Jim and Wanda returned to the table. Around them, people continued to clean the room while they slow danced in a tight circle with their bodies snugly wrapped together, oblivious to the commotion around them.

His chin nestled in her hair and his eyes gazed at the fine brown strands. Up close, he could see the sign of nature's course, a smattering of, not gray, but shiny tinsel-colored strands. A silvery promise of years to come. And he knew he held that promise in his arms; the woman with whom he wanted to spend the rest of his life.

When the song ended they began helping in the clean-up effort. By ten o'clock the lights were turned up and the tables cleared.

Momadou shook hands with Brax and Jim as Brenda stepped away for a few last words with Dae and Wanda.

"She's a nice lady, Jaws," Jim said. "I don't know what she sees in you, but you better hang on to her."

Momadou laughed.

Jim eyed him with a suspicious look. "She wouldn't be staying at your place tonight would she?"

A sly grin was Momadou's answer.

"Ah," Jim said. "Now I know why you're in a hurry to get out of here."

"Way to go, Jaws," said Brax.

"Hey," Momadou said, "if you don't get a charge every now and then, your battery will run down."

"You got that right," Jim said. "Hell, I could use a jump start myself, but I'd have to fall off the wagon and get knee-walking drunk to hook up with Miss Piggy over there."

Momadou smiled, stepped to the trio of women and escorted Brenda away.

A few minutes later, most of the room was empty. "Looks like the party's over," Jim said. "And they didn't even play my favorite Christmas song. I'd better get this young lady home before midnight so she doesn't lose a slipper."

Wanda giggled as the foursome exchanged goodbyes and Merry Christmases. Jim led her away crooning "Blue Christmas" in a voice that sounded more like Richard Nixon than Elvis.

"What a couple," Dae said after they were gone.

"Yeah, they're about as authentic as that cake he brought," said Brax.

"I loved the party," she said as they left the building. "Everyone seemed to have a good time and there was plenty of food. It was … perfect."

"Yes," he agreed. Now that they had taken care of Dae's husband, everything was perfect.

# 27

*It was perfect.* Dae's comment about the party lingered in Brax's mind after they left the clubhouse. As they walked to her place in the crisp night air, past houses with bright holiday lights, everything about the night did, in fact, seem perfect.

Entering her front door, she said, "Let's have a little Christmas cheer while we open our presents."

"Sounds good. You need any help?"

"No, I'll get it." A moment later she called from the kitchen. "Is white okay?"

"Sure." Same mouthwash, different color.

She returned with a glass for each of them and they settled on the sofa. "I enjoyed the party," she said. "Jim is such a card."

"Yeah, he's full of it but he's a good guy." He took a sip of wine and wondered how something could taste sweet and bitter at the same time. "Are you ready to open the presents?"

"Yes, let's do." Dae picked up the gifts next to the little tree, kept the one in the silver wrapping, and handed the other to him.

"Ladies first," he said.

She opened the package and spread the sweater in front of her. "It's beautiful. I love it. Thank you." She leaned over and gave him a kiss. "Your turn."

"There's something else," he said.

She rustled through the tissue inside the box and pulled out an unmarked CD.

"Don't play it just yet. It's for later."

"You've got my curiosity up now." She set the CD on the end table. "Go ahead, open yours."

Brax opened his present and kept the shirt neatly folded with all the pins as he admired the fabric and the Polo logo. "This is very nice. I can wear it on the plane tomorrow." He kissed her cheek, then leaned back against the cushion in the corner of the sofa and gazed into her eyes. "I'm going to miss you while I'm gone."

She leaned forward and put her head on his chest.

"I'll miss you, too," she whispered.

Putting an arm around her, he pulled her closer. "There's something I want to tell you. I think you know, but I've never really said it the right way."

She raised her head to look at him.

"I love you." His voice was soft and clear.

Her face gleamed with the look of unexpected pleasure. "I love you, too."

They kissed and held a long embrace.

Then he broke the silence. "While you're away I want you to think about ... us."

"It will be hard to think of anything else." There was a distant look in her eyes.

"When we were dancing, you said we fit perfectly together. I think that's where we belong—together."

"That's what we've decided."

He thought he detected the ring of duty in her voice rather than excitement, but he ignored it for the moment. "I want you to be absolutely sure how you feel. Marriage is not an option—we agreed on that—but if we're going to live together we have to make the same commitment. We need to think about where we're headed. We won't live forever, you know, and one of us will get sick before the other. I'm older than you—I'm seventy-one—and I've just had prostate surgery. That's something that concerns me and I don't want you to be burdened with two sick people. "

"Brax, I'm almost sixty-eight, so we're not that far apart. And, I have health issues, too, not the least of which is that I'm also a cancer survivor ... so far. You've already lost one loved one that way." Dae paused, absorbing the painful truth of possibilities. Lowering her voice, she said, "Neither of us has any guarantees."

Her age surprised him; he thought her to be younger. Nor had he given much consideration to the fact that her health might be as questionable as his.

"You're right. We don't know what might happen and we can only live for today. That's good enough for me and if you still feel the same way when we get back after New Year's, we can make plans. But I don't want you to worry about hurting my feelings or make a commitment if you're not absolutely certain."

Dae looked annoyed. "Brax, we've decided. You're moving in with me."

"Huh? When did we decide that?"

"Just now. I have the bigger place and you want to stay at Seaside don't you?"

"Yeah, but ... look, you'll be leaving in a couple of days and so will I. The next time we're together we can decide everything."

"Okay, but promise me we're going to stay at Seaside. I never want to leave this place."

"Even if this development goes crazy?"

"We can only live for today, remember?"

"Yes, dear, I remember." He looked at her with a grin. "Gee, we've already started."

She faked an exaggerated smile.

"I'll get us a refill," Brax said. Taking her glass, he went into the kitchen and returned with more wine for each of them. He handed her a drink and touched his glass to hers.

"Merry Christmas," he said.

"Merry Christmas."

"Would you like to hear the CD?" he asked. "It's different ... it's not Christmas music."

"Yes, I'd almost forgotten about it. My mind is a little off track right now." She leaned back and put her hands on her cheeks.

He touched her leg and whispered, "It can wait."

"No. I want to hear it."

He put the CD in the player and the smooth sound of a trumpet filled the room with the melodic strains of "Stardust." Sitting back down on the sofa, he put his arm around her as she leaned into him.

Dae tilted her shoulders back and closed her eyes. Swaying her head slightly, she appeared to be lost in reverie.

"I love that song," she said.

"It's the most perfect song ever written," he said.

The song ended and the next track continued with the mellow sound of a muted trumpet playing "When I Fall in Love." She opened her eyes with a glazed look and began humming along with the tune. "Hmm, Hmm." Then she sang a few lyrics " ... it will be forever."

When the song ended, Brax said, "That's all. There's only two songs." He stepped to the CD player, removed the disk and placed it back in the cover. "For a special lady," he said, handing it to her as he sat back down beside her.

"Thank you." She placed the CD on top of the sweater. "It's you, isn't it? That's you playing."

"Yes. And you can't listen to the notes without hearing the words. The words are always in your head."

"And in your heart," she said. "Did you fall in love forever?"

Brax put his hand to his chin and stared vacantly before he nodded. "Yeah," he said softly.

Dae's expression turned somber. She moved from his arm to pick up her glass. "If Jane were still alive, but in the same condition as John, you would still love her, wouldn't you?"

He didn't have to think about it and he was sure she knew his true feelings. Reaching for his wine glass, he gently swirled it before taking a sip. Frozen in the absence of a response, he felt a distance that had come between them with no warning.

"I promised to love forever, too," she said, not waiting for his answer. "I promised John."

Though sitting next to each other, they were no longer in an embrace and he sensed an undertow of regret tugging at her.

"I never asked you to break that promise."

"No, it's not your doing. I just don't know what's right anymore."

It happened in a flash. They had just spoken as if everything was certain and now she wasn't sure. When she asked him what he would do if the roles were reversed, he knew he wasn't sure either. The night wasn't perfect anymore.

"If you love John as much as I loved Jane, maybe what we're doing isn't right."

She took a deep breath. "What happens when love gets in the way of what's right?"

He shook his head. "I don't know." Trying to sort his thoughts, he put a hand to his temple. "I love you for who you are but that doesn't mean I love Jane any less or that I expect you to love John any less." He began to sense a tone of resentment in her change of mood. "You asked me how to choose between love and what's right and I can't answer that. I just know that love doesn't mix with what's wrong. "

"Is it wrong to want to be happy?"

He clenched his jaws and squinted his eyes. "Sometimes."

"You think I feel guilty, don't you?"

"I didn't bring this up. We were getting along just fine, thinking about our future and you started talking about the words to a song. Obviously, there's been some doubt in your mind all along and I don't blame you, or think less of you for having those thoughts."

"It's not the way I feel all the time. It comes and goes. Sometimes I know exactly what I want and other times I worry about being an unfaithful adulteress. I've learned my lesson about hiding the truth and, eventually, the word will get out about my marriage. I don't want to be judged and I don't want you to go through that either. But more than that, I have to live with my own conscience."

"And so do I."

Brax stood up. Trying to conceal his anger, he spoke with deliberation. "Look, we don't have to live together. But I can't be just a friend, living here practically in your backyard. If we decide not to go on together, I'll move from the island."

"No, I can't let you do that." She rose from the sofa.

His anger subsided as he regretted his words that sounded like an ultimatum. But he felt his future with her dangling by a thread. "Dae, it's all the way or not at all for me. That's just the way I am. If we're going to make this thing work, we both have to make a commitment."

"I have. Brax, I said I love you."

"And I know you mean it, but I remember something you told me once. You said that you wished John had loved himself as much as you loved him. And that's what I want for you. I don't want you to live with the burden of feeling selfish."

She moved forward and put a hand in his, an anguished look on her face. "I've messed everything up."

"No, it's not you. That's the way life is—it's messy." He squeezed her hand gently. "We'll both be leaving tomorrow and we won't see each other for more than a week. You won't have to worry about it during that time."

Dae sighed and wrinkled her forehead. Then she looked down as if to rid her mind of worrisome thoughts.

"Once you're with your family and away from me, you'll know what you have to do." Releasing her hand, Brax said, "The answer will come to you, clear as a bell." Maybe he was right but it sounded pretentious, as if he were some prescient mystic. He only knew he had no words to make everything perfect.

She gazed at him with a wistful look. He walked to the door and she followed him.

"I'll see you next year," he said. He wanted to hold her and kiss her, maybe for the last time, but it would only make things harder.

"Next year," she said weakly, as if speaking to herself.

He walked away and after a few steps heard Dae's voice from behind.

"Brax."

He turned to look at her and she stared back in silence. A part of him hoped she would ask him to come back and he knew he couldn't resist even the slightest plea. His pulse raced as if his whole future were at stake.

"Have a nice trip." Dae's voice trembled and she hugged herself tightly against a cool breeze.

"You, too."

Brax knew she was hurting as badly as he was but she had to have some time to herself. Time to get her mind clear like that stupid bell he told her about.

He needed to clear his mind, too, so he trudged on toward his house. But what he really needed was a cave to crawl into. A place to go to sleep and wake up when everything was perfect again.

# 28

The morning after the Christmas party Dae arose early, eager to get to Charlotte where she would spend the holidays with Julie and her family. Having arranged a ride with Julie's in-laws, she was glad to have their companionship during the five hour drive.

An hour before their scheduled arrival Dae was packed and ready to go. She gathered her luggage along with a bag of Christmas gifts and set them down at the front door. Staring through the sidelights, she caught a glimpse of Brax's car in the distance as he left the complex on his way to the airport. Seeing him drive away was a stark reminder of his abrupt departure from her embrace only a few hours earlier. It left her wondering if their relationship was over. Then she remembered how he had insisted that she make a final commitment the next time they met. *You won't have to think about it. It will come to you as clear as a bell.*

But she doubted her thoughts would ever be clear. Her mind was stuck in a bog as muddy as the nearby marshlands, and she couldn't separate her feelings for Brax from her marriage vows to John.

A half hour later George McAfee and his wife, Betty, arrived. Meeting Dae at the front door, they exchanged greetings and George took her luggage and bag of gifts to place them in the back of the SUV.

"What a lovely place," said Betty. "When we bring you back,

maybe you can show us around."

"I'd be glad to. I love it here and I've met a lot of nice people." It was Dae's standard mantra and she never tired of telling people how much she liked living at Seaside, as if reminding herself how lucky she was.

As she settled into the backseat, Dae tried to forget about the dilemma facing her. For the first few hours, the conversation centered on Julie and Ben and their two young daughters. Jenny, nine, and six-year-old Emma were the McAfee's only grandchildren. Engaged by the companionship of the other couple, Dae was able to forget about the worrisome question of her future.

When the conversation tapered off and the threesome settled into their private thoughts, Dae's mind returned to Brax. What would the McAfees think of her if they knew she was contemplating living with another man while John was still alive? It was just another smear on a blurry picture.

By mid-afternoon they pulled into the driveway of Ben and Julie's home. Dae had called ahead a few minutes earlier and, as soon as the three grandparents stepped from the SUV, they were greeted by the young girls.

"Gramma!" Jenny yelled as she rushed to hug Dae.

Emma followed close behind and snuggled to Dae's waist.

Dae bent down and gathered them in her arms. "Oh, you're getting so big," she said to the pair. Releasing the girls, she stepped to Julie for a big hug, then Ben.

The house, in an upper middle-class neighborhood of mostly two-story homes nestled among heavily wooded lots, was decorated for the season. The wreaths on the windows, green garland and red bows on the porch railing, and the unseasonably cold air created an inviting holiday atmosphere. The scene lifted Dae's spirits and, with her thoughts firmly in the moment, she felt as though she had found Christmas.

The McAfees were set-up in Jenny's room while she moved in

with her young sister. Dae settled in the guest room on the main floor, a room that had been called the Gramma room since the days when the girls were babies. The four-poster, canopy bed and some familiar keepsake furniture made her feel as if the room were her home away from home. As she put her things away, Jenny and Emma followed at her heels like frisky pups, trying to update her on everything they had done since her last visit. Being with them made Dae feel like a mother again and it rekindled the joy of being a mother with her children at Christmas.

The next day was Christmas Eve. Dae helped Julie prepare a big meal with turkey and dressing, giblet gravy, smoked ham, lots of side dishes and desserts. Ben's brother, Jeff, and his girlfriend drove over from their home in Hendersonville. With nine people in the house, it was like a beehive compared to what Dae was accustomed to. Being with her family for the big meal at Christmas was once the most exciting day of the year. But with John no longer around and Justin in a foreign land halfway around the world, now the family nest was reduced to just Julie and her.

As the women prepared the meal, the three men gathered in the family room to watch football, drink beer, and cuss politicians. Dae stepped into the room, and quickly realized she was out of her element. She imagined Brax sitting there, enjoying the company of the other men, and was reminded how much she missed having a companion to share times like this.

When the food was ready to be served, the women changed out of their house clothes into dressy-casual holiday attire.

"Mom, you look so nice," Julie said, as she entered the Gramma room. "That's a beautiful sweater."

"Thanks. It's a present."

"From your boyfriend?"

"Julie, he's a friend. We're not teenagers."

"Okay, your friend. Your good friend."

Dae felt uncomfortable, not knowing exactly what to call Brax, or if he was even still in her life.

Julie stepped into the doorway of the family room. "Guys, it's time to eat. Come on before it gets cold." She looked at Ben. "Record the game. You can finish watching it after we eat."

Grumbling sounds filled the family room as the men stirred to join the women in the dining room.

The atmosphere reminded Dae of past Christmas meals with her family and she felt the spirit of the season rise within her. Everyone, including the women, piled their plates full as if it were a challenge to get some of everything the first time around. The men ate fast and hearty, going back for second helpings.

Ben took a big swig of tea, then glanced around the table. "There's not a restaurant in the world that can cook a dinner like this. Ladies, this is like going to heaven without dying. You girls did great, too." He looked at his daughters sitting at one end of the big table.

"I second that," said George McAfee.

"And I third it," chimed in Jeff. "Here's to this good food and to those that prepared it." He raised his glass and said, "Cheers!"

The young girls raised their glasses and touched them with "Cheers," along with the adults. They smiled at each other, obviously delighted to be included with the big people.

After the meal was finished and the table cleared, the men went back to the family room to watch the rest of the game. The grandkids coaxed their Gramma McAfee and Jeff's girlfriend to the basement playroom for video games.

Dae and Julie retired to the living room, a place most often reserved for visiting preachers, lonely pieces of display furniture, and quiet times.

"Your friend's name is Brax, isn't it?" asked Julie.

""Yes, Braxton. Braxton Donovan.""

"Umm, that sounds so ... masculine. So ... Irish."

"Julie ..." Dae's inner struggle bubbled to the surface. "I'm not sure what to do. I'm still married to your father."

"Mom, we've talked about this."

"I know, but it's not just about what you and I think. Other people might not be so understanding. How would your girls feel?"

"They wouldn't think anything of it. They know Grandpa John is sick and we never talk about him."

"Maybe not now, but someday they'll learn the truth. I don't want them to think I abandoned my husband."

"They're bright girls and they love you to death. When they get older, they'll understand."

Dae looked directly into her daughter's eyes. "I considered getting a divorce, but I just couldn't go through with it."

"I'm glad you didn't. That wouldn't solve anything."

"No, there is no solution."

"But you still have your life to live. You can't let Dad's illness take that away from you."

"And I want to get my life back. When I'm with Brax, that's how I feel—alive. I haven't felt that way in a long time." Dae paused, reflecting on the emptiness of living alone. "I don't want to lose that feeling."

Leaning forward in her chair, Dae wiped moisture from her eyes.

Julie moved to her mother's side and bent down to embrace her.

"No one will blame you. You've stuck by Dad all these years and you've done all you can for him. I want you to stop beating yourself up. Brax sounds like a wonderful man and that's what you deserve."

Dae hugged her daughter tighter. "I love you."

"I love you, too." Julie straightened up and smiled. "This will all work out."

Dae felt comforted by her daughter's words and returned Julie's smile. Spurred by Julie's encouragement, she wanted to share more about Brax with her daughter. "I have a CD I'd like you to hear. Is there somewhere we can listen to it, just the two of us? I'd rather not play it in front of everyone."

"We can use the player in my bedroom."

"I'll get the CD and meet you up there."

Dae retrieved the disk from her room and joined Julie in the sitting area of the master bedroom. Julie put the CD in the player and the haunting strains of "Stardust" drifted from the speakers with perfect clarity.

"That's beautiful," Julie said as the song ended.

"That was Brax playing. He played in the band in college and some professionally."

"Wow, I'm impressed. He's very talented."

The next song began and Dae sang the lyrics softly. "When I fall in love ..." The music ended and she stared dreamily out a window. "... it will be forever," she whispered.

Julie let the moment linger quietly. Then she said, "Mom, I'm so impressed. I know I would like this man."

"I think so. I like the sweater, but this CD is something just for me. That makes it a very special gift."

"I'm glad you met Brax. I can tell how much he means to you."

Dae stood and hugged Julie.

"Thanks for being such a wonderful daughter."

"It's you," Julie said, holding the embrace. "You're the greatest mom in the world."

Julie stepped back, holding her mother's hand.

"How's the book coming?"

"It's at the publisher. I made all the changes they wanted. I was reluctant about a few things, but not enough to keep haggling over it. There are some illustrations and formatting to complete. I'll probably go to Chicago when all of that is done. Everything is on hold for the holidays, but I hope to hear something soon."

"That's exciting."

The book. Not long ago it was at the top of her to-do list but now there was something more important. And she hoped to hear about that soon, also. Waiting to hear a voice that would tell her what to do.

———————

At nine o'clock everyone gathered around the tree and each opened a present. Ben handed gifts to the girls to pass out one at a time. Afterward Jeff and his girlfriend excused themselves to return to Hendersonville where they would spend Christmas Day with her parents. Then Dae and the others changed into their good clothes to go to the candlelight vigil at the Methodist Church.

They arrived well before the start of the eleven o'clock service. The parking lot was almost full and they had to walk a good distance in the cold, drizzly air. Inside, the pews were filling quickly and they scrambled to find seats together. It was a large, impressive sanctuary with a huge stained glass window behind the choir loft. An organist played a prelude and the gigantic pipes pushed the notes out with lusty volume. Gold chandeliers hung from the domed ceiling high above and the white walls and woodwork created a bright ambience. The setting was uplifting to Dae and in total contrast to what she was accustomed. Her church in Savannah was made of solid granite with a long, narrow sanctuary and massive, dark wooden pillars and arches that evoked a much more solemn and timeless setting.

The service moved quickly. The large choir, clad in burgundy robes with gold trim, sang several hymns of the season and the congregation sang others from the hymnal. When a soloist sang "Oh Holy Night" a cappella, Dae lip-synced the words she had sung several times in her own church.

As the pastor delivered his sermon, Dae gazed at the altar. She recalled the time, forty-five years earlier, when she stood at a similar spot and pledged to love John "until death do us part." Sitting among a crowd of two thousand worshippers, she felt the pious eyes of judgment staring at her. Then she looked at the crucifix in the stained glass window and realized who she really answered to. *God knows who I am. He's my only judge.*

With midnight approaching, the choir began to sing "Joy to the World" and the sound of a hundred voices stirred the air with the powerful exaltation of faith. After the last refrains faded away, an aura of peacefulness surrounded Dae and she felt contentment unlike she had known for many years.

The service concluded with the lighting of the candles. The room was dimmed to near darkness and the flame was passed from one to another until everyone's candle was lit. Dae raised her candle along with the others and joined the congregation in singing "Silent Night." After the benediction, the overhead lights were turned up and she donned her heavy coat and gloves to walk out into the chilly night with the rest of the family.

Ben carried Jenny in his arms and his father carried Emma, both girls fast asleep.

"The service was beautiful," said Dae. "Very inspiring."

"I know," said Julie. "This is my favorite night of the year."

From above, the church bell began to toll.

Dae stopped and looked up in amazement at the steeple.

"It's the original bell from our old church," Julie said. "It still sounds good, doesn't it?"

"Yes, it sounds great," Dae answered as she resumed walking.

As they approached their car, the bell went silent after the twelfth ring.

"It's Christmas," said Ben.

Dae entered the car with a sense of peace. She felt the hand of God and she knew what she should do.

It was as clear as a bell.

# 29

Brax had plenty of time to think about things on the flight to Dallas. A change of planes in Atlanta stretched the trip to four and a half hours and, in the idle time, he couldn't help but reflect on Dae's attitude after the Christmas party. Even though he wasn't sure what might happen between them, he was determined not to let the uncertainty ruin his holidays.

Gazing out the window at the clouds, he thought about his sons. He never understood how three people, born of the same flesh and blood, and raised in the same house, could look at life so differently. They all had a part of him, but each went in their own direction like balloons released into the air. Mason, the oldest, was the brainy one, a career businessman caught in the corporate rush like a cyclist pedaling furiously to keep up with the peloton. Logan, in the middle, was the artistic one, perfectly suited to work part-time in a Seattle art gallery and perform in plays all around the Northwest. Dylan, the youngest, was the physical one, a high-school football coach near Atlanta, who spent his spare time hunting, fishing, and living out of a camper hooked to his pickup truck.

As he got older, Brax had grown closer to his sons, each in a different way. Or maybe it was they who had changed. They were their own men now and no longer bound by the authority of his ways. Having gone through a similar relationship with his own father, Brax felt a sense of déjà vu but with a reversal of roles.

In his mind Brax could still see them as boys, fresh faced and innocent, and sometimes he wished they had never grown up. If he could turn back the clock and start anew with them, he would do things differently. His sons would still turn out the same—a boy becomes the man he is born to be, he thought—but he would find a way to be closer to each of them.

Their youth came and then it was gone in a flash, only to be saved in photograph albums and stories that were told at family gatherings. Then the real world sneaked up on them and their innocence shriveled, like periwinkles at the first frost. The best he could do now was to know they were good men and that a piece of that goodness came from him. He hoped they had come to realize that somewhere along their journey to manhood.

During the descent to the Dallas-Ft. Worth Airport, he looked at the paper in his hand one more time. It was an e-mail from Mason with all the family members. Sometimes, he had to stop and think to remember the grandkids' names, and he had lost track of their ages. So he studied the list again. Eldest son, Mason, and his wife Sandy with son Kelly (17), and daughters Madison (14) and Heather (9); middle son, Logan, with his dog, Ren, and cat, Stimpy; and youngest son, Dylan, and his wife, Jeanne, with son, David (13), and daughter, Jenny (11).

He folded the paper and stuffed it into the travel bag under his seat. "Damn, I wish this shirt had a pocket," he muttered to himself. Thinking of the shirt, he couldn't help but recall the night before when Dae had given it to him as a gift. He tried to forget the way things had ended.

After landing, he walked from the secured area and, seeing Mason among the crowd, widened his eyes in acknowledgment.

"Hey," he said, reaching for Mason's hand.

"Hi, Dad," Mason responded with a firm shake. "How was the flight?" he asked as they headed toward the baggage claim area.

"Ah, the flight was okay, but everything else was a pain in the butt. It's such a damn hassle flying these days. I guess this time of year is the worst. Everybody in the world must be going some-where for Christmas."

"Yeah, it's crazy around the holidays, but I'm glad you could make it. How are you feeling?"

"I feel great. The doctor said I was in good shape. Or maybe he said sad shape. I can't remember."

Mason smiled. "You look good. Are you still walking every day?"

"Yeah. It's a morning routine." An image of Dae walking beside him formed in his head. *Damn it, stop thinking of her.*

"You said you started playing your horn again. That's cool. Are you playing with anyone?"

"No, I'm just screwing around by myself, killing time. I've got a lot of that, you know."

"I can't see you ever just sitting around doing nothing."

They grabbed the luggage and began walking to the parking lot and Brax thought about Mason's comment. It sounded almost like a compliment. He couldn't recall any of his sons ever telling him that they admired him for any reason. Maybe that was a part of him they inherited because he had never told his father how much he admired him either, until he spoke at the foot of his grave. That was a great regret he could never erase. Nor had he ever revealed to his sons how he felt inside. That was Jane's job. Maybe if he had a daughter it would be different and he could talk to her about how smart she was and how pretty she looked and what boys think about girls. Things that don't cause a man to reveal himself to another man.

On the way to Mason's house, they talked non-stop about foot-ball and family and politics, trying to fit a year's happenings into an hour.

"Dylan and Jeanne and their two kids got here this morning," Mason said. "I told them we could fit them in at our house, but they said it would be too hectic. All of the kids are sleeping here.

Dylan and Jeanne are staying at LaQuinta. It's not far away. Logan won't get here until tomorrow afternoon. He's in a play tonight. I got him a room at the hotel, too."

"I'm just glad everyone could come," Brax said.

"I had to beg them. Not that they didn't want to come, it's just not convenient since we're so scattered around the country. Especially this time of year when things get kinda chaotic."

"Yeah, joy to the world," Brax said sarcastically.

"It's been a long time since all of us have been together." Mason looked over at his father. "Merry Christmas."

"Ho ho ho," replied Brax.

There was a cynical side to Brax that sometimes led him toward the dark clouds instead of the rainbow. It was a part of his DNA that didn't transfer to Mason, a fact for which he was always grateful. Still, he never understood how a man could go through life without ever losing his temper or feeling so low that he had to look up to see over the curb. That seemed unnatural to Brax. But that was Mason and it was just another way in which he differed from his brothers. At Mason's home in Plano, a house full of Donovans shouted greetings as Brax walked in.

Dylan stood behind as the five young ones rushed to their grandfather. Then he stepped forward. "Hi, Dad."

"What's up, Big D?" Brax said, shaking his youngest son's hand.

"Nothing but the price of gas," replied Dylan.

Brax got the names of all five kids right, just as he had practiced on the plane. They gathered around him while he settled on the sofa in the family room in front of the big Christmas tree. Mason disappeared with his bag to an unseen room. Everyone chattered away for an hour until the newness of his arrival wore down.

"Do you mind if I rest up for a little while?" he asked. "I hate flying. It wears me out."

"No, go right ahead," said Mason.

"Come this way," said Sandy. She led Brax down the main hallway to a bedroom with pale green walls, cherry-stained furniture, a desk with a computer, and obvious signs of a young girl.

"This is Heather's room. She'll be sleeping with Maddy. She thinks that you're really special and she insisted that Granddaddy stay in her room. We'll have dinner about six," she said, closing the door.

Brax slipped off his shoes, loosened his shirt, and lay back on the bed. He closed his eyes and thought about how magical it was to have Christmas with family, even though it wasn't the same without Jane. Then he thought about Dae and he imagined that she was having the same feeling with her family. He wondered if she mentioned anything to them about their relationship or if it was something she was trying to forget.

When he awoke, he tucked in his shirt and splashed some water on his face in the adjoining bathroom. He walked into the den where Mason and Dylan were playing gin rummy and noticed the women in the kitchen setting food out for dinner. Pulling up a chair near the coffee table, he watched the men play cards for a few minutes.

After finishing a hand, Mason looked at Brax. "What's new Dad?"

"Not a lot." He hesitated. "Well, maybe there's something I need to let you guys know."

They put their cards on the table and leaned back on the sofa.

"Sounds serious," said Dylan.

"Don't worry, it's not about my health. I feel fine."

"Good," said Mason.

"I'm glad to hear it," said Dylan.

"I might be moving from the island soon," Brax began.

His sons looked stunned.

"Why?' asked Mason. "I thought you really liked living there."

"I do, but there's a big development project in the works and they're going to ruin the place."

"You'll still be in a nice community near the ocean," Dylan said. "It's a perfect retirement spot. Anywhere you move could be worse."

"Yeah, you're right. I haven't completely decided. I just wanted you to know so you wouldn't be surprised if it happened.

"Where would you go?" asked Mason. "Can you sell your home?"

"I haven't checked everything out. I'm so pissed off about what's going on that I'm still trying to figure out my options."

His sons tried to discourage Brax from considering a move. He played up the development angle, but he couldn't tell them that his decision really rested on his future with Dae. He didn't want to live near her if they weren't going to be together. The more the conversation progressed, the more he regretted bringing it up. He had promised himself not to think about Dae while he was away from her, and now she was back in his thoughts.

Brax felt relief when Sandy stepped from the kitchen. "Ya'll come to dinner."

The five grown-ups ate in the dining room and the five young ones ate at the "kids table" in the breakfast nook. After Mason said the blessing, everyone filled their plates and the light conversation began.

Shortly, Dylan looked at Brax and said, "Dad, this development might be a good thing for the island."

"Development?" Jeanne asked, looking at her father-in-law.

"Let's not talk about it anymore," Brax said with a stern face. He shoveled in a mouthful of mashed potatoes and washed it down with iced tea.

—————

Logan arrived from Seattle at mid-day on Christmas Eve. Dylan went with Mason to pick up their brother at the airport and by the time they returned it was after two o'clock. A deluge of handshakes and hugs met him as he walked through the door.

"Hi, Pops," he said to Brax. Logan was the only son who called his father "Pops" and Brax knew it to be a sly reference to a nickname for his trumpet playing idol, Louis Armstrong.

Brax grasped Logan's hand. "Good to see you. It's been a while."

"Yeah, it has been."

"Too long." There was a serious tone in Brax's voice.

Less than an hour later, Logan asked if he could be excused to take a nap.

"We didn't get out of the theatre until after midnight and I was at the airport at four-thirty. I'm feeling kind of washed out."

"Gosh, I can imagine," said Sandy.

"You can use my room," said Brax. "Excuse me—Heather's room. It's the best room in the house. Very comfortable," he said looking at the young girl.

Heather looked at her mother and giggled through a huge grin.

———◆◆◆———

After dinner, Logan put on his fleece and stepped outside for a smoke.

"I think I could use a little fresh air, too," Brax said. He grabbed his jacket and joined Logan on the patio. "I think it's been more than a year since we've been together. How have you been?'

"I'm well. And you? What's the latest prognosis?"

"Everything looks good they say. I might live another year."

"You'll probably live to be a hundred. Hell, you're probably in better shape than me." Logan snuffed his cigarette on the sole of his shoe and tossed the butt into a trash can nearby.

"You want to take a little walk?" Brax asked.

"Around here?"

"Yeah, just around the neighborhood, not too far. Just enough to walk off a little of that big meal. I usually walk about five miles a day on the beach."

"Okay."

*Michael K. Brown*

Brax opened the back door halfway and spoke to those in the kitchen. "We're going for a short walk. We'll be back in a little while."

They walked around the house to the sidewalk in front. It was a clear, crisp night and there were lots of spotlights and Christmas decorations on the nearby houses.

"This seems like a nice neighborhood," said Brax as they headed away from Mason's house.

"Yeah, a real slice of Americana," Logan said with an edge to his voice.

"I know, it's not for everyone."

"It's sure not for me."

"Do you still live in the same apartment?"

"Yep. Seven years now. Can you believe that?"

"That's a long time in an apartment."

"Tell me about it. There's a condo not far away I would love to buy. And they say it's a buyer's market now. But it would take almost everything I've got for a down payment, and acting's not a very reliable source of income. I doubt I could get financing and probably shouldn't do it anyhow."

"I could help you a little, but I'm not exactly loaded. You're better off not to get in over your head."

"I know." They walked a minute before Logan spoke again. "Pops, I know my lifestyle is a lot different than Mason's and Dylan's. I can't be like them, and I don't want to be."

"I understand that. But they are as different from each other as you are from them. I love you all the same."

Logan didn't say anything. Brax stopped walking and Logan stopped ahead of him, turning to look back at his father.

"Did you hear what I said?" Brax calmly repeated his words. "I love you. I've never said that before, but I think now is a good time."

"I can't help that I'm different." Logan sniffled and pressed his hands to his eyes. "I can't be anyone else."

"I don't want you to be anyone else. I'm as proud of you as your mother always was. Don't ever think otherwise. I'm your father and I'll never change the way I feel about you."

"Thanks." Logan took a deep breath. "I love you, too."

Brax nodded and resumed walking. "Come on."

After a short way, Brax spoke again. "I've been looking at some places on the internet and there're a couple of them in your area that look pretty nice."

"What do you mean—places to visit?"

"No, places to live."

"Mason and Dylan told me you might be moving. You're not serious ... are you?" Logan sounded incredulous.

"I don't know. Maybe."

"Dad, you said you love living on the island. And why in the world would you consider moving to Washington? Have you ever been to Seattle or anywhere else in the Northwest?"

"No, but I've heard good things. It's not something I've decided. I just wanted to check it out a little more thoroughly."

"Do you know anyone out there?"

"Yes, I know you."

Logan grimaced. "Dad, you need to be closer to people who can be with you if you need them. Mason and Dylan are a lot more prepared for that than I am."

"You mean when I start dying or losing my marbles?"

"Don't talk like that."

They rounded the last cul-de-sac on the way back to Mason's house. Though having only walked about a mile and a half, they had bridged a gap as wide as the three thousand miles that separated them.

———

In the family room, Brax leaned back in the leather recliner, Mason's TV chair, and admired the Christmas tree while the family gathered around reminiscing about old times. By nine o'clock the stories were winding down. With Christmas Eve fast disappearing, the kids retired to their rooms, leaving the adults to talk about things only meant for their ears.

Brax recalled a Christmas Eve when things weren't so cheerful. "Remember that night we got into a little tussle under the tree?" he said, looking at Dylan.

"Yeah, I remember," Dylan said, stone-faced.

Mason grimaced. "Dad, let's not bring that up."

"Ah," said Brax. "It's a part of our family lore. I think it's funny as hell."

"I think I've heard this story," Jeanne said. "But I want to hear your version."

———

As a youth Dylan had a bad temper and was fiercely anti-authoritarian. He was rowdy and he ran with a different circle of friends than his brothers. It seemed that trouble followed him around and he would get into situations that his mother would try to smooth over. Brax was more of a disciplinarian and was constantly at odds with his youngest son.

It was Christmas Eve and Dylan was sixteen years old. Brax could always remember that, one of the few benchmarks of time chiseled into his memory. Dylan came home late from his date and there was alcohol on his breath. Brax began scolding him and they got into a big shouting match. Jane tried to calm things down, but Dylan's temper, fueled by the alcohol, erupted.

"Go to hell," Dylan yelled, red-faced, at Brax.

"Don't you talk to me like that in my house!" Brax grabbed Dylan by the shoulders.

Dylan pushed back at his father and they stood clinched in a battle of wills and strength. Brax outweighed his son, but Dylan, a football player and wrestler, was wiry and strong,

"Y'all, don't start that!" Jane yelled.

Mason grabbed his younger brother from behind with a bear hug in an effort to calm him down. Dylan twisted his body violently and the three men tumbled sideways into the Christmas tree. The tree fell over, breaking ornaments and shedding needles, and the men lay atop crushed boxes of wrapped presents.

"Stop it!" yelled Jane. "Damn, you fools, look what you've done!"

Logan, who had stood aside passively during the fracas, said, "Guys, calm down."

Brax and Dylan separated at Jane's command and, along with Mason, the three men untangled themselves from the wreckage.

"Get this mess cleaned up," Jane said. "I'm going to bed." She stormed out of the room.

Brax and his three sons silently began to work on the damage. They straightened the tree, disposed of the broken ornaments, and tried to restore the crushed presents to their original shape. Thirty minutes later the four men left the room, three of them a little worse for wear.

The boys separated to their rooms. Brax got a blanket from the closet and went down to the basement to the comfort of the sofa in the rec room. He lay there in the dark with his eyes wide open and his heart still pounding. After a while he heard footsteps upstairs and knew exactly what was happening. Jane was talking to Dylan like a mother does.

He tossed and turned all night in the cold basement and, before he knew it, it was Christmas morning. The family gathered around the battered tree and opened their presents as if nothing had happened.

------

"That was an exciting Christmas Eve," Brax said. Then he let out a big laugh and the others smiled as if they saw the humor in the story.

"What are you up to now?" Brax asked Dylan. "Two-seventy, two-seventy-five?"

"Two-eighty and a little change," Dylan responded. "Maybe a little more after that meal we had tonight."

"You're a little over your playing weight aren't you?" Dylan had been a star linebacker at Middle Tennessee.

"I still kick those kids' butts. But there are some big ole boys these days."

"You could probably kick mine now, if you had a mind to," Brax said with a grin.

"You know I wouldn't do that. If I wanted to I could have done that a long time ago." Dylan grinned, but there was a swagger in his voice.

"You tried, but let's not ruin this Christmas tree."

"Yeah, let's not do that again," Mason said.

"No," said Logan.

"That's one of those Christmas memories we should probably forget," Dylan said.

"Not really. It had to happen," said Brax. He stood up in front of his son, the prodigal child of the family. "I'm glad you found coaching. It's perfect for you. I've always admired your spirit. I'm proud of you."

"Thanks." Dylan looked at his father awkwardly as if he wanted to say more. Then he rose from his chair. "Are y'all ready to go?" he asked, looking at his wife and Logan.

"Yes, we're ready," Jeanne replied.

Dylan started to leave, then turned back to face his father. "I'm proud of you, too, Dad."

They locked hands with forceful grips and looked each other straight in the eyes, their faces frozen in expressionless stares. It was the only way they knew to say "I love you."

Mason and Logan looked on intently as their father and brother finally closed the loop twenty-five years after a fight one Christmas Eve.

A few minutes later, Dylan pulled out of the driveway and headed for the hotel with his wife and Mason.

Brax went into the kitchen for a glass of water before going to bed. Sandy joined him and poured herself a glass of wine.

"You want a cookie?" she asked.

"No, I'm good," he said.

"Yes, you are."

He looked at his daughter-in-law and she looked back directly at him.

"They all think the world of you," she said.

"What makes you think that?

"I know it, because I live with one of them. And I see how the other two are when you're around. You should be proud of your family because they all love you."

She set down the wine and moved to him with an embrace. "And I feel the same way."

"I love you, too, girl."

He patted her on the back and they separated.

Sandy's words meant a lot to him and he hoped his meant a lot to his sons. It had taken him a lot of years to pull that love from his heart and express it out loud. And he couldn't say "I love you" without thinking of both Jane and Dae. He wondered how such simple words could describe things that were so complicated.

Brax went to his bed and the clock on the dresser told him it would be Christmas in a couple of hours.

The house was alive with the sound of people moving around when Brax awoke. It was still dark. He put on some clean clothes and tidied up the room before joining the others.

"Merry Christmas!" he bellowed. A chorus of voices echoed the greeting.

"Would you like some coffee?" Sandy asked from the kitchen.

"You bet." As she filled his cup he said, "Just black is fine."

"Everybody is here now," Logan said. "Are we ready to open the presents?"

"Yes!" shouted the kids.

Everyone gathered in the family room around the Christmas tree. Dylan, Jeanne, and Logan were sitting with the rest, already back from their night in the hotel.

"You sit here, Brax," Sandy said.

Brax sat in the big leather recliner with the coffee cup cradled in his hand. In front of him, five big stockings hung from the fireplace, each monogrammed with a different first name of Mason's family. On the side of the mantel were six smaller stockings with names of the visiting family members. All of the stockings were stuffed with fruit and nuts and candy.

"It looks like Santa knows where Texas is," he said.

The presents were passed out one at a time to delighted rounds of "thank you." When all of the gifts were open, the floor was covered in wrapping paper, empty boxes, and piles of presents.

"Okay, time for breakfast," Sandy said.

Everyone moved toward the kitchen and edged in as space allowed. There they filled their plates with eggs, waffles, biscuits, grits, and sausage for a morning feast. They waited for Mason to say the blessing and, right after the "Amens," they dug into their food like it was the Last Supper.

His meal finished, Brax rose from the table. "I'm going for a walk. Mason, do you want to go?"

It was clear to the others that only the oldest son was invited.

"Sure, let me change my shoes. We can go to the park, it's not far away."

Mason drove five miles to a large park. There was a small lake, scattered trees and shrubbery, and a two-mile, asphalt trail. A few children rode the trail on their new bikes with parents close by and some older kids wiggled by on skateboards, but otherwise the area was relatively free of activity. The two men set out at a leisurely pace.

"I walk every day," Brax said. "We pound sand on the beach a lot, but there are other places on the island that are good for walking."

"I'm glad to see you stay in good shape."

"I walk with a lady on most days."

"Good."

"Her name is Dae. D-A-E. We've become very close."

"That's great."

"There's a problem though. She's married."

"Really?" Mason eyed his father with a look of surprise.

Brax told Mason about Dae. He explained how he had become attracted to her assuming she was widowed, then learned of her husband's dementia.

"That was a real bummer," Brax said.

"I'll bet."

"I met the man in the assisted living place where he lives. He's out of it and doesn't know who Dae is. He's been that way for a while and she's taken good care of him. She doesn't want to be unfaithful, but she needs companionship and we get along real well."

"You want to be with her, don't you?"

"I enjoy her company but I don't want her to go against her own convictions."

"I'm sure you don't."

"Your mother was the love of my life and always will be."

"I know that."

"I didn't go looking for anything; she just came out of nowhere. For some reason, we connected from the beginning. There's no explanation for that, it just happened. I don't think Jane would blame me."

"No, of course not. Mom would want you to enjoy your life." Mason stopped beside the path, picked up a small rock and tossed it into the lake. Then he turned back to Brax. "Dad, whatever you do, we'll all stand behind you. Don't ever worry about any of us questioning your character."

"Thanks."

Brax had told Dae that the answer would come to her as clear as a bell. It was a brash bit of unfounded wisdom and he could only hope it was true. The possibility of spending the rest of his life with her was clouded by the possibility of losing her altogether. He thought about calling her on his cell phone and wishing her "Merry Christmas." Maybe the sound of her voice would give him a clue to what she was thinking.

No, he couldn't do that. It might ruin the holidays.

# *30*

Brax sat in the empty clubhouse at Seaside Village on his first day back from the holidays. Looking up from the crossword puzzle, he set his pen aside, took off his glasses and leaned back in the chair, awaiting Dae's arrival. He knew she was home because he had seen the light in her living room when he walked past her house the night before. Now it was time for their morning walk.

In the idle minutes, his mind wandered back over the last few months. Not long ago, he had resigned himself to living out his last years in comfortable solitude. Then it seemed as if his life had gone from coasting to full throttle with no warning. His prostate cancer, Jim's heart attack, the start of the massive island development, the foolish gun incident with Jim and Jaws, and renewal of playing his trumpet all happened at a dizzying clip. But those things paled in comparison to meeting Dae. Since their very first time together, he had looked forward to getting out of bed each morning to walk the beach with her.

Learning of John Whitehead changed everything.

Brax's worst fear in growing old was the possibility of losing his mind before his body was ready to go. After visiting Dae's husband, he dreaded that possibility even more. Yet he now found himself hoping to take that man's place, as if he no longer existed. At times, he felt guilty for that desire but the guilt withered when he thought of his role in filling the void in Dae's life. Or was he more concerned for the void in his own life?

In putting the burden of decision on Dae, maybe he had taken the easy way out. But she had to be true to her convictions and, whatever she decided, he wouldn't try to convince her otherwise.

He looked at his watch and it was almost seven-thirty. *Is she coming?* The dim light of day had crept into the sky. If he walked from the clubhouse slowly, a sliver of sun would creep from behind the horizon by the time he reached the beach.

It was a good day for walking. There was a strong wind blowing from the east and the sea would rumble with a noise that always calmed him. No hurry, though, so he picked up his glasses and pen and peered back down at the crossword puzzle.

He filled in a couple of words but his concentration slipped away again. He should leave now. If he stayed much longer, people would begin to drift into the clubhouse and he wasn't in the mood for chatter.

He picked up the newspaper and scanned a few articles, not retaining anything he read. There was no more time to waste, so he folded up the paper and straightened in the chair, ready to leave.

Then Dae walked in.

Wearing a cobalt blue cardigan she appeared to have a fresh glow about her, but no outward sign of emotion as she approached. He sat silently as his heart pounded furiously.

She took a seat in front of him and looked directly into his eyes without speaking.

He knew then what she had decided and he felt numb.

"I can't," she said.

Choking back the lump in his throat, he clinched his teeth and nodded.

She buried her head in her hands and then looked up. "I'm sorry," she said, as a tear rolled down her cheek.

He took a deep breath and the tension faded from his body. "No," he said. "It's for the best." His voice was strong and resolute.

Dae stood first, then Brax.

She stepped into his arms and buried her face in his chest, her cries muted by the soft cotton of his sweatshirt. Lifting her head, she started to speak. "I lo—"

"It's okay," he said, halting her words. "You don't have to say it. Neither do I. We'll always know."

He wanted to hold her tighter and never let her go. Kiss her passionately like a young lover. Beg her to change her mind. He wanted to do all of those things, but instead he wiped her tears with his fingers and released her.

"This is hard for both of us," he said. "But you've done what you had to and I respect you for that." Struck by the finality of it all, his body began to quiver and he forced the only words he knew to say. "Take care."

Dae sighed deeply and gazed into his eyes. "Bye," she whispered.

She walked from the clubhouse and he watched through a window as she drove away in her car.

Brax walked alone on the beach that morning. His windbreaker billowed in the gusty air and his hair swept wildly over his forehead as he shuffled along beside the white-capped breakers. Over the roar of the surf, he could still hear her say, "I can't."

Strangely, he felt calm in the midst of the turbulence and his thinking became clearer as the shock of Dae's words wore off. He thought about the morning when he had first met her on the same stretch of pristine sand. And he remembered their times together; how she had given his life meaning, even taught him to love himself once again. It was the gift from her that would always be with him, a gift he would never forget.

The memories helped soothe the pain, yet his heart still ached.

He knew Dae was hurting, too, but he could never blame her for being true to her conscience.

And he would love her forever.

# ACKNOWLEDGMENTS

The inspiration for this story came from the late-in-life marriage of my aunt and uncle, Nita and D.C Scivley. Having lost their spouses to cancer, Nita and D.C. met while attending grief recovery sessions. Soon they were steady partners and a couple of years later married, she at age seventy- two and he at seventy-four. For the next seventeen years, they enjoyed a full life and loving relationship until she passed away after a brief illness.

This book would have never been written without the help, support, and friendship of my critique partners in the Atlanta Writers Club. Barbara Connor, Mary Anna Bryan, and Casi McLean of the Fiction Crafters group read every word of every revision, patiently guiding me along until I felt the manuscript was reasonably presentable to a publisher. During that same period, I also received invaluable feedback from the AWC on-line critique group, notably Lianne Simon, Brenda Way and Mary Hall. Additionally, close friends Ron and Nancy Williams provided a sounding board and encouragement that kept me grounded as I plodded along.

Special thanks also go to the following people who provided invaluable personal insight in specific areas: Dr. Adam Hayes, Assistant Professor of Music at Berry College and master trumpet player; Diane Shearer, Chairperson for the Initiative to Protect Jekyll Island; and Ruth Wright, Betty Noland, Era Clemons, and Kim Copeland, caregivers for loved ones with Alzheimer's disease.

Any success this novel might achieve is a direct result of support from the Ingalls Publishing Group. Bob Ingalls has been an encouraging advocate and guiding force while Judy Geary has provided editing expertise that I find nothing short of amazing.

Finally, I have to give affectionate thanks to my wonderful wife, Judy, for putting up with me for days on end as I sat glued to my chair in front of the computer. Besides managing our small business and keeping the house running smoothly, she's a darn good proofreader. I'm either lucky or blessed; I like to think both.

Meet the author:

*Michael K. Brown* lives in Loganville, GA, where he and his wife, Judy, own and operate a flooring business. They have three sons and three grandchildren. A graduate of the University of Alabama, Mike has also held management positions in three major corporations. Several of his personal interest articles have appeared in newspapers in the Atlanta area as well as the *Wall Street Journal.* This is his first published novel.

For more information about the author,
his current projects and appearances, visit his website:
**http://www.michaelkbrownauthor.com**

For more information about Ingalls Publishing Group,
*Bringing readers great stories by Southern authors
of historical fiction, mystery, romantic suspense
and adventure!*
Visit the website:
**www.ingallspublishinggroup.com**

Made in the USA
Charleston, SC
25 March 2014